It's 2002, and South Dakota third grade teacher Ellen Jeffers has signed up for a photography summer course and assistantship at an art academy in Minneapolis. Thirty-three, divorced from her college boyfriend for nearly a decade, she's not seeking major change. She just hopes the course will enhance her teaching skills and her resume.

Aaron Brewster comes from privilege, and he has used that status to flaunt his family's values and carve out a successful career as a photographer specializing in black and white erotic portraiture. Has he ever loved? His love is for beauty, sensuality, eroticism. His new uptight teaching assistant will never fit that vision. Should he send her packing? For reasons he cannot fathom, he takes her on as a challenge.

Aaron's frontal assault shocks Ellen, but it also triggers something deep inside she's never been willing to acknowledge. Is her beloved prairie a safe refuge, or will it become a crucible for transformation? The choice is not merely Ellen's.

Through the Lens
Copyright © 2020 Adriana Kraft
ISBN: 978-1-4874-2956-0
Cover art by Martine Jardin

Published by eXtasy Books Inc or
Devine Destinies, an imprint of eXtasy Books Inc

Look for us online at:
www.eXtasybooks.com or www.devinedestinies.com

THROUGH THE LENS

BY

ADRIANA KRAFT

CHAPTER ONE

"I wish you'd change your mind and tour Europe with me this summer."

After putting away the last of the third-grade workbooks, Ellen Jeffers glanced up to smile at Angie Graham, her best friend on the Washington Elementary faculty. "Maybe next summer," she quipped, "if you're still single by then. I enrolled in my photography summer program before your divorce settlement came through."

"And I plan on toasting that bastard in every large city and tiny hamlet across France and Switzerland. Can you believe it? I gave him five years of my life." Angie tossed her head to the side, her curls bouncing. "At least I got a trip to Europe, and if I save my money, I'll have another trip for next summer. I'm counting on you joining me then. You can make it a photo shoot of some sort."

"Right. We'll see." Ellen started looking in each child's desk to make certain none of her charges had left anything behind. "You're still on that post-divorce high. You know at first it's a downer, and then when it's finally settled there's a euphoria — and then reality sets in."

"Don't tell me about reality. I'm not ready for it. How long has it been for you?"

"Nine years."

"And no other serious guys?"

Ellen shrugged. "Nothing serious. A couple guys were interested in more, but I wasn't."

"So, you're satisfied with the way things are." Angie shook

1

her head. "I'm so goddamn horny, I may screw my way across Europe."

Ellen laughed. "That's different than looking for a serious relationship. My post-divorce horny period lasted six months, one week and two days. I had eight guys during that stretch and probably not that many since."

"You don't know for sure?"

Ellen grinned. "I haven't been counting lately."

"At least you're getting out of Graystaff, South Dakota, for the summer. Maybe you'll find true love in the big city."

"I'm not holding my breath. I need the continuing education credits, and maybe if I ever tire of teaching, I'll have some other options."

"Speaking of options . . ." Angie stepped to the classroom door and closed it before turning to give Ellen a quizzical look. "Have you ever been with a woman?"

"What?" It was Ellen's turn to be shocked.

"You know what I mean. Have you ever slept with a woman?"

Ellen shook her head and took a step backward.

Laughing, Angie clasped her hands at her waist. "Don't worry, I'm not about to hit on you — here."

Ellen's breath caught in her windpipe. She hadn't missed the emphasis on *here*.

"I tried it a few times in college and found it surprisingly satisfying. But I was faithful to Allen — the bastard who swept me off my feet with his glibness. Too bad you can't come with me. We could've had a beautiful summer. Apparently, I could've introduced you to some new erotic experiences."

Ellen swallowed. She'd never noticed this side of her friend before. Angie could be flip and scattered. Sometimes her raunchy jokes were too much, but she'd never talked about being with other women or implied she had any interest in Ellen.

2

Ellen frowned. She'd been pretty much out of the dating game for the past three years, but she still recognized sexual banter for what it was — an invitation for more. Maybe the fact that they both were leaving the next day had triggered something in Angie. Maybe Angie was simply priming herself for her European adventure.

"I've got a lot of packing left to do tonight," Ellen finally volunteered, "before I can head out in the morning."

Angie gave her a knowing smile. "I didn't expect a sleepover invite. I've got a lot to do, too. I am so excited I probably won't be able to sleep anyway. You really think your summer is going to be all work and no play?"

"The program looks intense on paper. I'm not sure which will be more time consuming, the courses I'm taking or my teaching assistantship."

"Well, you have plenty of years teaching. Your professor should appreciate that. Maybe that's why he selected you."

"Probably. I don't know how any of us were assigned. And he's not a professor. He's an instructor. It's a private academy that offers photography and art instruction. It sounds more hands-on than many college programs. I don't want to spend the whole summer buried in theory and esoteric stuff. Though I do wish he specialized in landscape photography."

"What's his specialty?"

"Portraits."

Angie giggled. "Maybe he does nudes."

Wincing, Ellen shook her head. "He probably does weddings, graduation pictures, kids, and animals."

"Boring. Nudes sound much better. I hope you can stick out the summer."

"I'm sure I'll manage. I always do."

"I'd better run. Give me a hug goodbye, and good luck to you and your summer."

Ellen stepped easily into Angie's arms. Angie hugged her

tight and kissed her cheek. In turn, Ellen kissed Angie's cheek.

Before she backed away, Angie tapped her rear lightly. "I'll miss you. Have a good summer. And make time for some fun, for a change." She gave her a half smile. "And at least think about coming with me next summer."

Ellen nodded. "I'll think about it. Have fun, and be careful."

A smile split Angie's face. "See, we would be perfect travel companions. You'd keep me safe, and I'd pull you out of that shell of yours. Maybe we should plan a fall camping trip to northern Minnesota to see the changing colors."

"Maybe. Send me an email now and then when you can find the time — and a cyber-café!"

"I will. Bye." Angie blew her a kiss and left.

Ellen exhaled, looking around her classroom through clouded vision. Why hadn't she simply said no way to a fall trip? She loved Angie, but not in that way. She hadn't wanted to offend her friend and colleague.

Wasn't that just like her? Now she'd have to deal with that issue in the fall. Maybe with any luck, Angie would return with a lover, or maybe she'd be completely sated for a year. No way would Ellen think about spending the next summer traveling with Angie.

She wasn't repulsed by the idea of a woman being with a woman. She had a distant relative who'd lived with a woman for years, but she'd never seriously thought about that for herself — probably because she'd never been attracted in that way to a female. Inhaling sharply, Ellen tried to ignore her aching nipples.

She couldn't help but envy Angie's freer style, and she knew their four-year age difference didn't account for it. At thirty-three, she'd never been so free or felt she had the extra resources to consider barnstorming across Europe. Dale had been her high school sweetheart whom she'd dutifully put through college by clerking at two stores while cramming in a community college course here and there. He'd dumped her shortly after graduating from college without even a thank you. They really hadn't owned much to argue over — but he didn't have to leave her for one of her old high school friends. Nor did he have to tell her repeatedly she was cold and sexually uninteresting. She'd been warm enough while he was in college.

She grimaced. That wasn't even true. After they'd split, she learned he hadn't always been studying for exams when he stayed late at the library. Maybe that was how he discovered his wife was so inadequate in bed.

Ellen pursed her lips. Maybe it wouldn't be completely terrible to find a guy in Minneapolis for a summer fling. Small town South Dakota hadn't been very fruitful for her in that department — not that she'd spent much time looking recently. She and Angie had talked frequently about checking out teaching possibilities in the Twin Cities, but neither of them had done anything about it.

Taking one last glance around her classroom before turning out the lights, Ellen couldn't help but wonder if inertia had become her favorite sleeping companion. At least she'd taken the leap to rent her house out for the summer, and she'd found a beautiful place in Minneapolis to lease while a professor and his wife were abroad.

And she was excited about the photography program. She hoped she'd strengthen her skills so she could begin to introduce photography to children. The middle school principal had already talked with her about offering a class or two — it might be in school or after school. From the course descriptions, it looked like the Academy considered photography as one more genre of the art world, and that appealed to her a lot. She'd taken an art minor in college and French as her language, so she thought she had a fairly good background for what she was setting off to do.

It was unlikely that her French would've gotten her far in Paris. Probably best not to let Angie know she might have a working knowledge of the language.

A last glance told her she'd left the class calendar on the bulletin board. She walked over and removed it — 2002, a decade since she'd first taught third graders in this room. Those children would be graduating high school in a week

She flipped off the classroom light switch. Inhaling deeply before leaving, Ellen tried not to wince at the rather barren, spartan classroom. It had been so full of life only two days earlier with screaming children on their last day of school. There had been some tears, too. But now the room looked so stark without kids.

She squared her shoulders and left her classroom, ready to embrace the world of photography and whatever else might come her way. She had no doubt Angie would keep her appraised of her summer ventures — and probably her conquests.

Fixing his gaze on the rather stoic woman sitting across from him at the small table in his academy office, Aaron Brewster tried his best to get a good read on her. He'd spent much of his life reading women — their moods and their desires. He'd developed a reputation for being adept at capturing feminine subtleties in black and white.

Ellen Jeffers was one of those rare women who defied immediate description. She vacillated between projecting an air of haughtiness — which he supposed came with being a schoolteacher who seldom believed her audience understood her — to projecting an air of innocence characteristic of a girl from the South Dakota prairie making her way in the unfamiliar big city. And in between those poles, he witnessed prim and proper, mystery, smugness, disdain, awe, shyness, self-censure, and thankfully a spark or two of humor.

If she was going to work with him, he'd have to get her in front of the camera. It was through the camera lens that he could best sort out the nuances of a woman and his own feelings about her. Keeping his smile to himself, he wondered if his summer teaching assistant had ever posed in the nude.

He needed help with his tits-and-ass study, but the way Ellen Jeffers blanched at some of nude pics hanging on his office walls, he wasn't sure she'd be helpful with that project. He'd take a wait-and-see position about her usefulness. At the very least, he needed an assistant comfortable enough in her own skin to help models prepare themselves for the scrutiny of the camera.

"Do you only do nude portraits?" Ellen asked, glancing quickly from one photo to another and back to him.

"Some subjects are partially clad," he said dryly. "So does nudity bother you, Ellen? Is it okay if I call you Ellen? Given how close we'll be working together, first names seem more natural."

"Of course, please do."

"And nudity?" He arched an eyebrow. "You are comfortable with nudity, right? You've been married. You've hung around art students, and you applied to this program."

"My undergraduate college didn't allow nude modeling." She didn't blink. "I had hoped to expand my knowledge of landscape photography or taking action pictures of children."

"I see. You're avoiding my question, but that's okay. In case you're wondering, I didn't select you as my teaching assistant. You were the only person available when I returned from a conference. So if you want to blame someone for your misfortune, blame my colleagues. This is sort of like going on a blind date." He paused. "I've only been on one. I didn't like it."

Ellen's laughter came quick and a little harsh. "At least we can agree on that." She swallowed. "So I guess it's safe to assume that you don't do weddings, family portraits and such."

He shook his head. He'd love to have a window into the strawberry blonde's brain as she appeared to check off her options. She didn't have many, and he knew it. She could go back to South Dakota, but he'd already witnessed her grit. Ellen Jeffers wouldn't run if she could manage at all.

She smacked her lips. "I haven't spent much time around nudity"—she gave him a wry smile—"and much of that was in the dark. It may take me a while, but I'm sure I'll be comfortable enough."

"We'll see. I do appreciate your honesty and spunk. I apologize in advance, because too much of your job will be that of a gopher, but I promise to try to help you hone your skills behind the camera. You'll make arrangements for some of our work outside the academy. I'll want you helping students with the basics. I am pleased that you have some darkroom experience. Our inexperienced students will need help with such fundamental things as cropping." He chuckled. "You may be surprised how many will forget to turn off the lights."

Ellen matched his chuckle and smiled genuinely. "Sounds like some of my students."

"Fortunately, we only have eight of them for the summer. That'll give us plenty of opportunity to get you involved in some of my other projects. That's where you'll best see the merging and interaction of art and photography." He peeked at her application. "If we introduce you to action photos, it won't involve children at play."

She remained passive, giving no indication she had any clue what he'd alluded to.

He'd let that pass for now—no need to press her prematurely. "I will want you to do some modeling."

She sat up straighter.

Good, he'd shocked her. He smiled. "That's the best way to get a feel for what's going on with a model when you're behind the camera. Much of this work is about feel and sensitivity. We'll be honing your observation skills as much as anything else. You must be able to envision a finished product while remaining open to the magic of the process, to being surprised by what you had not envisioned."

Seeing a look of confusion on her face, he shrugged. "This will be clearer as we proceed. We're dealing with an art form here, not simply with a skill. I only work with film. No digital cameras allowed. I'm well aware of the sharp rise in the sale of digital cameras — anybody can get one now. I don't believe photography should deteriorate to a crapshoot. That might be okay for taking snapshots at home, but it has no place in undertaking photography as a serious art form. Understand?"

"I think so." She narrowed her eyes. "You do seem to have strong opinions."

"So you are observant." He chuckled just as his cell phone rang. Glancing at the caller ID, he shook his head. "Sorry, I have to answer this. It won't take long."

Ellen took advantage of the interruption to catch her breath, study the office more thoroughly, and consider her instructor. Several black and white photos of nude women decorated his office walls. She had to admit the photos were tasteful. Two focused on breasts and taut nipples. One highlighted a black woman's backside. The two she found most fascinating were only headshots. Each woman was so expressive, with eyes sparkling and lips set provocatively. She tipped her head to the side and studied them closely. She was unable to decide whether the photographer's intention was depicting a moment of seduction or a woman mimicking the moment of orgasm. Maybe if she had more experience with those, she'd know for sure.

She returned her focus to Aaron Brewster. She considered herself a fairly good judge of character. That was a helpful skill when it came to working with parents. She'd had the impression that Aaron was trying to be straight with her about his expectations, yet he was withholding something. She was certain of that.

He wasn't hard on the eyes. His nearly shoulder-length dark hair was almost as long as her own. His dark eyes seemed to snap with every emotion—be it humor or annoyance. The phone call had clearly irked him. While she tried not to listen in, she couldn't help but hear that he had a problem with a model. Apparently not for the first time, the model was not going to make her scheduled photo shoot. That must be one downside to this photography business.

Ellen had only posed for artists a few times back in her undergraduate days, which was years ago, and clothed. She wasn't about to pose in the nude for her new instructor, but she didn't question his logic. It had been her experience that to learn anything, you had to put yourself in the role of the other, whether a child, a parent, or a teacher. Now she'd have to add photographer and model to that list.

She grinned. Maybe she would agree to pose in the nude—discreetly—if he let her photograph him in the nude. That sounded like the kind of deal Angie would make. He did have a nice square jaw. His shoulders and chest filled out the dark tee he wore very well. Her mouth watered, surprising her. She didn't think about men like this.

Still, she had considered a summer fling. But not with Aaron Brewster. She had to work with him. Work and pleasure did not mix. She knew that for a fact. She shook her head—better not let her mind spin out of control.

"Did I say something wrong?"

Ellen flinched. When had he gotten off the phone, and how

long had he been smirking at her? Surely he wasn't a mind reader. "No, no," she said quickly. "I was just thinking of the unpacking I have left to do to get organized for the summer."

"I expect being organized is very important to you."

She didn't detect any sarcasm in his statement. "That's right. If you have thirty-some third graders to teach, you'd better be organized."

"I suppose. I'm sure your organizational skills will come in handy here. So do you have any questions for me?"

She nodded, feeling her cheeks warm. "Is there a good reason why I have to be tested for sexually transmitted diseases on a monthly basis?"

His disarming chuckle came without hesitation. "It's not you personally. Everyone who works with me, staff and students, are tested monthly. No one has to work or study with us. It's always a matter of choice."

His look flashed from menacing to mirthful, and she nodded her understanding. No one had put a gun to her head to walk in the door. And she'd have no compunctions about leaving, if it came to that. She could always pick up continuing education credits elsewhere. But she couldn't fight the notion that she'd been drawn to the academy because of its hands-on orientation, and she was getting a glimmer of just how hands-on it could be. "But why the testing?" she insisted.

He nodded. "Fair enough. You've been around models before, and as I've told you, we do work a lot with nude models — women and men."

Men. That caused her breath to catch. She'd only teased herself with the notion of photographing him in the nude.

"There are times," he continued, "when posing a model in the exact position the photographer wants, that there may be inadvertent touching of the genital region. It's highly unlikely that anyone would be exposed to STDs, but our lawyers tell us in these litigious days we'd better play it safe. So everyone

11

is tested. There are no exceptions, including me. Are you going to be okay with that?"

She nodded. She didn't have a problem with the testing—but what did *incidental touching* involve? She chewed on her lower lip. Her sink-or-swim attitude might yet get challenged, but she had no desire to bail yet. "How do we begin?"

"Good. We'll meet our students tomorrow. I've already scheduled a tour at the Minneapolis Institute of Art for the end of the week." He hesitated and scrunched his mouth. "I see you have classes Tuesday and Thursday mornings. The rest of the time, you're mine."

She winced but didn't bother to point out that her time wasn't exactly his.

"As you probably gathered from that phone call, my model for Wednesday's photo shoot is going to be out of town. Maybe we can use that time to get you a little experience in front of the camera."

"So soon?"

He shrugged. "Better sooner than later, don't you think?"

"Okay," she sighed. "Do you have a studio here?"

"I rarely use the one here. I have my own a half dozen blocks from here. That's where I do most of my indoor shoots."

"Then you do some outdoor photography?"

His smile split his face. "Oh yeah, various landscape settings add a certain eroticism of their own, don't you think?"

He did seem to ask her opinion a lot, usually about things she knew little about. Oh well—he was the expert. "I'm sure I'll learn."

"I'm quite optimistic about that. You do appear to have an eye for this sort of work. Wait 'til you get behind the camera and learn that from that position, you can see even more than you ever thought possible."

She pursed her lips. He did have her intrigued with her

summer work, and she knew that was part of what he was trying to do. After all, they were going to be working together as colleagues. He wouldn't want someone who didn't have an ounce of curiosity about his passion.

"Sorry, but we really don't have much office space at the academy." Aaron shook his head. "I do seem to be apologizing a lot to you. That's not my style." He shrugged. "Anyway, there's a small bullpen office space down the hall shared by our TAs, or you can use the desk over there in the corner. That'll be more private and more convenient. I'm seldom in my office. And I expect you won't be either." He checked his watch. "I have to get over to my studio for a shoot. Why don't you settle in the rest of the day? And I'll see you in the morning."

"Okay. I'll check out the office down the hall, but I'll probably prefer being in here. I do like having my own desk and space."

"So be it. See you."

Ellen sat and stared at the door closing behind Aaron Brewster. What had she gotten herself into? The man seemed so sure of himself — and of her. That was what disturbed her most. He seemed more confident about how she'd adapt to his world of portrait photography than she was. He did have a way of making her feel comfortable. He exuded confidence and assurance. That probably came from spending so many years working with models.

Ellen ran fingers through her hair. How many years? She was quite certain he was younger than she was, but then increasingly that had been her experience with guys — when she bothered to look. They were either too young or bouncing off recent divorces. She'd learned not to be the first woman after a guy's divorce. That had disaster written all over it.

Frowning, she couldn't help but wonder if Aaron Brewster was married or had a live-in partner. She blinked. Cripes, the guy could be gay. Maybe that explained his comfort level with talking to her about nude women.

Glancing around the small semi-circle of students, Ellen guessed that only one woman was older than she was. She'd been a little surprised to discover two of their eight students were male. Like her, five of them were elementary, junior high, or high school teachers. One was a college teacher. And two were stay-at-home moms. Two of the women were black, and one was of Asian descent. The remainder appeared to have that mix of backgrounds that made them Caucasians.

What had actually surprised her so far was Aaron Brewster. He was much more dynamic in the classroom than he'd been when interviewing her in his office. His passion for photography as art formed the cornerstone of the introductory lecture — he preferred to think of the classes as a series of seminars, but there'd be plenty of room for lectures. He had a knack for taking off into several areas from a single student question. She smiled. He could teach third graders, because apparently he'd never encountered a stupid question. Maybe that was why he was teaching at the academy. Their instructor was no stuffy professor type.

"Now then, if Ellen would step forward."

Ellen snapped to attention at the sound of her name. Now what?

Aaron motioned her to a stool. "Let me demonstrate a little what I mean by perspective and how it changes what the observer is seeing and feeling. That understanding will become sharper for you when you're looking through your cameras, but this will do for now."

Ellen sat on the stool facing the class with her hands folded at her waist. She'd deliberately chosen to wear a blouse and skirt that came nearly to the knees because she didn't want to stand out in the class. She tried not to grimace. So much for that.

"You've all been introduced to Ellen, and I'm sure you've chatted with her at break, so we've established some mutual comfort. Being comfortable with your model is extremely important when you're doing portraiture. While you remain in overall charge of the setting and the photo, you must be tuned into your model — to what she is thinking and feeling. Many won't tell you or can't tell you.

"Now then, let's take Ellen as she is." He smirked. "Tell me what you see. What's her mood? Who is she? Who might she want to be, and so on? Spit it out. One word or two. No more than three. Quickly now."

"Pensive," the college teacher said.

"Good. More. Don't take time to reflect. You don't have a lot of time to react in a sitting."

"School teacher."

Aaron laughed. "Yeah, I see that."

"Shy."

"Genuine."

"Determined."

"Capable."

"Great! Now I'm going to pose Ellen as I want her. Swivel on your butt so you're at a right angle to most of the group. Good. Now look back over your shoulder at them. That's right. Hold that. Now what do you see?"

"Goodness. Mystery," one of the stay-at-home moms said.

"Fun."

"Temptress."

"Almost sexy," one of the guys said.

Holding her pose like she knew she was expected to, Ellen wanted to hop off the stool and bop that guy over the head. She tried not to wince. Had the simple change in direction made that much difference? Given the look on the faces of the students, it must have. Aaron had proven an important point.

Never accept the obvious front-on position as the best or only perspective.

If she looked that different, maybe she should walk around the city with her chin resting on her shoulder.

"Go ahead and pout." Aaron chuckled.

Without thinking, she did.

"As I thought. Even more sexy."

She knew she must be blushing now. It was one thing to have one of the students describe her as sort of sexy — but she was supposed to be working with Aaron, not reacting to him.

By the time Aaron finished having her pose one way and then another, the students were all chattering, seemingly quite happy with their choice of instructor and class. Actually, Ellen was rather pleased, too, even if she hadn't chosen him in the first place. Clearly, she could learn a lot from him.

CHAPTER TWO

Pursing his lips, Aaron peered through the lens of his camera on a tripod at his newest assistant, who sat perched comfortably atop a tall stool. Dressed in a long calico skirt and white blouse, Ellen projected that determined air he'd quickly come to expect from her and which he thought reflected quite well his idealized image of the prairie woman. She might as well have stepped out of the tall prairie grasses into his studio. That she sat there barefoot at his suggestion only enhanced that fantasy.

She seemed more comfortable and confident in front of the camera than he'd expected, but then from experience he knew he saw more deeply looking through a camera than with the naked eye. Uncharacteristically, his mind spun in several directions. Usually, he was calmer behind the camera. But he had to decide what to do with this woman.

She had an air of innocence he'd not often seen. Was that part of her prairie spirit, or was it his imagination? Something pinged in the back of his mind — a long-standing dream of creating a photo series on prairie women as determined and hardworking but also equally sensuous and provocative. Ellen would probably flee back to the prairie if he asked her to help with his more erotic projects, but this might work. Still, his prairie woman would have to be much more forthcoming than her current pose suggested. He liked mixing up photos of the same woman fully dressed, partially clad and completely nude. The progression invited the viewer to participate in the total process. It might take time and patience, but now he had a woman who—with his help—could fill that image.

The tip of Ellen's tongue slipped out to wet her lips.

Damn, he knew she wasn't trying to provoke him, but he couldn't help but wonder how her face would contort and light up in the heat of orgasm. Getting her involved in his orgasm series seemed highly unlikely. He smiled. But he could wonder. Too bad she wasn't his type—then he could find out how expressive she could be climaxing without the camera. But he liked his women much more experienced and edgy than his prairie woman. An elementary school teacher? She'd never keep up with him.

Still, he needed to loosen his schoolteacher up. "Take your bra off for me, please."

Ellen blanched. "What?" she said as if she hadn't heard him correctly.

"I said remove your bra. I like the image you're projecting. It's very real. Very grounded. Very earthy. But I need something a little more sexy. A view of shielded nipples may help." He stood up and glared at her. "I'm not asking you to pose in the nude." He deliberately withheld the words he figured she'd heard—*not yet.* "You're supposed to be getting the feel of modeling for me so you can assist our models. Most of them have given up on modesty."

"For their art?" she said caustically. Her fingers flexed as if she was still undecided.

"Look it, Ellen, you came to me wanting to learn. It's your choice. And I do think I'll want you to work in front of the camera more than I'd originally intended. You're very expressive in subtle ways. I've been doing research on the possibility of a prairie woman photo series. You may have fallen in my lap at just the right moment."

"I have no intention of being in your lap." She turned around and reached for the buttons of her blouse. "But I would like to hear more about this prairie woman idea. I've done a lot of historical work on the pioneers in the prairie states. They were remarkable people — especially, I think, the women."

"From what I've read, I tend to agree with you." He walked around the tripod as she turned to face him. "Just as I expected," he said, grinning, "you have very expressive nipples. They'll add just the right hint of seduction to this little photo series. "Can you pinch them to make them a little more perky, or do you want me to?"

When her fingers suddenly flew to her nipples and pulled on them, he chuckled. "Excellent. Doubt that I could've done that better."

"Do you try to drive all your women crazy?" It looked like she was having some difficulty breathing.

"You mean my models?"

"Of course." She scowled. "What did I say?"

"My women, but no matter. I want my models to exude sex. Sometimes subtle. Sometimes raw. Some women can climax by simply twisting their nipples like you did."

"I don't," Ellen said sharply.

"Others require much more coaxing. You must be one of those." He did his best to ignore her irritation. "Let's get another button or two undone."

Slowly he reached for the top button of her blouse, holding her gaze, watching her swallow hard. He undid it deftly and moved down to the next button. When he had it undone, he parted the blouse to better show off her cleavage. Almost accidentally, the back of his hand grazed the rise of a breast. She gasped, but he headed back to the tripod before she had a chance to say anything.

Whatever she might've said remained unspoken. She gave him a curious look and then settled back into her pose.

"You have the kind of breasts I wanted in my idealized

prairie woman." He clicked pictures as she frowned, then gave him a tiny smile.

"What do you mean by that?"

Perhaps she did have some vanity—not surprising. She'd had to devote a fair amount of time to develop her deep tan. Again, that fed into his image of the windswept prairie woman, though Ellen didn't have leathery skin by any means. Her tan had come from carefully timed exposure to the sun, or maybe a tanning bed. Did she tan in the nude? He'd find out, but not today. "Your tits are full, but not huge. They slope just enough to project a maternal quality."

"They slope too much." Ellen quickly clenched her teeth, as if trying to bite back her words.

"I want to see them in their glory."

She shook her head.

"But not today. We have time. Plenty of time. Can you see how important it is to take your time with a prospective model?"

Not waiting for an answer, he stepped from behind the camera. "Let's set you in a three-quarter pose. Hike your skirt up above your knee. Use both hands. That's right. You do have sculpted legs and thighs. I assume you work out."

"That's right. I'm not going to go to seed prematurely."

He grinned at her. "I don't see that happening anytime soon."

He stepped back to get an overall view of her. "Perfect. Keep your hands on your skirt like that. The viewer will have to decide if you're pulling it down to protect your treasures from a would-be suitor, or if you're lifting it in invitation."

He stood in front of her. "That's right. Wet your lips for me." Before she could blink, he reached out and tapped a finger on her nipple. It rose immediately.

She gulped. "What . . ."

"Keep your hands on your skirt, please. Your nipples need

a little more attention." He locked his gaze on hers as he reached for the other nipple. "I'm not hitting on you, Ellen. I'm trying to make this photo the best we can make it. You may have to do the same for someone else. You wouldn't want that model to think you were hitting on her, would you?"

She shook her head.

He nodded, cupped each breast with a hand, and grazed each nipple with a thumb. Satisfied, he stepped back. He couldn't read the silent plea in her eyes. Did she want him to stop or continue?

"Beautiful," he said from behind the camera. "That's exactly the look I hoped for. We won't know for sure until it comes out of the darkroom, but you're quite photogenic."

"In an earthy sort of way," she said, seeming to find her voice.

"There's nothing wrong with that. If I wanted the sophisticated chic look, I've got hundreds of models to choose from." He chuckled. "Your makeup budget is probably a tenth of what most of my models spend. And for the most part, it works for you. We may want to experiment with a few things, but I wouldn't want to lose your naturalness. Okay. That's it. How are you doing?"

Ellen stretched and stood, apparently unaware of how her tits rose and fell with every move.

Aaron winced. What if she wasn't unaware?

"I didn't come here to join your stable of models."

"But it does intrigue you."

She shrugged, blushing a little. "Doesn't every little girl dream at one time or another of being a model?" She shook her head. "But I guess you're right. I am getting a better feel of what it's like being in front of the camera. Do you pose?"

He tilted his head to the side and then laughed at her serious question. "I have in the past. Yes."

"In the nude?" She eyed him levelly.

"At times."

"Good."

He frowned. "Why is that good?"

"I'm a teacher, Aaron Brewster. I know how to coax and cajole students into doing things they never thought they could. This posing was only a taste. You work primarily with nudes. It's no huge leap to figure you're trying to get me easy with talking about nudity while posing with you touching me in intimate" — she arched an eyebrow — "but non-sexual ways."

"Maybe you're too smart for all of this," he grumbled. "Maybe I should've simply told you to take your clothes off and been done with it."

"That wouldn't work, and you know it." She gave him a half smile. "I am surprised, but I'm actually quite pleased with how you're seducing me into posing nude. There's something very breathtaking about the process." She reached out and tapped his chest. "But if you ever do get me to pose nude, I can assure you that won't happen until I've taken pictures of you in the nude."

Aaron practically bellowed. He grabbed her hand, trying to control his own response. She'd called him at his game. He hadn't fooled her at all. Where the hell had this woman come from?

He blinked. Maybe she could help with his other projects — or maybe she was bluffing. It didn't matter. He wasn't about to call her bluff this soon. She might not even know whether she was bluffing. They had time. And, in any case, he had his prairie woman.

"You can put your bra back on, if you want." Aaron busied himself with the camera. "See you tomorrow at the Institute of Art. We'll want to take the class through at least the photo gallery and Impressionist sections."

She nodded. "I'm looking forward to that. The Impressionists are my favorites, and I've never been to the Minneapolis Institute. I was sick when my art class took a trip there."

"Too bad. You'll love it, I'm sure."

Looking rather nonplussed, Ellen reached under her blouse to put the bra back in place. "Why the Impressionists? Certainly some of the Dutch painters created more realistic art, more like a photograph."

"Very good. You do know your art history. The Impressionists are important to me because I want our students to see the world through multiple lenses — sometimes sharp and clear, sometimes a soft focus is needed, sometimes a fisheye, and so on. The Impressionists leave the viewer with a feel for what is happening, and that's what I'm often after."

"Ah. You do seem to be into feel."

The catch in her voice made him grin. "If I can feel what's happening in a photo, then I have a much better chance of helping transmit that feeling to the viewer."

She nodded. "I'm beginning to get a clearer understanding of what you mean. When the academy's literature speaks of hands-on experience, I wasn't quite aware of how much that implied."

"And you're still not. Try to keep an open mind. Art often stretches our senses by asking a lot of us."

"We'll see. I'd better go. As you said, we've gone far enough for one sitting." She waved and grinned over her shoulder. "See you tomorrow."

Aaron hummed to himself. Did she really think she knew what he'd ask of her? No way, but she had sharpened his interest. He would've been satisfied with her being his prairie woman model, but now he wanted more. He wanted to add her amazingly expressive face to his orgasmic woman study.

Once he had her committed to participate in that photographic study, he didn't doubt she'd share his passion for authenticity. He'd never let any of his women get by with faking orgasms.

Having difficulty getting to sleep, Ellen pulled on her nipples. She still couldn't believe Aaron had been so nonchalant about perking them up earlier as she'd clutched her skirt. Or that she'd let him get by with that.

She closed her eyes. For a moment, he might've gotten away with much more than that, but then, as he'd explained, there was nothing sexual about his actions. He'd merely been trying to get the best photos he could from her.

Once she'd realized that was true, she'd relaxed and gotten into the entire photo shoot. She'd seen through his game right away—and a part of her enjoyed being seduced, even if it was only to improve the art.

There was something very freeing and exhilarating about being seduced by a gay man. You could enjoy all the byplay without wondering about the endgame.

And he was gay. He'd proven that for her. He hadn't been aroused even when he was twisting her nipples. She knew enough about male physiology to know that any man intent on getting her nipples tight and taut would also be experiencing some tautness in his crotch.

Not Aaron Brewster. He hadn't shown a hint of being turned on. His eyes smoldered occasionally, but that was probably because he liked to play the marionette. She must've given him some pause by insisting she'd have to photograph him in the nude before she'd ever pose nude for him.

She's never seen a naked gay man. She pursed her lips. Would he get hard for her if she was behind the camera? She chuckled. Maybe he'd require some assistance.

She'd never stopped to wonder if a woman could get a gay guy hard. She chuckled again and hugged a pillow. Her parents had often told her she was too curious. Maybe she'd satisfy her curiosity, if the opportunity came about.

"I'm glad I came along on this tour," a woman said beside Ellen.

Caught up in Aaron's detailed presentation at their third painting in the Minneapolis Institute of Art, Ellen hadn't heard the woman's approach.

"I'm Tina Chambers. Aaron has told me about you, but he didn't do you justice."

Ellen tried to return the tall dark-haired woman's smile. Tina Chambers was a beauty. Ellen vaguely remembered the name—one of Aaron's models. What had he said? Sophisticated, chic. Ellen tried not to be envious. Even dressed casually in a tunic and pants, Tina exuded sex. The stiletto calf-high boots suggested she knew she could conquer the world whenever she chose.

"I don't know what you mean," Ellen said as they followed Aaron and his small band of scholars. Institute personnel knew him on sight, and he seemed to be on a first-name basis with everyone. And this was more than a little tour. Aaron would gather the group around him in front of a painting of particular interest, then proceed to give the group a small background lecture on the painting and how it demonstrated what he wanted them to understand about their work with photography as art. "I understand you model for Aaron."

"That's right. He wants me to come into his seminar from time to time, so this is a good opportunity for me to meet the students and for them to meet me."

"Comfort."

Tina smiled broadly. "Yes, one of Aaron's first principles."

"So you must be quite comfortable working with him."

"Oh, yes. We've worked together for years. Me and my husband."

"You're married?"

"Don't look so shocked. Even models get married. Well, at least some of them. Happily so, I might add. How about you?"

She shook her head. "Was married. Not happily."

"Oh. Sorry."

"It happens."

"I look forward to working with you." Tina squeezed her fingers. "I'm sure as Aaron's new assistant, you'll be helping me some."

Ellen swallowed hard. After yesterday's experience in front of the camera, she wasn't sure what would be asked of her next. What would Angie say if she knew about this change in her responsibilities? *You go, girl!* She stifled a chuckle. "I'm sure you're an expert at modeling. I'm more of a klutz."

"It takes time. And I assume you want to work behind the camera, since you're enrolled at the Academy. I never have been able to fathom f-stops, meter readings—and I doubt I have the required patience. Anyway, we'd better catch up with the group before Aaron comes looking for us."

"Isn't that the most lewd, despicable painting you've ever seen?"

Aaron looked up sharply from his notes. He hadn't even begun to talk about one of his favorite Impressionist paintings—Caillebotte's *Nude on a Couch*.

Ellen was standing with her arms crossed under her breasts, glaring with disdain at the painting.

"What's your problem, Ms. Jeffers?" He'd purposely called her Ms. Jeffers to try to snap her out of her tirade, but it didn't work.

"It's so huge. The woman is begging for attention, for sex. The painting must be life size. No wonder it's under glass.

Someone might claw it to pieces."

Aaron gulped, trying to hold himself in check. Who would even think of such a thing? "This is one of Caillebotte's most famous paintings. We're quite fortunate to have it here."

"I've never heard of Caillebotte. He must be a third rank Impressionist."

"Well, you're wrong, Ms. Jeffers." Aaron saw Tina grab Ellen's arm to warn her, but Ellen pulled away. "Caillebotte was not only an impressionist of the first rank—it was through his financial support and considerable influence that the group was able to attain recognition and stature in its own time. What is your problem? We looked at other nudes in the last corridor, and you didn't begin to flip out."

Looking at least somewhat chastened, Ellen sniffed, seemingly unable or unwilling to let it drop. "The others weren't in our face. She's too bold. Good grief, she's playing with a nipple. She's trying to seduce us." Her eyes widened. "She must've been a prostitute. Only such women would've posed like that during that era of French history."

"And you know that for a fact?"

"It was the custom of the time. Upper-class women wouldn't go out unchaperoned."

"Do tell." He gathered himself as best he could. "That might've been the norm at the time, but even the upper class of the Victorian era had its libertine members. There are plenty of accounts in England and France of upper-class ladies being escorted to a rendezvous with a paramour by a maid or manservant. After successfully completing her liaison, the woman would be escorted back to her house to await her husband as he returned from another lover's arms. Does that upset your sensibilities, Ms. Jeffers?"

To her credit, Ellen kept her lips tightly sealed and this time did not shake off Tina's supporting hand. She shook her head, but he knew everyone knew she was lying. According to what he knew, the woman in the portrait had become Caillebotte's mistress. There remained some debate whether she'd been a prostitute. Many models of that period were, but he wasn't about to let Ellen know he was aware of that. "Our reclining nude might've been a woman of the working class trying to put food on the table. Had you thought of that possibility?"

Ellen shook her head cautiously.

At least she knew he was upset with her. "And you'd never consider lowering yourself to pose like that or to take on lovers as indiscriminately as you seem to presume our fallen angel did."

She shook her head vigorously. "I have my limits."

He smirked. They'd see about that, but this wasn't the time or the place to continue this little tangent. "Now, if you can gather yourself enough to listen, I will proceed with my lecture on this painting."

"There are three principle interpretations of this work," he began. "Though as I share these, I don't want to impose any particular viewpoint on you. The first is that she's simply being coy while pleasuring herself. It's difficult to determine whether her eyes are open or shut. One eye is obviously blocked from our view. And if she is involved in self-pleasure, we have to wonder what she will do next.

"Second, she may be trying to seduce a favorite lover— male or female." He smiled when he saw Ellen startle and Tina squeeze her arm. "Perhaps her lover is already nude ready to join her."

"Third, she is pleasuring herself to seduce someone she's watching through shuttered eyelashes. Perhaps her prey has unexpectedly stumbled across her nude on the couch. Perhaps she's whimpering little oohs and ahs to further attract. Her raised knee arching away from her body draws the attention of her lover to the obvious invitation. Although completely nude, our woman remains subtle." Aaron looked around his little group to settle on Ellen's flushed face. "But not too subtle.

"Now then. If we were to stand at the edges of this room and watch people studying this Caillebotte work, we'd be struck by three responses. First, there are those who gawk and can't quite draw their eyes from the thick pelt between this woman's thighs — though even it doesn't look quite complete. Second, there are some, like some of you when we entered the room, who saw the portrait and looked quickly away only to glance back furtively. We wonder if we should be looking. This seems like such a personal, intimate moment. And third," he sneered at Ellen, "there are those who are repulsed by the painting's intimacy and its clear in-your-face disregard for so-called morality. This woman is no prude and challenges that part of us which might be prudish."

He saw Ellen whirl away from the group and duck into the next room. Tina hurried after her. He was a little surprised Ellen had hung in there that long. Maybe he'd been too harsh on her in front of the others, but she'd brought it on herself. Tina would console her. Tina was as good with women as she was with men.

He let out a long slow breath trying to collect himself. "Why don't we all spend a few more minutes with this work and the others in the room, and then we'll move on."

Aaron walked over to the far corner and stared back at *Nude on a Couch*. It always seemed to him that no matter where he stood in the room, she stared at him intensely — at no one else, only at him.

His teaching assistant thought she'd never succumb to posing like that or make herself so available to lovers. He snorted. Ellen Jeffers might be his perfect prairie woman, but she'd just thrown down a gauntlet for him — wittingly or unwittingly. She'd be begging for more than one lover before he was finished with her. And she'd find herself on a couch — he nodded at the painting—in the exact same pose as his favorite nude.

"That bastard tried to embarrass me in front of our students," Ellen said through clenched teeth, standing in the women's room looking at her reflection in the mirror. She glanced at Tina, who stood next to her. The woman seemed so self-possessed.

Tina gave her a tiny smile and nod before speaking. "I do believe you brought much of that on yourself. You didn't have to have an outburst before Aaron even began to discuss the painting."

Ellen sighed. She knew she'd overstepped. But the painting had insulted her so. She couldn't understand why it hadn't insulted everyone else. And then Aaron had begun to defend the painter and his mistress.

"Look at me," Tina said. "Let's get you straightened up."

Ellen swallowed as Tina used a tissue to swipe at the corner of her eyes. "Guess I was over the top. Do you think he's going to fire me?"

Tina's face lit up. "Not hardly. You've only become a bigger challenge for him."

"Me? I don't understand."

"No matter. You will." Tina slanted a finger across her lips. "Oh, Aaron is really pissed at you. That painting is one of his absolute favorites here at the Institute."

"Great! And I stomped all over it. Why?"

"I'm not completely sure. But Aaron comes from a very wealthy family who does not approve of his line of work. He knows the inner workings of the upper crust and how people can bend things pretty much any way they want."

"His notion of the upper-class French or English woman being escorted to a lover?"

"Exactly."

"So is he angry at me because of my art criticism, or because I said I would never do what that woman was so obviously doing?"

"You're very bright. I'd say about fifty-fifty. You about ready to go back and deal with our lion?"

Ellen nodded. "Sorry to have gotten you in the middle of this little spat."

Tina grinned. "I'm used to being in the middle. Now let me smooth out your shirt and give you a hug."

"Thank you," Ellen said, letting the woman gather her in her arms. She hugged her as if she were hugging Angie—close, but not too close.

Tina hugged her tighter and let her hands drift down her backside and over her rump. "Oh, we do fit together nicely. We're going to have so much fun."

Looking a little flushed, Tina backed away and took her by the hand. "Come on, we'd better hook up with our group. You still look a little lost." Tina pecked at her cheek. "Everything will be okay. Aaron won't fire you. He may give you a hard time for a day or two, but he's really a very sensitive guy. You can learn a lot from him—if you're willing."

Ellen wet her lips and hurried out of the restroom, matching Tina stride for stride. "I'm trying. It's not easy for a teacher to suddenly become a student again."

Tina squeezed her fingers. "I understand, but you're in good hands. Believe me."

Ellen remained silent as they hunted for their group. She tried to take in enough air. Tina still clung to her hand. Ellen knew that city people and especially people in the art world did things differently, but she wasn't used to walking around in public places holding on to a woman's hand. Not even in private places.

She blinked her eyes quickly open and shut. Tina Chambers was a happily married woman, so there couldn't be any meaning to the model's touches other than one woman reaching out to comfort another. Comfort. There was that damn word again. She gripped Tina's fingers tighter. Was she simply becoming more comfortable with human touch? She hadn't realized how uncomfortable she'd been with touching until now. She'd never had trouble hugging children, but adults were another matter.

Tina had helped her a lot. And she didn't have to face Aaron and the group alone. Tina would be by her side, and that was comforting.

CHAPTER THREE

On the following Monday morning after a restless week-end, Ellen warily entered the seminar room to find Aaron already checking several cameras and tripods. He looked up when she entered. His stare was blank, giving away nothing about how he might treat her after the Caillebotte fiasco.

"Good morning," she said softly, putting her notepad on a chair. "What can I do to help?"

"Double check the cameras on that table," he said, pointing to a table on the far wall. "Make sure they're loaded."

Remaining rooted in place, she watched him walk over to drape a white sheet over the stool she'd sat on during their first seminar session.

"Don't worry," he said, "I have Tina coming into to pose for us today. I didn't want to offend your tender sensibilities."

"Look." She gritted her teeth. "I'm sorry about the other day. I didn't mean I wouldn't pose for you or for our students. I just . . ." She glanced away from him. "Are you giving up on your prairie woman project so quickly? I'll leave, if you want. You don't have to fire me. I'll just leave."

"No." Aaron quickly closed the distance between them. He grazed her cheek with a finger.

She didn't flinch.

"I didn't say I wanted you to leave. But I won't subject you to posing in front of the seminar. They need to see models who are comfortable with their nudity. You're not." He arched an eyebrow. "You may get there, but you're not there yet. Right?"

She nodded. "I may never get comfortable with letting strangers see me naked."

His lips curled into a small smile. "I'm betting you will. For now, I'm reducing your responsibilities with the seminar. I'll want you spending more time at my studio. We'll move forward with the prairie woman project, if you're willing."

She nodded, not quite able to hold his stare. "I'd like that."

"Good. I have some other projects I'll want your assistance with, too, but we can discuss those later. Today I want you concentrating on Tina and how she handles herself in front of a group. Later, you and I will divide the class in two. You'll take four of the students to darkroom A and help them develop their pics, and I'll take the other four to darkroom B. You okay with that?"

"Sure. I'm just introducing them to darkroom basics, right?"

"That's right." He gave her a genuine smile. "Don't be surprised if someone flips on the light switch in the middle of the process. Some students require more than one try at this."

She inhaled. "Thanks for giving me a second chance. I'll try not to go over the top again."

"You were something to see. I wasn't aware of that until yesterday after I'd processed that little scene in my head dozens of times." He reached out to cup her chin in his hand. "You have loads of passion, as my prairie woman should. I wouldn't want you to bridle it, but we may want to channel that reservoir of passion in more positive directions."

Ellen shuddered slightly as Aaron walked back to the posing stool, clearly ending their conversation. At least he hadn't given up on her. And he'd been worrying over their spat as much as she had. And he liked her passion. She'd spent so much of her life bottling her urges—channeling them into teaching, into gardening, into fitness.

She studied Aaron's back muscles highlighted against a

dark tee. Her nipples began to tighten. For a moment, she'd forgotten the man was gay. Wasn't that a hoot? Her ex thought of her as cold, too mechanical in bed. And here she was responding to a gay man. She knew now that Barry hadn't known how to prepare a woman for loving. He'd only cared about getting off. And they'd managed that for too many years.

Aaron clearly had the patience and skill to prepare a lover. Ellen looked quickly away and busied herself with checking the cameras. She wouldn't allow herself to be jealous of Aaron's male lovers.

Making small talk with the students as they arrived, Aaron kept an eye on his assistant. He couldn't begin to describe the relief he'd felt when she walked into the room. He'd spent much of the weekend wondering if she'd already fled back to her prairie. She wasn't the only woman who could fulfill his image of the prairie woman, but he hadn't found another one yet. And he did rather like her mood swings. A lot of guys didn't like being around women with such changing emotions. But for him, such a woman kept him on his toes. This one had completely unbalanced him in front of the Caillebotte. Was she aware of it? She'd seemed quite contrite this morning. She probably would've done most anything he'd asked.

He grinned as she joined a couple students in conversation. She'd be doing what he asked, but not out of a sense of contriteness. She had the passion of a zealot. Hadn't anyone helped her direct that passion to the pleasures of sex?

He glanced at the door and waved at Tina as she entered dressed in a white robe and carrying her fans. It was time to introduce his class to another photo genre. Ellen's mouth parted slightly as she took in the day's model. Yes, it was also time for his assistant to stoke her subconscious yearning for a new playmate.

He hadn't been at all surprised at the Institute to see Tina offering Ellen a shoulder to cry on. Ellen's outburst over *Nude on a Couch* provided a propitious entrée for Tina. By the time they'd caught up with the group, Ellen had been clutching Tina's hand like it was a lifeline.

If Tina had tried, she probably could've coaxed Ellen into going home with her. He peeked at his assistant. Given the look of confusion on her face, she was probably still warring with emotions she might not have yet realized or named. Tina had kept herself in check, knowing that he wanted to capture her seduction of Ellen through the lens of a camera.

"Okay, class. Why don't you sit down, and let's get started? This morning Tina is joining us. She will be posing for us in the nude." He grinned as several students fidgeted. Ellen sat up ramrod straight. "You may have been wondering, but I'm not going to ask any of you to pose naked. We have too much to try to accomplish in a four-week course to add that kind of modeling. It takes time to become an accomplished model of any sort. To be a nude model requires an amazing amount of confidence and creativity. If you'd like to pursue that venue for yourself, you might want to enroll in a full-length course we offer on modeling for photography, or," he grinned at Ellen, "you might want to apply to be my assistant for one of the upcoming quarters. As you know, that position is already filled for the entire summer by Ellen."

All heads turned to look at Ellen, whose cheeks had suddenly turned red.

"Now then. Ellen and I have introduced you to the basics of the cameras you'll be using today. You've done some photos of each other. This will be a little different. We'll have a professional model who will be switching her poses. Usually, the model works under the direction of the photographer.

Because this is a class, we have multiple photographers, and since Tina is the one with the experience, she will do what feels right for her. In other words, you won't be able to take all day to set up a photo. This won't be like trying to take a photo finish of a horse race, but there will be movement.

"When we're finished here, we'll go to the darkroom to see what you've got. Ellen and I will each work with half of you. What I'd like you to do is begin to identify three photos that you'll eventually present to the class — a small portfolio, if you will. It may take several trips back to the darkroom before you're satisfied that you have what you want.

"Remember, photography is a process. It's not about either-or. It's about engagement. Think of your result as a continuum that has no end. Okay, I'm going to have you each working with cameras mounted on tripods, including one for Ellen."

"This has two purposes. If you were working with free-held cameras, you'd likely get in each other's way. And this way, when you actually present your portfolios to the group, replication is rather unlikely, given your different angles. Again, keep in mind process, continuum, infinity." He narrowed his eyes at Ellen. "There are no limits to creativity.

"Go ahead, Tina. We're all in your hands."

Ellen stretched her neck muscles, trying to reduce the strain. Tina had beamed her a warm smile as soon as she'd strolled into the room. And that was what she'd done — she'd strolled. Clearly, she knew she had the group's attention. No one would be nodding off during this class.

Ellen had tried to listen to Aaron, but she'd had to struggle to not keep her focus locked on Tina. And now Tina was moving to the stool — her workbench.

She never spoke a word. She half perched on the stool and

raised her arms above her head with a fan in each hand, then held that pose and pouted at the class.

"Remember to look through your cameras," Aaron said. "This isn't a strip show."

Ellen gasped and ducked behind her camera. By the time she had Tina in focus, Tina had placed the fans in one hand by her side, and her other hand was tucked in under her robe, probably covering a breast. Ellen swallowed as she heard cameras clicking around her. Tina smiled at her as she snapped a picture.

Ellen tried to breathe as Tina worked through a series of poses showing leg, lifting her long black hair above her head, sliding a hand suggestively under the robe and up a thigh.

Tina's eyes sparkled. She stuck her tongue out at the group before turning to face away from them. Slowly the robe slid down to her waist. Tina held that pose as cameras clicked, and then the robe fell to the floor.

Ellen inhaled sharply as Tina bent over the stool, showing off a tight rump and sculpted thighs and legs. Before she could focus, Tina had moved a fan to shield her butt from view. There was a groan from the class.

"Sometimes subtle is more erotic," Aaron pointed out. "And sometimes not."

Tina turned around to face the group with the fan hiding her loins. Her long hair hid one breast. The other stood free and open to view. Its nipple stood at attention. Tina teased it with a strand of hair. Ellen focused her lens on the nipple until it nearly filled her viewfinder.

"Goodness," she muttered under her breath. It was as if the nipple winked at her. It was still tightening. Did that fleshy nodule know it had her entire attention? She clicked off several shots. Her own nipples were straining.

"You doing okay?"

She didn't trust herself to take her attention off the camera to look at Aaron. "I'm fine," she muttered, ignoring his hand on the rise of her rump.

He moved on to one of the students, and she redirected her full attention back to Tina, who had flipped her hair over her shoulder to reveal the second breast. Tina grinned as she lightly pinched that nipple. Ellen blinked. Did everyone in the room believe that Tina was only looking at them? She moved often, giving them different angles to work with. She turned and looked back over a shoulder at Ellen.

At last, Tina stood. Maybe they were done and they all could breathe again. Adroitly, Tina raised the fan from her loins, concealing her breast.

Ellen gulped, trying to keep her eyes open. Tina was bare. She'd never seen a bare vulva—hell, she'd seldom seen any vulva.

"Remember, you're photographers, guys," Aaron reminded. "Take pictures."

Ellen nodded. She took a couple pics before focusing in on Tina's vulva. Jesus. Had Tina's clit been exposed all that time? Ellen shook her head. She rarely creamed anymore, but she was now. She'd never done so thinking about another woman's pussy, though. She squinted. Tina's vulva began to glisten.

Cripes, it wouldn't take much for Tina to orgasm. Was she going to touch herself? Ellen swallowed hard and blew air through her nose. Did everyone in the room want to help Tina?

Ellen refocused her lens for a full-body view. Tina shook with laughter. She pouted and tipped her chin. "Later," she said softly, then put down the fan, donned her robe and quietly left the room.

Had she spoken to the group, or to Ellen?

Exhausted, Ellen backed away from the tripod and plopped down. She glanced around the room. Everyone looked like they'd just been hammered. Thankfully, she wasn't alone. Maybe Tina had been playing to the whole group without singling her out.

"Okay," Aaron said with a trace of humor. "That's probably enough for camera work. You may want to take some time to collect yourselves before going to the darkroom. The relationship between a model and the photographer can be very intense. Just as with a painter. I'm sure Tina is as exhausted as you are. Let's say we'll meet in the darkrooms in an hour."

Ellen gathered her stuff, hoping she could still put one foot in front of the other. She looked up to see Aaron eyeing her curiously.

"Looked like you got into being behind the camera. You want to talk about it?"

She shook her head. "Not now." She glanced away. "I really have to go to the bathroom."

His laugh came quick. "I won't keep you, then. Meet me at my office tomorrow afternoon at two. We'll give you more opportunity for working in front of the camera. Okay?"

She nodded and scampered out of the room to avoid any further questioning.

Would she ever get any sleep before going back to South Dakota? It was past midnight. She closed her eyes to try again. Like so many times before, the image of Tina's elegantly bare vulva emerging before her eyes in the fixing tray of the darkroom gradually reappeared to keep away sleep.

She couldn't decide which was more erotic—peering at Tina through the lens of the camera, or watching her come to life square inch by square inch in the darkroom. Ellen exhaled through tightly compressed lips. She'd always been a sound sleeper. She'd never been bothered by unwanted images or by erotic dreams.

She had concluded that Tina had not been playing to her

specifically, but that the personal connection was part of the repertoire of a superior model. There were times when she forgot Tina was happily married.

That left her with her gay instructor. What was he expecting tomorrow? She hadn't missed his jibe that his assistants, unlike his students, were expected to want to learn about nude modeling.

She groaned. That wasn't in the contract or the description of responsibilities, though there had been considerable allusion to hands-on experience. Things were escalating fast — maybe she'd better get back on birth control, just in case. Who knew what might happen next? Maybe she'd have stories to share with Angie after all.

She shivered. She felt like she'd been half turned on ever since she began at the academy. Was that why she was almost looking forward to what Aaron Brewster would want from her next? She smiled into a pillow. Would tomorrow be the day he posed for her?

"Feel free to examine the photos more closely," Aaron said, watching his assistant as she wet her lips and moved nearer to the private studio wall where he'd hung a series of black and white close-up photos of pussies. Below that row was a similar series featuring cocks.

"Amazing," she whispered, leaning closer to a photo of very full vulva lips. Ellen peered at the photo.

Did she recognize that as Tina? "You do seem to be more interested in the pussy photos than in the cocks."

She gave him a curious look. The corner of her mouth turned up slightly. "I'm more familiar with cocks than I am with pussies." She cast her gaze back at the photos. "I had no idea they came in so many shapes and sizes. I knew penises varied some. But some of these vulvas are small, like rosebuds, and others gape. Some are puffy and some not. Some glisten like . . ." She shook her head and didn't complete that thought. "And some don't even show a hint of a clit, while others are engorged but covered. And then" — she returned to the photo of Tina—"there is one in full bloom. It's odd to look only at sex organs. I wouldn't think this would be particularly erotic. And then there are the differences in hairlines, and some are entirely bare."

"Like Tina," he interjected.

She nodded and moved on to another row of pictures of head shots—women and men. She stood back and studied them intently. He knew when the subject matter began to dawn on her. Her shoulders tightened and then relaxed.

She turned her head to look at him. "You really are into this from an art perspective. Those men and women are faking orgasms for you, aren't they?"

He shook his head. "I'd never settle for anything fake."

She stared back at the photos. Her hand came to her mouth but couldn't smother her giggle. "Oh my God, they're having . . ." She peeked at him. "They're actually having orgasms."

"Absolutely."

"Incredible. When did you finish this work?"

"It's not finished. It's a work in progress. This series is another project where I'll need your assistance."

"Me?"

He ignored her squeak. "That's right. After we finish the current seminar, we'll devote our full time to this series, the prairie woman series, and other things."

"Other things?" She shook her head. "Is there a market for this art?"

"You'd be surprised. And sometimes I multi-task."

She frowned.

He shrugged his shoulders. "Every artist probably has to

do something over and above to sell his or her art. I have some customers who want to pose for sexy photos. Some couples want to have pictures taken while they're engaged in various sex acts."

"That's how you get the pictures of orgasms? Why in the world would people want those kinds of pictures?"

"That's one way I get pictures of folks climaxing. And my customers prefer to have a professional job. I don't know exactly what they all do with the photos. I know some hang them in their bedrooms. And some use them for advertising."

"Advertising?"

"Swingers like to know what they're getting before identifying themselves directly."

"Swingers?"

He grinned. "You do know what swingers are about?"

"I didn't come from another planet." She glanced back at the photos. "But I never realized people actually advertised or would want their pictures taken while . . ."

"Fucking, I believe, is the word you're searching for. Maybe we should head across the hall to the first sitting room." He squeezed her arm to get her to move. "I'm glad you wore the same outfit as the first time. That long calico skirt is perfect. One of these days we'll want to try some different wardrobes, but we have more to do with this one. Oh, I've asked Tina to join us."

"Tina?" Her eyes widened.

He nodded. "As you're already finding out, it's hard for a photographer to pay attention to everything at once. She'll be assisting us with the prairie woman project. Is that okay with you?"

She dipped her chin. "Why wouldn't it be?"

"Oh look, a real spinning wheel," Ellen squealed as soon as

she entered the room. She waved briefly at Tina, who stood by in jeans and tee, then she dashed to the wheel. Rubbing her fingers over the wheel and the seat, she couldn't stop bubbling. "This is so much like my great-great-grandmother's. My mother has the wheel, and it will be mine someday. It is so lovely."

"I didn't know you came from original pioneers," Aaron said, working on the tripod and camera. "I found the spinning wheel over the weekend. I thought it might work for our project."

"It's perfect." She grinned back at him. "I can do some spinning, if you like. I do know how."

He shook his head. "That won't be necessary, at least not today. Why don't you kick off those sandals and let Tina get you in position?"

Self-consciously, she kicked her sandals aside and peered at Tina. "Hi, I didn't mean to ignore you."

"No problem. It's always good to see a model excited about her props."

"Let's try a couple simple shots with Ellen standing behind the wheel."

Ellen let Tina guide her by the hand. Soon she was standing behind the wheel.

"Why don't we have a hand on the wheel," Tina said, placing Ellen's hand where she wanted it. Tina looked back at Aaron.

"That's a good start."

Tina stepped away, and the camera clicked. Ellen swallowed, trying to remember to breathe normally. It seemed like she had a hard time breathing, no matter which side of the camera she stood on.

After several tripod and free-held shots, Aaron glanced at Tina. "Let's make this prairie woman a little more provocative."

"That's what I thought was needed, too," Tina said, stepping back to her.

Tina's smile warmed Ellen. "What do you want me to do?"

"Just hold onto the wheel. Let's open some buttons on this blouse to give more hint of your beautiful cleavage."

Ellen nodded and focused on Tina's skilled fingers as she undid three buttons.

Tina parted the blouse, grazing each breast with the backs of her hands. "I'm glad you didn't wear a bra. They only get in the way at photo shoots."

"That's what Aaron said the last time."

Again, Tina stepped away, and Aaron took more shots.

Struggling not to tremble, Ellen tried to smile. Were they nearly finished? She wet her lips. She hoped not.

"Unbutton the rest of the blouse and bare one boob," he said to Tina.

Tina stepped forward and reached for the next button. She paused as if seeking permission.

Ellen inhaled, then nodded.

Tina beamed a smile and undid the button. She took a half step back before parting the blouse to display Ellen's left breast.

"You have gorgeous tits. Isn't that beautiful, Aaron?"

Aaron didn't speak. He'd been taking free-held shots throughout. Ellen knew he'd been trying to capture her changing facial expressions as Tina exposed her to both of them.

"That nipple could use a little attention." Tina pursed her lips. "May I?"

Ellen remembered how Aaron had pinched her nipples to get them fully aroused. She nodded at Tina.

Tina leaned forward and drew the nipple and part of Ellen's breast into her mouth and began to suckle.

"I didn't know you meant . . ." Ellen whimpered. No one

had ever suckled her breast so deliciously. She tapped Tina's shoulder lightly before grabbing her and pulling her closer. Her eyes widened — Aaron was snapping more pictures. She didn't care. Tina had her climbing a wall of ecstasy. That was all that mattered.

Ellen gulped for air and began rocking back and forth on her heels. She grabbed Tina's hand and pushed it down to her crotch. A muffled sound came from her breast as Tina worked her hand up under her skirt to caress her panty-clad vulva.

"Oh my God," Ellen murmured to no one in particular. "I haven't come in ages."

She bucked against the fingers sliding along her panties. She pulled Tina tighter still as the woman continued working miracles on her tit, and then she soared. "Oh, hell," she whimpered. She slammed against Tina's fingers one last time, and then she simply clung to her for support.

No one spoke. Ellen fought back from semi-darkness and let out a long slow breath. Her wet breast felt the slap of chill as Tina dropped it from her mouth and covered it with the blouse fabric. Blinking at the light, Ellen let Tina help her sit on the spinning wheel.

"You okay?" Tina asked softly.

Ellen nodded, not yet trusting her voice.

"That's probably enough for today. You look rather beat," Aaron said.

Surprised by the concern in his voice, she looked up at him. "Exquisitely beat."

"Next time," Tina said, kissing her cheek, "don't wear panties. Our prairie woman doesn't have to wear panties, does she, Aaron?"

"Of course not. If she doesn't want to."

"I won't," she said to Tina. "But I thought you were a happily married woman."

Tina laughed out loud. "Oh, I am. I'm also a happily

married bi woman."

"Oh my." She turned to Aaron. "You won't use those pictures?"

"I'll develop all of them. We'll only use what you consent to. You could sue my ass and bring down this studio if I used any without your consent."

Regaining her equilibrium, Ellen looked from Tina to Aaron. "I have a feeling this was your plan all along."

Tina smiled and Aaron shrugged.

Ellen bit her lower lip. "Surprisingly, I'm okay with this." She shook her head. "That was splendid, actually, but I'm not sure how far I'll go."

Tina slanted a finger across Ellen's mouth. "You only do what you want to do, girl."

Ellen nodded at Tina and looked back at Aaron. "Remember, I'm not posing in the nude until you've posed for me."

Tina roared with laughter. "You really do have spirit. Maybe I can show her how we sometimes have to assist guys."

"Tomorrow afternoon," Aaron groused. "I doubt our pioneer woman will be able to keep her clothes on next time. Oh, by the way, I don't want you two hooking up on the side — at least not yet."

Ellen shook her head. "I'm not ready for that." She wet her lips and looked at Tina. "I'm not sure I ever will be. Doing it in front of the camera seems so surreal. I'm not sure . . ."

Tina pressed a finger across her lips. "Don't worry about it. Just like photography, you have to trust the process. For now, let's just think about it as exploring another art form. Okay?"

Ellen nodded.

Tina quickly brushed her lips across Ellen's. "See you tomorrow." She grinned. "Who knows, maybe after you shoot Aaron, you'll be up for a little more exploring of your inner prairie woman."

When she heard the door close, Ellen sighed and glanced up at Aaron, who continued eyeing her with concern.

"You really okay?" he asked.

"I'll catch a second wind in a moment." She smiled softly. "I may find the strength to button back up." She drew the blouse over her breasts, which she hadn't realized remained fully exposed.

"Don't hurry on my account. Your breasts surpass my expectations for my prairie woman." He coughed. "Tina wasn't too much for you?"

She shook her head slightly. "You having second thoughts? You set us up."

He lifted one shoulder. "I knew she'd hit on you. I didn't know she'd move that quickly." He arched an eyebrow. "Though you did seem quite encouraging after you adjusted to her suckling your breast."

She grinned and cupped the breast that had been so thoroughly loved. The blouse fell away. "This tit is still humming, I can assure you."

Aaron reached down and covered the nipple and rising curve of the breast she held. "Yes, I can feel you humming." He jerked away and quickly retreated to his camera equipment, his neck flushing

Would she ever understand gay men? He'd seemed so unaffected by her—even by Tina seducing her. Yet brushing his fingertips over her breast had nearly sent him into a panic. She'd gotten another unexpected jolt from his touch. Maybe he sensed that and it had embarrassed him.

Partially restored, she began to button her blouse. "I need to talk to you about something."

"What now?" He gave her a sharp look. "Isn't that the language women use when they're dumping a guy?"

She shook her head. "I don't know if I'll ever understand

you. But this is about me. Seeing and touching the spinning wheel overwhelmed me with feelings and memories." She wet her lips. "I know why I overacted to *Nude on a Couch.*"

That got his attention. He came around from behind the camera and flopped down on the floor in front of her. "What about the spinning wheel?"

"The spinning wheel I grew up with first belonged to my great-great-grandmother, Clarissa Forbes."

"The woman of the prairie."

"That's right. She moved to south central South Dakota with her husband and three daughters in the spring of eighteen eighty."

"Whoa, just ahead of the harsh winter that started in the fall of eighty and didn't let up till late spring."

She nodded. "You do know your pioneer history."

"You don't have to do much research on pioneer history before learning about that particular winter. But I interrupted."

"Not a problem. And that winter was critical to my great-great-grandmother's story. Her husband had gone to Brookings between blizzards to get more supplies. He never made it back. The story is they found his bones and a few articles of clothing during the spring thaw.

"Clarissa did everything she could to keep their little homestead going and her three girls safe. Apparently, their soddy was sufficient shelter, but the few vegetables she'd planted produced little. The story is she tried several enterprises, none of which worked, and finally the following spring, she began to earn her living on her back."

Aaron gasped. "You mean?"

She nodded and swallowed hard. She hurried on, needing to complete her story. She wasn't looking for sympathy — not anymore. "The soddy wasn't that far from a small town, and the railroad had just gone in, so there were travelers of all kinds — mostly men. Again, the story that survives suggests Clarissa had some sort of working relationship with a hotel keeper. She met some of her men at that establishment. Others could be seen renting buggies and heading out to the soddy. The girls were either at school, or she'd send them out to play until she finished entertaining. And they all survived."

"Damn, she was one gutsy lady."

Ellen snickered. "True enough, but few neighbors or townspeople called her a lady. Her daughters must've received the brunt of the shame. One can only begin to imagine what they knew or felt.

"In eighteen eighty-three, Clarissa became pregnant with another daughter, to whom my family traces its roots." She pursed her lips. "We have no idea who my great-great-grandfather was."

"Jesus."

"Right. Apparently, that was the last straw for Clarissa's oldest daughter. She married at the age of sixteen and took her younger sisters to live with her. Supposedly, they soon moved to California. We have no idea what really happened to that part of the family."

"To this day?"

"Shame stretches across the generations. Annabelle, the daughter out of wedlock, passed along the spinning wheel and some quilts."

"So did Clarissa die young, remarry or what?"

"That's the funny part of the story. Not long after Annabelle was born, a woman named Hazel Washington showed up at the soddy. She came with money. The two women lived together for decades. At first the scandal was like a prairie wildfire, but apparently, it burned out. The women were written off as eccentrics involved in the woman's suffrage movement of the period. They owned one of the first brick and wood homes on that part of the prairie and had one of the very first one-horse carriages. And they supported several local charities."

"Ah, money can gloss over much. So how did Hazel make her money?"

"No one knows. Rumors were passed around that she had been part of a bank robber gang, that she'd been a madam at a Chicago whorehouse, that she'd been cast out of her wealthy family with her trust fund when it was discovered she liked women. It doesn't matter anymore and probably didn't matter much then. She became my great-great-grandmother's benefactor." She exhaled. "Not unlike Caillebotte taking on his mistress."

Aaron blinked and rotated his neck. "So seeing *Nude on a Couch* must've touched a lot of deeply held stuff for you."

She nodded. "I wasn't conscious of that in the moment, but the spinning wheel helped me connect the dots . . . yeah. I was flooded with shame for my family and with anger at those who castigated her for trying to survive."

"Damn"—Aaron stood and reached down to her and then took a step back—"and I had to throw it in your face that the model might be a working-class woman trying to put food on the table."

She shrugged. "And you may be right. No lasting harm done." Ellen stood. "I felt I owed you some sort of explanation, now that I'm sort of aware of what happened."

He gave her a quirky smile. "Thanks for telling me. You come to this bisexual possibility quite naturally."

Tucking the tails of her blouse in her skirt, Ellen winked. "Must be a recessive gene." She stepped into her sandals. "Strange, isn't it—Clarissa and Caillebotte's mistress were contemporaries. Worlds apart, but contemporaries."

"Maybe not so different. I'm glad it worked out for her."

Ellen smiled and headed for the door. "I'd like to think the mistress fared as well. Don't forget, I'll see you tomorrow in all your glory."

Aaron groaned. "How could I forget?"

CHAPTER FOUR

Fidgeting, Aaron tried to remain calm and collected. He tugged the sash of the white robe tighter about his waist. He'd posed nude often enough, but never for Ellen Jeffers. She'd struck a deal, and he'd honor it. She'd take pictures of him in his so-called glory before posing nude for him.

Dressed in denim shorts and a tee, Ellen set up the photo equipment the way she wanted it. He could see she hadn't worn a bra. He tried not to think about her being commando under those shorts.

He glanced over at Tina, who was waiting nearby. She wore a short beige skirt and orange tank top. He didn't have to wonder what she had on underneath. Nothing. She gave him a ribald wide grin. Tina enjoyed her work.

He nodded at her. This photo session was about more than meeting his end of the bargain with Ellen. They'd also be demonstrating what might be expected of her with some male models.

"I'm ready, are you?" Ellen announced.

"Anytime. What would you like first?"

"I'll begin with some shots of you in the robe. Some acclaimed photographer once told me to think in a sequence of shots, and that partially clad can be even more sexy than naked."

"Sounds like a wise man," he said with a smile. At least she listened to him some of the time.

After taking several free-held shots from several angles, Ellen returned to the tripod. "Why don't you undo that sash,

53

but leave the robe on for a bit?"

"All right." Counting to ten and trying to focus his thoughts on a favorite northern lake, Aaron began to undo the sash. His body had to cooperate for this session to work. He did everything humanly possible to ignore Ellen's appraisal.

"Oh my," she gasped. "Look at him. He looks soft. So unaffected. I want to get several shots of him flaccid," she said, already clicking the camera and refocusing for close up shots. She peeked around the camera. "Will he get hard for me?"

Aaron groaned and glanced quickly at Tina. She'd better get to work quickly, or Ellen would talk him into an erection.

Likely sensing his dilemma, Tina moved swiftly to kneel beside him. "We'll get him hard for you, Ellen." Tina bounced his balls on the flat of one hand and curled the fingers of her other hand around his shaft.

He responded immediately but kept himself in some sort of reasonable check.

"Wow!" Ellen groaned while clicking off more shots. "Do all male models require that kind of help?"

"Not all," Tina chirped. "Happily, many do."

Ellen's jaw fell. Forgetting the camera, she gawked at him. "And you expect me to do that."

He grinned. "Only if necessary. We all do whatever is necessary for our art."

"He's still only half mast." Ellen scowled. "Doesn't he get any bigger than that?"

"With the proper attention." He placed a hand at the back of Tina's head, and she quickly took him in her mouth.

"Oh my God." Ellen gulped but had the presence of mind to resume clicking off photos.

He chewed on his lip as Tina worked her miracle. He didn't attempt to stop her. She knew him well enough to know when to back off.

He concentrated more fully on Ellen as a photographer.

She surprised him with her ability to keep herself together. He'd had some assistants crumble when they began to realize what was really in store for them. Not his prairie woman. She was a woman on a mission.

"Don't make him come, Tina."

Tina dropped him from her mouth and kept a hand skimming his shaft. "I wasn't going to. I know what I'm doing. Trust me."

"Good. Why don't we have you move out of the picture? I want you, Aaron, to let the robe drop to the floor and turn so I have a profile view of this gorgeous fellow of yours."

He did as she asked.

"My, he did get big, didn't he? Don't go too far away, Tina. We may need your help again if he begins to soften. I want to take my time with this study of male rigidity."

Tina's laughter filled his ears. "You really are getting into this, girl. I'll be ready when either one of you needs my help."

"Thanks. I'm beginning to understand why the photographer needs an assistant. There's too much for one person to keep track of and do. Aaron, can you place your hand on him?"

He arched an eyebrow. "You mean on my cock?"

Her cheeks colored. She held his stare. "That's right. I want your fingers around your cock, as if you're jerking off for me."

"If that's what you want." He began stroking smoothly and then more quickly.

"No. Don't come."

He stopped and glowered at her. "What do you want?"

"I don't want to force you to come in front of me." She blew bangs off her forehead. "I'm doing a study of your cock, not of male orgasm."

"Okay. Maybe another time."

For several minutes, he let her guide him through various poses, often with Tina's help. Did she have any idea how badly he needed to come? His cock screamed for release.

"That about does it," Ellen said. "I'm almost out of film. Now what?"

Tina didn't wait for him to respond. She dropped to her knees to relieve him of pain. He held her head between both hands as she bobbed quickly up and down. His thighs burned. He swallowed hard. He failed to hold back a groan as his balls tightened, preparing for release.

He forced his eyes to remain open. Ellen gave him the oddest look before she ducked back behind the camera. He heard the clicks as he began spurting down Tina's throat. He closed his eyes.

Tina stayed with him until she had claimed everything.

Sighing with satisfaction, he backed away from Tina and reached for his robe.

Tina winked at him in the silence as he donned his robe.

"Powerful," Ellen said with awe. "I guess you're right. You will do anything for your art."

He frowned, unable to decipher what wasn't being said. He hadn't heard judgment. It was something other than that, but Ellen hadn't said everything that was on her mind. "I'm going to need a break. You two want to get back together in front of the camera later this afternoon, or do you want to wait until tomorrow?"

"This afternoon," Ellen said quickly before Tina could answer. "I'm so damn horny I could burst."

Tina laughed. "Me, too, girl. I've got plenty of time, and my husband knows where I'm at."

"Plan on being back in an hour, then." Aaron narrowed his eyes in warning. "Don't start without me."

Tina nodded.

"We wouldn't think of starting without you behind the camera." Ellen stuck her tongue out at him. "You were very photogenic and cooperative. And you're right, the world does look quite different through a camera lens. We'd better get out of here" — she shot a glance at Tina's flushed cheeks — "or we won't wait for Aaron. Or at least I won't."

"There is something to be said both for eagerness and patience." Tina took her hand. "Why don't we grab a cup of coffee and go out and soak up some sunshine?"

A few minutes later, Ellen sat next to Tina on the lawn in front of his studio. "It is so pleasant out here. I do love the sun."

"I can tell. You have a very nice tan."

"I must confess, tanning is one of my few vanities. After my divorce, I made a pledge to take care of my body, whether anyone else liked it or not. I tan in natural light when I can, but artificial works fine when I can't. And I exercise routinely."

"I try," Tina chuckled. "I noticed you didn't use the *try* word, so you must really exercise regularly."

Ellen sipped her coffee. She peeked at Tina. "How can you be comfortable walking around with that short skirt and wearing no panties?"

Tina chuckled. "So you noticed."

"How could I not, when you were going down on Aaron?"

"If anyone is looking that closely at me and catches a glimpse, then they're only seeing what they fantasized about seeing. So maybe fantasies can come true."

"You do have a gorgeous pussy. You know" — Ellen giggled — "I've studied it for hours in the darkroom. I'd recognize it anywhere."

"Really? Did you recognize it on the wall in Aaron's office?"

"Of course I did. It was the last photo in the row."

"That's right. Maybe yours will hang next to mine. Wouldn't that be right?"

Ellen closed her fingers around Tina's. "I never said I'd allow such pictures to be taken or exhibited."

"But very few people can identify a woman from a picture of her pussy."

"True enough. Unless they're connoisseurs. We'll have to wait and see. But if I do consent, I definitely want to hang next to you."

"I'm pleased."

"So your husband really knows what you do at the academy?"

"Of course he does. We don't keep secrets, at least not those kind."

"Does he know about me?"

"Uh-huh. He'd like to meet you sometime, but not until you and I get much better acquainted."

"I am looking forward to that." Ellen squeezed Tina's thigh.

"Careful, girl. Maybe we'd better head back inside before you get us arrested."

"What?" Ellen stared down at her hand. "Oh. I didn't realize what I was doing."

"So did the Aaron shoot meet your expectations?"

"That, and much more." She shuddered. "I'm not sure I'll be able to assist like you did."

"Don't worry about that. If the need is there, you'll probably respond appropriately. If not, it's not like the entire world is going to cave in around you."

"But I wouldn't be living up to Aaron's expectations."

Tina gave her a curious look. "And that's important to you."

"It is. I've never had an employer complain about my work."

Tina rose to her knees and then to her feet. She reached down to help Ellen stand. "You are a breath of fresh air, Ellen

Jeffers. Aaron may want to bring you on staff full-time."

Feeling her cheeks warm, Ellen shook her head. "Not a chance. I'm a small-town South Dakota girl. I have a classroom of thirty some third graders waiting for me come fall. Besides, I don't even think Aaron likes me."

Tina shook her head. "I admit Aaron can be moody and unpredictable, but I think you challenge him in ways he's not accustomed to. That doesn't mean he doesn't like you. And it's getting more difficult by the day for me to imagine you as an elementary school teacher. Don't you know you're exploring a new way of being, girl? Do you really think you're going to be able to crawl back into your former self when the summer is done? That none of this matters?"

"Everything matters," Ellen countered. "I know that, but I'm not going through some sort of metamorphosis." She smirked. "Though I might have to think about coming back next summer, if there's an opening."

Tina tugged on her hand, leading them back into the building. "I'm wagering there'll be an opening for you, if you want it."

Ellen smiled coquettishly at the camera. They'd taken her to Aaron's studio B, which was set up like a bedroom, with a bed, a couple easy chairs, a couch, dressers, and several mirrors. She'd wondered where couples went when they wanted lovemaking pictures. She hadn't been asked to assist with any of those yet.

She sat at the foot of the bed, dressed only in her calico skirt. Since this was a continuation of a series, they'd agreed to dispense with her blouse immediately. Though Ellen had changed into her prairie woman outfit, Tina still had on her tank top and beige mini.

Aaron worked calmly behind the camera, making suggestions now and then, but more and more he let her exercise some control over her posing. He'd given her a sheaf of dried wheat stems which she held so she could rub her chin against the seed pods.

"Excellent," Aaron crooned. "Spending time on this side of the camera also makes you more natural when you're in front of it."

"Speaking of natural," she said, giving Tina a half smile, "aren't we in studio B for you and me to get to know each other a little more naturally?" She set the wheat sheaf aside and held out her arms in invitation.

"And you don't think you're going through a metamorphosis?" Tina came to stand before her.

"A little one, maybe." Ellen took Tina's hand and brought it to a breast. Tina lowered her head, and Ellen wrapped her other hand around the back of Tina's head, drawing her lower until their lips met. Ellen drew air through her nose as she settled into the kiss — their first kiss.

Her eyes fluttered when she saw Aaron, who had moved in for a close-up. Tina's tongue parted her lips to explore her mouth. Ellen chuckled and suckled the delightful intruder.

She drew back to peck at the corners of Tina's mouth as she worked her hands under the orange tank top. Her heart skipped a beat as her fingers curved over a breast.

"Suckle me, girl," Tina pleaded, pulling her tank up over her breasts.

"I'd love to." Ellen ducked her head to a breast, laved it, and then slowly took some in her mouth.

"Jesus. You sure you haven't done this before?"

Ellen shook her head, thrilled with Tina's response. She closed her eyes and reveled in the texture of nipple and tit. So firm, and yet so soft. She didn't want to stop. She wanted — she needed more. To hell with Aaron's sense for stages. She wasn't about to wait for him to set up yet another scene. Reluctantly, she pulled away from the breast and silently pleaded with Tina. Her eyes had to be the size of quarters.

Tina's eyes shone. "I'll guide you, trust me."

Tina stood and tugged the tank over her head. Her hands dropped to her waist to undo the mini. Tina's bare pussy was only a foot or so away — Ellen swallowed hard.

Tina leaned closer and lifted the calico skirt above Ellen's waist. "Oh, my," Tina purred, "look at this, Aaron. Isn't she beautiful? Neatly trimmed and so puffy, so eager for me. Right?"

Ellen nodded. "I haven't gotten the nerve to shave it bare like yours."

"I'll help you, if you want. Why don't we let Aaron get a couple close-ups of this pussy untouched by a woman? And then later, after I've fully sated you, you might want him to take some follow-up shots."

Ellen looked at Aaron, who hovered over Tina's shoulder. "Hurry."

Chuckling, Aaron began a quick sequence of shots. "The lady doesn't like to wait."

She ignored his comment by focusing on Tina. Somehow the camera gave her permission to dig into her character. She wasn't questioning that. Maybe someday she'd explain it.

"Can you part her labia for me? Just a little."

"I'd be happy to," Tina said. "And she is so primed. Why don't you lean back with your hands on the bed to give us a better angle?"

Us? Ellen nodded and leaned back so her hands supported her weight, and Tina spread her knees further apart. She must be gaping. Aaron seemed in his element as he chewed on his lower lip and snapped off more shots.

"You are so open for us." Tina dragged a finger down the parted lips. "So wet."

Ellen gulped as a finger entered her, slowly but surely searching her depths. She whimpered, arching against the finger.

"So ready. You want a quick one?"

"Please. Don't leave me like this." Ellen shuddered. When had she become so brazen? And then she closed her eyes and focused her entire being on that single digit working wonders in her channel. Quick? More like instantaneous, electrifying. She lurched forward to hug Tina as the finger dove in over and over until Ellen lost track of it and everything else but her soaring to the far reaches of space.

When she finally cracked an eye open, she saw Tina kneeling before her, beaming brilliantly. Aaron stood behind her with camera in hand. He, too, had a strange look of satisfaction. Was he getting off vicariously watching? Ellen blinked. That hardly mattered.

She held out a hand to Tina. "I don't want to ignore you."

"I do appreciate a thoughtful lover." Tina rose to her feet and inched closer, lowering Ellen's hand to her vulva.

"So soft," Ellen murmured.

"You can take your time with me later. Right now, I need you inside me."

Tina's urgency fired every cell in Ellen's body as she allowed Tina to help her find the portal through which she could satisfy her lover.

She held her breath as she sank her finger into Tina's heat.

"Yes, that's what I need." Tina flexed her hips, driving her channel along Ellen's finger, taking it deeper with each stroke. "That's right, girl, join me. Fuck me. I've been looking forward to this since that day at the Minneapolis Institute. Put in another finger."

Ellen groaned and slid another finger in beside the first one.

Tina locked gazes with her, then bit down on her lip and lurched as Ellen tried to keep pace with her.

"Close, so close. Dig. Dig. That's it. Don't stop. Oh,

Aaron—this so good. Thank you. Thank you. Both of you. Scoot back on the bed, girl. I can't stand up much longer. No, don't pull out of me."

Ellen did her best to scramble back across the bed without dislodging her fingers. Tina rocked against them a few more times before she lifted off them.

"We're going for a ride, Ellen. You and me." Tina's nostrils flared. "I want to take my time to taste you, but that'll have to wait. You still have me clinging to a cliff."

"What do you want me to do?"

"Taste me," Tina said, raising Ellen's caked fingers to Ellen's mouth. "There will be more later. Much more."

Ellen curled her tongue around her fingers, delighting in Tina's taste and scent that filled her nostrils. More. Why not now? She glanced down as Tina dragged a finger along her slit and made a show of tasting her.

"She's a delicacy," Tina whispered, lowering her body to settle atop Ellen. "Now for that ride I promised. Raise your knees. That's right."

"Oh my God," Ellen whimpered as Tina ground her bare pussy over and across hers.

Tina paused to kiss her open mouth. Ellen wrapped her legs around Tina's buttocks.

"You like?"

Ellen nodded, tapping Tina's rear with her heel, trying to get her to move.

Tina chuckled. "I'll get there. You are so wonderfully expressive when you want something and when you come." Tina pecked her lips. "You don't have to be quiet when you come. I like to hear my partner squeal and scream. Understand?"

"Yes," Ellen screeched. "Ride me some more. Please."

"I also appreciate a lover who tells me what she wants." Tina brushed her breasts across Ellen's and then slowly grazed their pussies.

Ellen's eyes sprang wide as Tina added more pressure and quickened the pace.

"Tell me," Tina demanded. "What's happening for you?"

Between gulps of air, Ellen muttered, "You're setting me on fire down there."

"Are we going to go up in flames?"

"Yes," Ellen squealed, wrapping her arms tight around Tina's shoulders. "Oh. Oh." She pounded her heels against Tina's rear. "Fuck me, Tina. I can't hold on."

"Don't try. Let go. If you thought that was fire . . ."

"Oh my God, you're riding my clit."

"Shout it out, girl. I'll come with you."

Ellen tossed her head from side to side. "Almost," she screeched. She dropped her feet to the bed and let Tina do all the work. She arched her back. "I'm coming," she yelled. "So hard. Come with me."

"I am." Tina giggled near her ear.

Tina's weight crushed her to the bed, but Ellen didn't mind one bit. Feeling giddy, giggling in turn, she kissed Tina's open mouth. Their loins continued doing their own push and pull game, creating a sticky bond of promise. Too bad Aaron wasn't into women—between the two of them, they likely had enough juices to go around.

Aaron! Ellen broke off the kiss to glance toward the tripod.

He looked up and nodded at her as he put away camera equipment. "Welcome to our world. You two were really in sync." He inhaled deeply through his nose. "I've got some super pics." He raised his palm to stop her protest. "We'll talk about those later. Enough work for one day. I'll leave you guys alone. Take your time. The janitorial crew doesn't come in the building until after midnight."

With effort, Ellen raised her hand to return his wave. Suddenly she was alone with a naked woman in her arms.

Tina lifted her head. "We are going to have so much fun. I believe it's a shame to let good pussy juice go to waste."

Ellen watched Tina's head lower and felt her lips trace a wet trail down her ribcage and abs until they settled over her vulva. "Jesus, I don't know how much more I can take. No. Don't stop." She wrapped her legs around Tina's back, ignoring the muffled laughter coming from her loins.

Tina burrowed her tongue into Ellen's channel, coaxing yet one more orgasm. It was already building.

Ellen turned her head and caught a glimpse of the empty tripod. She tugged on her nipples and arched against Tina's tongue. She no longer needed to use a camera as a ruse to love a woman. Was that why Aaron had left?

CHAPTER FIVE

Scrutinizing the drying photos closely later in the week, Aaron grinned at the image of Tina's finger entering Ellen. He'd managed a couple close-ups and a couple full-length shots before he'd focused in on Ellen's face as Tina brought his prairie woman to overflowing.

Tina was damn good, but Ellen was also very receptive. In some of the pics, her mouth contorted as if she were trying to strain her climax through a tiny sieve. In another, her mouth fell agape as she peaked. In the last photo, she'd opened her eyes and stared dreamily at him, exhibiting not one bit of embarrassment. She struck him as a woman who had quite pleasantly surprised herself.

Tina was right, and he had the evidence in black and white — Ellen could be incredibly expressive. He smiled grimly, remembering how Tina had encouraged Ellen to be more demonstrative with her sounds. He examined the photos of the two women grinding against each other. Ellen's darker tan showed up nicely in contrast to Tina's more pale skin. He doubted Tina had ever spent much time trying to get a tan. The last photo was one in which Ellen was indeed howling praise to the gods.

That was when he'd decided he'd had enough and begun gathering his stuff. A guy could only take so much torture. He couldn't even remember for sure anymore why he thought it necessary to avoid fucking his assistant senseless. It'd had something to do with her response to the Caillebotte painting. He was supposed to be teaching her a lesson. He peered at the drying photos. It looked like she was having all the fun—she and Tina.

From some of Ellen's reactions, he was pretty sure she thought he was gay. That bought him time. He wasn't certain he wanted more time, but he had it.

She was in the darkroom next door, developing some of her own photos. They could've worked side by side, but he hadn't wanted the distraction. Ellen Jeffers was indeed becoming a distraction. He straightened his arousal. A big-time distraction.

The darkroom door opened and shut softly. He hadn't anticipated she'd drop by uninvited—but a quick glance over his shoulder told him it was Tina. "Oh, it's you."

"I saw the outside light was off so figured it was okay to come in."

"It's safe."

"Sounded like you were expecting someone else."

"Nope. What do you think of these pics?"

Tina whistled softly. "Very artful and tasteful. That first afternoon seems so long ago, and yet it's only been three days. Ellen can be surprisingly seductive, don't you think?"

"I've noticed."

"That's a stunning photo from yesterday with her on her back teasing the camera framed by her feet. It's almost like her head is resting on her pelvic bone. But look at that pussy slit separating, and even her asshole is slightly open. You've done a very good job capturing her invitation."

"Umm." He saw no need to tell Tina that one was his favorite pic. He hadn't gotten around to printing the others from that sheet. That single pic had attracted his attention, and he'd played with it in various intensities, dodging, and sizes. The one drying was the only one he'd kept. He planned on framing it for his private collection. It was rare to get a photo that pulsated with such vivid invitation.

"Do you suppose that's a virgin asshole?"

He looked sharply at Tina, who grinned. He'd asked himself the same question and assumed the same response. And he had little doubt about the cock best suited to test out that virginal channel. Said cock strained against fabric as he stared at his favorite photo of the collection.

"I was her first woman," Tina continued in a throaty tone. "Maybe I should save her ass for someone else."

"How magnanimous of you."

Tina leaned closer to one of the earlier photos of her finger fucking Ellen. "She looks so serene. You sure have a feel for anticipating how a woman spirals toward climax. I don't know how you do that."

"You should know that's a forte of mine."

Tina curled her fingers around his erection. "In the flesh as well as through a camera. Thank goodness."

Aaron arched against her fingers. It had been too long. And he'd been in nearly a constant state of arousal since Tina parted Ellen's labia for him. They'd been going at it for three days, and neither woman seemed at all concerned about his wellbeing.

Tina tugged on his jeans zipper. He did nothing to stop her from freeing his erection. This wouldn't be the first time they'd fucked in the darkroom. He doubted it would be the last.

He groaned as she rubbed his cock head with her thumb. He let her lead him by his cock as she backed toward the sink.

Deftly, she lifted her mini and widened her stance, pulling his cock forward until she could run it up and down between her wet pussy folds. She placed its head at her entryway and stood on her toes, easing it in with one hand and grabbing his waist with the other, helping him seat himself fully in her heat.

"Damn, you're always so hot."

"Umm," Tina purred in his ear. "That's nice. Wait a moment. I'm still adjusting to you." She nibbled on his ear. "I believe Ellen may have turned up my temperature a degree or two."

"I don't doubt that."

She placed both hands on his hips and wiggled. "Now, what are you going to do about Ellen?"

"What? You want to talk about Ellen with me buried in you?"

"I can't think of a better time. Wouldn't you like to be up to the hilt in Ellen's pussy? Or maybe pushing into her puckering asshole for the first time?"

He remained quiet. He thought he could hear both their hearts beating.

"Ellen may not see you lusting for her, but I know your little tricks at trying to stay in control. You hardly even look at me. You're so focused on your assistant." Tina clucked in his ear. "I should back off you and leave you with blue balls."

He cringed and dug his fingernails into her backside.

"But I won't. I'm a nice girl. And I do like to share. But it's difficult to share if you're not willing to join in." She backed off his cock a few inches only to take him back in. "What's your hang-up, Aaron? I've never seen you this gun-shy around a woman."

He shrugged, backing out and driving back into Tina's channel. Her gasp and her fingernails raking his back told him she wasn't nearly as unaffected as she'd like him to believe. "Ellen's different," he grunted. "She's not like us."

"I think she's proving you wrong. And with your encouragement, I might add."

He kissed her nose. "You see too much."

"I've had a good visual teacher."

"At first, I wanted her to know she wasn't so far above Caillebotte's mistress."

"None of us are." Tina clutched his ass and slammed against his loins, nearly knocking him off balance. She made a guttural sound and eased back, establishing a slower pace gliding over his cock. "So, now what? She's demonstrated she has the capacity to love a woman. What are you afraid of? And you do, at times, look afraid."

Suddenly Tina stopped moving. She grabbed his shoulders and stared at him hard. And then she started to laugh. "You're afraid she could be the serious one. That's why you're so distant, so hesitant." She squeezed his cock with her inner muscles before resuming her pace.

"Jesus, can't we talk about anything else? Why do we even have to talk?" He placed his hands under her butt and hoisted her away from the sink. She locked her ankles behind his back and held on tight as he began to thrust purposely, taking them both toward the climax he needed desperately.

"I feel you expanding," Tina howled. "Fill me, big guy."

He rocked on the balls of his feet on automatic pilot as he began to explode. "I am."

"Christ, you're good," Tina whimpered into his ear. "You're going to be wonderful for Ellen. She needs a man like you, and you need a woman like her."

Gasping for air, Aaron let Tina slide down his frame until her feet found the floor. Unceremoniously, he withdrew his cock. "Why can't you leave Ellen out of this? It's just the two of us."

Tina shook her head. "It's never just the two of us, Aaron, and you know it. Whether my husband is with us in the flesh or not, he is with us. And whether you like it or not, Ellen was with us just now and would've been whether we named her or not. She's part of our ménage — at least for a while. You may not like it, but you'll have to decide what to do with Ellen Jeffers.

"And" — she tucked his limp cock in his shorts and pulled

his zipper up—"you won't be getting any more of this from me unless Ellen is at least watching."

"That's blackmail!"

"Call it what you want," Tina chirped, kissing his chin. "That's the way it will be. She doesn't even think you like her." She scowled at him. "She must think you're gay."

"She can think what she wants."

"Don't be a stubborn ass," Tina huffed. "I should've left you hanging." She smoothed out her short skirt and stalked out of the darkroom.

So much for Ellen not joining him in the darkroom. She had, but she didn't even know it.

Feeling totally exhilarated, Ellen delighted in watching the image of Aaron's cock emerging from the solution. It started fuzzy, and then faint outlines appeared, and then gradually she could discern the ridges and veins of the handsome specimen. She'd never spent so much time examining a cock—not even her ex-husband's.

She'd gone back to the negatives several times just to re-experience that subtle appearance in the tray. She realized she'd taken shots from most every conceivable angle with one exception. There was no direct head-on shot. She didn't have pics of the tip of his cock head with its slit.

She giggled. She'd have to get that before her study of male rigidity was complete. How different might it look if Aaron pulled back on its shaft? Or if Tina did? Or if she did? Would it open and close like her labia had? Was it possible for her to skim his cock and take a picture at the same time? Of course it was. That was why the cameras had timers, or maybe attaching an extension to the shutter would meet her requirements better. Then she wouldn't have to hurry the pose.

Noises from the darkroom next door threatened her

concentration. Aaron must've dropped something.

Carefully, she started to hang up her latest photos next to some of the full-body shots that were already dry. She still couldn't get over how Aaron had stayed so flaccid until Tina began to skim her fingers over his shaft. Ellen blinked at the first photo of his fully erect rod. She started to laugh. Aaron's rod. She couldn't quite remember the biblical reference to Aaron's rod, but she knew there was one. Maybe she should check with her mother.

She ran her tongue around her cheek, remembering Tina finishing Aaron off at the end of their session. She couldn't think of a reason why gay men wouldn't get blue balls, too. Tina had done the humanitarian thing.

Would she have the courage and compassion to do the same if needed?

"Thanks again for bringing me to this funky place. I like it. We don't have anything close to this in Graystaff." Ellen smiled down at her plate. "I haven't gotten out much at all this summer."

Aaron winced. "Guess our work is crimping your style — sorry about that. But I thought wrapping up the seminar deserved some sort of celebration."

"Now we can devote full attention to the studio."

"That's right."

"So, I assume there'll be more nipples to pinch and more cocks to heft." She didn't miss the slight rush of color to his cheeks. Smiling, she continued, "I'm quite amazed at how detached I've become about that. But like you say, whatever it takes for the art."

"You do seem to be enjoying your studio work."

"Oh, I am." She pursed her lips. She hardly had to conceal her delight with her work from Aaron. He'd documented it thoroughly. She'd seen some of the prints. He was very good.

Some of the expressions he'd caught had even surprised her. She doubted any photographer could catch the full extent of her elation at orgasm, but Aaron was close.

She smiled brightly. "You do have a commitment to authenticity that I've grown to appreciate."

He looked genuinely pleased. "I hoped you might. But then you were pretty quick at figuring out the photos on my office wall weren't faked. Are you ready to release any of your photos?"

She shrugged. "I'd be booted out of school if any of those ever got back to my school board." She chuckled. "But I guess I'm vain enough to want to be on your wall. You may hang a pussy shot next to Tina's. Pussy only."

"Absolutely. I'll take care of it. Thanks. You have a very photogenic pussy and ass."

Ellen sipped her after-dinner coffee before responding. "Most women would probably be offended that you didn't say their faces are photogenic, but I've come to appreciate what you mean. I never thought much about the shape and look of pussies and assholes until I met you."

"Or cocks, apparently."

"Or cocks," she echoed, smiling broadly. "Which reminds me. I want another photo session with your cock fairly soon. I missed some possibilities that first sitting."

"Understandable," Aaron said. "We often don't know what we have or what've missed until we're in the darkroom."

"Ironic, isn't it? We have to go into the dark to discover what we have. When can we arrange another sitting?"

"Tomorrow is Friday. We're quite booked already. How about next Monday or Tuesday?"

"Let's plan on Tuesday morning. I'll see if I can get Tina to assist."

Aaron smiled devilishly. "If not, you may have to manage

on your own."

Ellen swallowed, unable to hold his challenging stare. Was he reminding her that he was gay? There were moments like this when she didn't want to be reminded. They'd been having such a nice time reviewing the seminar and talking about the studio work. Things had felt so — so comfortable. Even the banter.

She sighed. "So . . . when do you think you'll be releasing me and Tina from our commitment to only have sex at the studio in front of your cameras?"

Aaron stiffened. "I leave you alone often enough when I've finished with the photo shoot."

"It's been two weeks, Aaron. How much more do you want? You must have pictures of every angle and position imaginable."

"There's more," he groused. "There always is. There are always different vibrators to try. You've not tried a double dildo yet. Nor has Tina brought in a strap-on."

"Strap-on?" Ellen gasped. "I just want to know how it'd feel to make love with Tina in my bed or in hers."

"I believe her husband occupies her bed."

"Jesus," Ellen muttered. "It's so easy to forget there is a husband." She tapped the table with her right hand. "I don't want to be restricted the entire summer to having sex at the studio."

Aaron nodded and covered her hand, stilling her fingers but jolting her pulse. "I'll think about it. I'll talk to Tina. I just want to be present when you experience something for the first time. Those are the moments I need to capture."

She saw him swallow hard, but she remained silent. At least he was finally thinking about all of this from her perspective.

"No more than another week." He gave her a pained look. "Okay?"

She nodded. She withdrew her hand from under his. "That'll be okay." She gave him a tiny smile. "Who knows, once Tina and I are alone in my bed, I may want to only do it at the studio. I do get turned on knowing you're watching."

"Christ," he mumbled. "So how far do you live from here? In South Dakota. And are there any restored prairie lands nearby?"

The sudden topic shift made her blink. She'd never thought Aaron was particularly uncomfortable watching her and Tina engaging in sex. He'd frequently offered suggestions. But he was certainly done talking about that for now.

"It's about a four-hour drive from the Twin Cities. There are some efforts at prairie restoration close by. My uncle has set aside a small portion of his ranch for restoration. Actually, one of the largest such undertakings is north of Des Moines, Iowa. I've never been there, but I've read about it."

"Me, too. Maybe we should run down and look at it some-day. But I think I'd prefer your native land."

She frowned. "What do you have in mind?"

He grinned genuinely. "I want to expand our prairie woman series to include shots of the prairie. Maybe of you and your own spinning wheel."

"You're striving for authenticity again."

"Always."

"I visited an old soddy on my uncle's property when I was a little girl. I assume it's still standing." Ellen tried to contain her own excitement. Did she share his zeal for authenticity? Maybe this would be a way to lift up the memory of her pio-neer ancestors. "I doubt we could get inside it anymore, but there should be some outside shot opportunities."

"Excellent."

"None of the prairie woman series involves nude poses."

"Of course not. Though we'll want to depict some of that pioneer spirit the best we can." He winked. "That's a thought.

We might want a few nude shots in the tall grasses."

"We might, huh? Do you imagine all those pioneers were running around buck naked in the tall grasses?"

"Some of the time. Maybe. They did manage to have a lot of kids. But that doesn't really matter. The audience we cater to wants to see nudity, but they want it layered in both fantasy and reality. That's one place where the artist can exercise license. We attempt to project a mood, to convey perhaps in soft focus a spirit of determination and passion. That's the best we can do."

Ellen nodded. "That's the best we can do. I'll work on the logistics. If you want to examine your prairie woman's roots, I'll help. Maybe we'll both discover something that will surprise us."

Aaron nodded, giving her a crooked smile. "The true artist is always open to surprise."

"Do you suppose Caillebotte knew the nude on the couch would become his mistress when he painted her? Or maybe she was his surprise."

"And vice versa. We'll never know the answer to that question. Like some impressionists, history has a way of glossing over facts that might be of interest to following generations."

She lifted her wine glass in a toast. "So, we unite to discover and embrace the spirit of the prairie woman."

He clinked his glass against hers. "I prefer to think of this as a continuation of our work on the prairie woman. You embody so much of that adventurous spirit."

"Ah, the notion of continuum again. You are a process sort of guy." She shrugged. "I've never thought of myself as particularly adventurous."

He ducked his chin and eyed her. "I've witnessed a very adventurous woman these past four weeks. Bold. Tentative. Vivacious. Shy. Demanding. Giving. And usually in good humor."

"That can change at any moment."

"I said usually. I have noticed the occasional flare-up." He squirmed on his chair. "We'd better call it a night. Busy day tomorrow. Let me know when you have some possibilities for a little venture back in time out on the prairie."

She nodded, pushing back her chair. "I'll work on it."

Aaron thrashed around, trying to get some sleep before dawn. It was already well past midnight, hours since he'd dropped Ellen at her place. She hadn't bothered to invite him in. Why should she? He hadn't given her any reason to.

If he had it to do over again, he'd handle his summer assistant very differently. He had painted himself into a box. And the box was getting increasingly uncomfortable.

He flipped the bedstand light on to stare at her photo once again. There she was on his wall, with her pussy and asshole begging for attention. For *his* attention, but she didn't know that.

He'd give her one more week before letting her and Tina go at each other with abandon out of his sight. Maybe she'd have a plan for them to travel to South Dakota by then. Wasn't that one of his reasons for wanting to take his prairie woman to Dakota — to wrest her out of Tina's arms?

He clenched his stiff cock in his fist. Damn, he hated being deceptive with Tina. She hadn't done a thing he hadn't encouraged her to do.

His fist squeezed his cock as he worked it up and over its entire length. Tina had better not touch Ellen's asshole. That was his.

He absolutely had no difficulty imagining his cockhead disappearing into Ellen's seductive ass. He'd imagined that so many times before.

His focus on the photo softened as his hips pumped his

cock in and out of his fist. He groaned hoarsely and jerked. But he wasn't filling her ass. He was spewing over his own abs and chest.

Aaron squeezed out the last drop and settled back against the pillows. She'd reduced him to this. *No.* He flung an arm across his forehead. *He'd* reduced himself to this. And it wasn't enough. It was good, but not nearly enough.

He had to devise some way to come out of his closet while saving face. Enough was enough. If not before their South Dakota trip, then definitely while they were on the prairie.

CHAPTER SIX

Resetting lights and tripods, Ellen tried not to stare too directly at the male model Aaron had introduced as a long-time buddy from college days. Apparently, they'd been football teammates. The black man with short-cropped hair had a massive bronze chest, even larger than Aaron's, which she'd thought looked as solid as a rock. Both men had distinctive abs and biceps that could grace a magazine for women. Mike had stripped down to his pants. She tried not to think much about what lay behind that zipper. Aaron hadn't said whether this was to be a nude shoot.

Ellen cranked her neck from side to side. It had already been a long day. Thankfully she'd dressed for comfort, with a tank top and shorts. She wouldn't be center stage, so her apparel didn't really matter.

The first model had taken forever. Even pinching the woman's nipples hadn't been enough. She'd become the only woman other than Tina that Ellen had fingered to orgasm. Ellen smiled, remembering how the woman seemed to be trying to hold back, probably trying to find out how far Aaron's new assistant would go, but she'd learned from Tina about g-spots. Once she'd found the model's g-spot, she had her gushing in moments, and Aaron had his pictures. She'd made a point of handing the model a towel to clean herself up.

The couple who'd come in just before noon were actually quite cute. They stayed until mid-afternoon. They'd wanted a series of pics of the two of them engaged in various acts of sex. Initially, they'd seemed quite shy. Why, she didn't know.

The pics were their idea.

Aaron had been very patient with them, as she'd been. While she'd never been required to touch either one of them sexually, she'd helped them get into various positions. Aaron had guided them through an initial series of foreplay options. The young man had come right away in the missionary position. After that, the couple seemed to settle into a rhythm.

Ellen couldn't help being a little envious of the girl. She'd lost count of how many times the young woman had come. Her husband came two more times before they were finished. Husband and wife went away quite satisfied and eager to see the finished products.

For herself, she was still reeling from that experience. She had never witnessed a couple having sex before — other than when Tina blew Aaron after his photo shoot. They'd used multiple cameras, so she'd been quite involved with an array of shots. It looked like when they worked with couples, Aaron would be drawing on her skills as a photographer, not merely as an assistant with posing.

Would she ever get to the point of being so totally unaffected by this process, like Aaron was? Her entire breasts ached. There were moments when she'd wanted to reach inside her shorts to relieve her stress. She glanced at Aaron often. His crotch never tented with need. Weren't gay men stimulated at all by being so close to the sexual act? The heavy scent of sex still clung to her nostrils. Maybe she should've taken care of herself when taking a break to go to the bathroom.

She shook her head, making one last adjustment to a light. Tina was expected to join them before they quit for the day. Ellen smiled. Tina would help her with her little problem.

"You about ready with that light?"

She snapped her head to see Aaron unable to hide his frustration. It had been a long day for him, too. "That should do it," she said, walking back to where he stood at the tripod.

"Good. We'll take several shots with Mike standing in front of the table. Okay, Mike. You know the routine. Try to look sexy, man. Let the ladies know you want them and know exactly what they need."

"Right." Mike winked at her. "How's this?" he asked, grabbing a wrist with one hand and pumping his bicep.

"Works for me," she quipped, joining the men in their banter.

"Now a couple profile shots. Good. Excellent." Aaron stood and stretched. "Let's cut the light back a little, Ellen."

She did as he asked.

"Now, Adonis, kick off those pants and we'll show the ladies what you really have."

Ellen stood halfway between the light and the tripod as Mike slowly removed his trousers. He wasn't wearing underwear. She gawked at his inert penis lying between his legs. It might be larger limp than the erect cock she'd seen earlier in the day, but it showed no signs of life. Not even the faintest interest.

"Christ, man. Can't you ever get it up without assistance?"

Ellen looked sharply at Aaron. Was this typical? He looked at her with a raised eyebrow, and she shrugged in response. "I'll see what I can do."

Mike smiled at her as she approached. "Sorry. My guy can be stubborn at times."

"Aren't all men?" she quipped, curling her fingers around the dark shaft. Her fingers skimmed lightly along its length. Silence filled the room as she tried to puzzle out the key to the man's cock. She reached beneath to heft his balls.

"Careful—you have the next generation at your mercy."

She laughed easily. "I'll be careful." She rolled his cock between her palms.

"Nice," Mike said softly.

She detected life, but not nearly what they wanted.

She looked back at Aaron. Aaron grimaced at her.

"Ah hell," she said huskily, before ducking down to quickly take him in her mouth.

"Whoa!" Mike groaned. "Now you're talking, girl."

She felt Mike's cock stiffen in her mouth. She backed off a little, giving him room to expand. Placing one hand around the base of his cock and the other under his balls, she proceeded to bob up and down, pleased with his response. She breathed through her nose as she inched more of him into her throat. And then she suckled, hollowing her cheeks, working him like she hadn't done anyone in years.

She sucked harder and faster and reveled in his moans and squeals. He rocked on his feet, thrusting with her.

"Jesus, she's a suction pump. Orgasm shot, Aaron. Sorry, man."

His words sounded garbled to her as he folded his large hands over her ears, helping her pump him to completion. She swallowed quickly and rapidly. His howling ebbed and flowed, matching her efforts. At last he shuddered and pulled away from her.

"Jesus, woman," he mumbled as he hoisted her to her feet to cuddle her close. "I wasn't expecting that."

"Neither was I," she muttered into his hard chest. She turned enough to catch a glimpse of Aaron. "I'm sorry. I guess I got carried away."

Looking beet red, Aaron nodded. "I could tell. Christ, that's the end of this session. I didn't take a single shot since you got into the picture."

The door opened and Tina entered the studio.

Ellen looked up—she still hadn't found the strength to move out of their cuddle.

Tina's eyes narrowed and then a grin split her face. "Ah, I see you've met my husband."

Ellen jerked out of Mike's arms. "Your husband? Mike?"

"That's him," Tina said, stepping over to run a thumb over the corner of Ellen's mouth. "I believe you left a little. Don't be embarrassed. We've wanted you to meet Mike anyway."

"But . . ."

"As I told you early on, my husband and I share most everything."

"Me?" Ellen squeaked.

"Why not? We're all consenting adults. Mike is straight, but he doesn't mind me being bi. I believe it has a few perks for him."

Ellen whirled on Aaron. "Why didn't you tell me he was Tina's husband?"

He held up his palms. "I figured you knew by now. I'm surprised you women can keep anything secret."

"I wasn't trying to keep Mike a secret — I just hadn't figured out how to introduce you two and get you to be open to him." Tina chuckled. "Hopefully, both have been accomplished now."

"I can't believe this," Ellen began. She didn't blame Mike. She didn't blame Tina. But she did blame Aaron. He had to know she'd been clueless about Mike's relationship to Tina when she went down on him. But then she'd only done what was required by the art. She'd had about enough of Aaron's deceptive ways. He might not have out-and-out lied to her, but he sure had no qualms about letting her make her own discoveries.

"So now that you've met, maybe you'd like to spend the weekend with us. I've been wanting to invite you over, but Aaron wanted us to stay here, and Mike doesn't like having sex at the studio with Aaron snapping pictures all the time."

"I can understand why he wouldn't." She cast Aaron a defiant look. "Yes, why don't we spend the weekend together? I need to be reminded that there is life outside this studio."

"I'm sure we can help you remember that, Ellen."

Ellen glanced back at Tina's soft-spoken husband. "I believe you can."

"If that was a prelude"—Mike blew air through pursed lips—"this is going to be one hell of a weekend. I may forget there's a reality outside our house."

"It's settled, then." Tina tucked her arm through Ellen's. "You'll be staying with us."

Ellen took a step toward the door and looked back over her shoulder at Aaron. "You okay with this?"

"What I feel doesn't matter. You go ahead and have a fun weekend." He glared at Tina and then at Mike. "Save her ass for me." He stormed out of the studio and slammed the door.

"What?" Ellen gawked at Tina, who had draped an arm over her shoulders. "Why is he so mad? He was going to relieve us of our commitment in less than a week anyway."

"Sometimes Aaron can be fairly rigid with his expectations."

"And what in the world was that barb about my ass?"

Tina chuckled. "Don't worry about it. He doesn't want either of us to touch your asshole unless he's present."

"My asshole." Ellen gasped.

"Don't get ahead of yourself, girl. I'll explain more later. Let's just enjoy this breath of fresh air. I'm so much looking forward to showing you where we live." Tina grabbed Mike by the hand. "And to sharing my husband with you. You only got a taste. A delightful taste, I hope."

"Delicious." Ellen giggled. "I can't believe I did that or that I'm doing this, but let's go before I start to think too much."

Banging his head against the office wall, Aaron tried not to scream. The damn woman was a witch. She'd blown Mike like it was an everyday thing. He'd been with Mike enough to know his buddy seldom came that quickly. Had she been holding out on all of them? She sure as hell had developed some oral talents somewhere.

What would she have done if he'd invited himself along for the weekend? Tina and Mike had been aware of his discomfort. Neither of them had intervened to put him out of his misery — but then that misery had been of his own making.

They knew he would've happily shared Ellen with them eventually, but he certainly hadn't planned on Mike getting to her before he did. Son of a bitch, they'd been competitive in the army and in college, but they'd never been competitive over women. Sharing freely had taken care of any need for competition.

He glared out the window at his two best friends escorting Ellen down the sidewalk toward their lair. And he was left behind to nurse his wounds. It was going to be one hell of a long weekend.

This entire charade was out of hand — at least out of his hands. He'd have a plan together by Monday morning. He knew he couldn't hold off until traveling to the prairie to let Ellen know he was as straight as an arrow. Son of a bitch. How had he gotten himself into such a morass?

Ellen stopped bouncing up and down Mike's cock to squirm and wiggle against his loins. She beamed a smile at him, then at Tina, who lay beside her husband. Their intertwined light and dark fingers toyed with Tina's vulva.

Ellen bent down first to kiss Mike and then to run her lips across Tina's. "This has been the most incredible weekend of my life."

She laid her cheek on Mike's solid chest. He ran a large hand down her backside and raised his knees until his hips nestled against her bottom. He levered in and out of her slowly. Her inner sheath stretched with each inward stroke. She beamed at Tina. "How long will you loan me your husband? I think he could do this for days."

Tina giggled. Clutching Ellen's hand, she brought it to rest on her own pussy so three hands covered it. "I'm quite sated," Tina said. "You two really did a number on me the last time, but Mike is only on temporary loan. You may want to come back for more installments."

"Oh," Ellen moaned as Mike slammed his hips against her buttocks, driving his cock deeper, as if she needed a reminder of what she'd be missing if she didn't take Tina's offer. "I'll definitely want more installments." She pushed back against Mike's corded thighs, then wiggled her fingers over Tina's vulva and nipped at Mike's dark nipple. Mike grunted. Smiling, she squeezed his encased cock. "Speaking of installments. Are you about ready to leave me with something now?"

"Oh yeah, babe," Mike gasped. "He's been cooking in your heat for nearly an hour. More than ready." Mike wet his lips and nodded. "Hold on."

Quickly she let go of their joined hands to curl her fingers around his shoulders. "Go for it!"

The first thrust drove her six inches up his chest. He waited for her to scoot back down and lock her knees at his sides, and then he drove back in. She grunted, maintaining her perch. Biting down on her lower lip, she watched his eyelids close. And then he began a relentless barrage on her pussy. She fought for balance, for air, for sanity. Her whimpers turned to screams.

She couldn't recall when it happened, but he'd released Tina's fingers to clutch her buttocks firmly, as if he needed to secure his target. "Jesus!" she shouted. She'd become his rag doll. "Oh my God. He's so deep."

Tina rolled to put an arm around her. "Steady, girl. Don't hold back. Let it happen."

She nodded. Who was trying to hold back? She was exploding everywhere. Between her toes. Between her ears. Christ, everywhere. Especially her pussy. Relentlessly, Mike pounded a tiny nubbin in the hidden recesses of her womb. "Hurry," she screeched. "I can't take much more."

"Almost," Mike grunted, pulling her butt cheeks wider, compressing her vagina even tighter around his cock. "You're like a heated vise. Here's your latest installment."

Laughter bubbled from Ellen's mouth as she felt him deposit payload after payload into her depths. His entire body wracked with shudders as he finished. Mike flung his arms out from his sides and dropped his knees to the mattress.

Tina kissed Ellen's hair, her forehead, her eyelids. "Take your time, you two. I'll go down to the kitchen and brew us some tea. Come on down when you're ready."

Floating, Ellen wasn't convinced she'd heard right. She wasn't even certain she could move. Why would she ever want to?

"I'm surprised I could make it down the stairs," Ellen quipped, glancing between her two hosts, now seated at their kitchen table. "I wasn't sure I'd ever walk again."

"Was I too much for you?" Mike said, with a hint of a smile.

"You know you weren't." Ellen inhaled deeply. "But I've missed so much sleep this weekend, I'm not sure I'll manage to get to work tomorrow morning."

"You'd better," Tina warned. "Aaron is already pissed as hell."

"That's his bad. He doesn't own me. I was supposed to get two days off after the first four weeks. I hadn't planned on taking them." She tipped her head to the side and smiled. "But I may have to take one."

"Aaron can deal with it," Mike snorted. "He's a big boy."

"What is it with him?" Ellen narrowed her eyes. "He can

be a slave driver. Sometimes he's so pretentious about his art. I don't know whether he likes what I'm doing or not. I thought gay guys gushed with praise."

The room suddenly turned quiet. Mike scowled at Tina. Tina shrugged as if she didn't know what was going on.

Ellen tried not to back away from Mike's withering glare.

"Aaron is not gay," Mike said quietly. "Who told you he was?"

"Not gay!" Ellen looked at Tina. Did she look as horrified as she felt? "Not gay? But . . ."

"Did he tell you he was gay?" Mike insisted.

"No. No one told me. I just . . . assumed he was."

"Well, you assumed wrong, girl." Tina covered her hands. "Why didn't you ask me? Why didn't you ask him?"

"But he's never even noticed me. He's never gotten the slightest arousal around me."

Tina nodded. "He can wield incredible control over his cock, like Mike."

Ellen glowered at Mike. "You did that on purpose in the studio—staying flaccid. You wanted me to go down on you."

"Of course I did. How else were we going to meet? Tina seemed to be prepared to keep you to herself forever." He arched an eyebrow. "Are you complaining about the weekend?"

"Of course not." She gave him a plaintive smile. "You're forgiven. Good God, my entire body is still humming from the last round." She turned her glare on Tina. "But I'm not about to forgive that bastard Aaron Brewster. Can you believe he's been leading me on like that? So he doesn't want me."

"I never said that," Tina interjected quickly. "You were talking him into an erection by the end of your photo shoot with him just before I went down on him."

"You were part of the conspiracy?"

Tina shrugged. "Not as explicitly as you're thinking."

"So when you swallowed him down your throat, you knew you weren't blowing a gay guy."

Tina laughed, and Mike couldn't hold back a chuckle.

"Let me fill in the picture for you," Tina said. "I've been fucking Mike and Aaron for years. Often together and sometimes not. When you were working in the darkroom the other day, Aaron was trying to fuck me senseless. Though I expect he was thinking of you at the time."

Ellen covered her mouth. "I heard noises. I thought he'd dropped something."

"He nearly did. Me."

"Jesus, he's not gay."

"Does it take this long for information to sink into all South Dakota women, or just you?"

"Just me, I suppose. And" — she swallowed — " — you fuck them at the same time."

Tina grinned. "Now you're getting the picture. So far, you've only had half a loaf. Believe me, girl, you may think you were fucked this weekend. Wait until you have one of my guys in your pussy and the other in your ass. Then you'll know how glorious fucking can really be."

"Ass? Both at once. Aaron isn't gay." Ellen fought to stay rational. She pushed back her chair. "I've got to get out of here. This is too much. I must be in way over my head."

She glanced from Tina to Mike — they both looked shocked. She'd better say something. "None of this detracts from what we shared this weekend. But I've got to get my head around what to do about Aaron. If he wants to play games, I can do that. I'm good at playing games."

"You're not going to run back to South Dakota?"

Ellen exhaled through pursed lips. "That'd be too easy for me — and for him. Do me one more favor?"

"Of course." Tina reached for her husband's hand. "What is it?"

Seeing that simple gesture of husband and wife holding hands, Ellen nearly crumbled. She'd given up on that fantasy for herself, and now she was embarking on who-knew-what to give a guy his comeuppance. "Don't tell Aaron about this conversation?"

"Of course not. You two are adults." Tina gave her a quirky smile. "Aaron no doubt deserves whatever punishment you're scheming for him. If you'd like a lesson in the art of using a whip, I could coach you."

Startled, Ellen took a half step back. "Is there anything you don't do? Don't answer that question," she said, with a half-smile. "I might want to take you up on that later. One more thing?"

She eyed Mike closely. "When we left the studio Friday afternoon and Aaron told you to save my ass for him, he wasn't simply talking about being around to take pictures."

Mike shook his head. "That's not how I understood him."

"He wants my virginal ass."

"I think that's a safe assumption."

"So I've got something he wants?" She eyed Tina as if she'd found the secret to a hidden treasure.

Tina nodded. "Something he really wants."

"And the edge goes to Ellen," she said, hugging herself. "Now that I know the game we're playing, I may have some fun after all."

"You do have the edge," Tina said, smiling broadly. "This may yet be fun to watch. What do you have in mind? You'll only be able to push Aaron so far."

"I'm not saying he won't deflower my ass . . ."

Mike coughed, trying unsuccessfully to hide a smile.

"But if he does, he will have to pay a very high price."

"And what might that be?" Tina asked.

"I have no idea, but I'm working on it." She smiled brilliantly. "He likes to talk so much about continuum and process. He'll have to work through a very long maze to claim my ass."

She stepped over to kiss Mike's cheek and then Tina's. "I expect to be back. Thanks for leaving my asshole alone. You know you could've had it on several occasions. I was so turned on you could've tried anything."

"That was clear," Mike agreed. "But I owe Aaron."

"I can help you get ready by introducing you to anal play with vibrators. Your openness" — Tina paused, a mischievous grin on her face — "to adventure is very appealing."

"Funny. Aaron said something like that." Ellen gulped. "You were serious. Two guys at once?"

Tina flashed an eyebrow. "Don't knock it until you try it."

"We'll see. First things first. I have some business to take care of with Aaron before I can think beyond that. And that may take a while."

She started to head out of the kitchen, then stopped. "Oh, I've got a session set up with Aaron for Tuesday morning to take more nude shots of him."

"I know," Tina said, "he told me."

"I won't need your assistance. You might want to find something else to do." Ellen chuckled. "Like you did when your husband came for his session." She waved over her shoulder. "Bye, wish me luck."

"Sounds like Aaron may need the luck," Mike said as she left the kitchen and headed back to her place to flesh out a game strategy.

CHAPTER SEVEN

"You didn't come in yesterday," Aaron challenged Ellen as soon as she entered Studio B.

"I had things to do," she said levelly, tossing her bag on a chair. "Did you miss me?" She began setting up the lights and cameras the way she wanted them.

He felt like a fool standing by the couch as she worked. Tugging his tee over his head, he said, "You could've called."

He didn't add that he had missed her, had actually worried about her. She'd never missed a day of work. Since he hadn't seen Tina either, he figured the three of them were still locked in a lovers' clench.

"I was making arrangements for us," she explained, "for our prairie woman trip."

"Oh." That was good news. He'd get her away from the Twin Cities after all. "When do we leave?"

"It's not quite set yet, but probably by the end of next week."

"That long." He scowled. That was a long time to wait.

"Like you often say, anything worthwhile is worth waiting for."

"I don't recall saying exactly that," he grumbled. "Now where do you want me? And when is Tina getting here?"

She smiled at him pertly. "Tina won't be joining us this morning. Something came up."

"You're going to do everything by yourself?"

"That's right. Everything. Why don't you get rid of those trousers? This is a nude shoot, you know?"

"Shit," he muttered half under his breath as he unbuckled his belt and kicked the trousers aside.

"Leave the shorts on," Ellen ordered as he began to slide them down. "I didn't have the chance to take any scantily-clad shots last time." She ducked behind the camera on the tripod. "I hope you won't be uncomfortable without Tina helping you."

"I'll manage," he grunted, doing his damndest to keep his cock from responding to Ellen's teasing voice. What the hell was she up to?

"Why don't you turn around? That's right. Flex some muscles. Fantastic. You have a very strong looking back."

"I'm glad you like it. So how was your weekend? Thought maybe you'd fled back to South Dakota."

"It was fabulous," she said, walking up behind him and jerking his shorts down.

"What the hell?" He started to wheel about.

"Don't. I didn't think about backside shots the last time. Like you said, it takes time to realize what one didn't consider during initials shoots."

She squeezed his butt, and he flinched. "A very tight ass. That may explain a lot."

As she retreated back to the tripod, he caught a breath or two. Whatever game she was intent on playing this morning, she hadn't clued him in. He heard the camera click twice.

"Now bend over. I want a picture of your asshole."

Aaron bent over and grabbed his knees.

"Oh my. I've got your balls, too. Amazing how your thighs are pulsing and framing those seedpods."

"Seedpods?"

"Okay, turn around." She shook her head at him like a third-grade schoolteacher. Stepping closer, she said, "I can't say I thought much at all about assholes until this past weekend."

His heart skipped a beat and he gave her a withering stare.

She giggled. "Don't worry, mine is still virgin. I have asked Tina to join us tomorrow afternoon. I checked that neither of us is booked. I want her to start preparing my ass. I understand it might take some doing before I'm ready for Mike's cock, but I'm sure you wouldn't want to miss any of the preparation."

He shook his head and swallowed hard. She was preparing to take Mike's cock in her ass? He'd see about that. He glanced toward the door and then down at Ellen's fingers, now curling around his soft cock. "What are you doing?"

"Trying to get you hard. You don't seem to be doing a very good job of that on your own. Does this bother you?"

"Of course not. Just take it easy with him."

"Poor boy," Ellen cooed, bending over to plant a kiss on his cock. "Your master thinks I might hurt you. I'll try to be as careful with you as he has been with me."

He nodded as she worked her fingers up and down his shaft. He lost control of his breathing first. He wanted to grab her head and pop his cock into her mouth and let her have at him as she'd done with Mike the other day, but he kept his arms locked at his sides.

"There, that may do. Hold that," she added, placing his hand around his cock.

She turned away and bent over to pick up a camera.

His eyes nearly popped out of his head. "Good God, she shaved you!"

"Naughty boy." Ellen chortled, turning around to grin at him. "You peeked." With the camera in one hand, she lifted the mini skirt with the other. "So what do you think? Use your artistic eye. Both Mike and Tina like it better bare. Before Tina shaved me, Mike kept getting hairs caught between his teeth."

"Jesus," Aaron moaned, nearly squeezing his cock in half. "It looks fine. I'm sure it's better."

Ellen lowered her skirt. "I'm glad you approve. You may want to get an updated pussy shot for your wall."

He nodded. *Both* walls — office and bedroom.

"Okay." Ellen's cheeks showed a little color. "I have plenty of angle shots. What I'm missing are head-on shots. If you'll move your hand off him and let him find his own equilibrium . . ."

He did so quickly. Suddenly he wanted this photo shoot to end. Her words had been unsettling. Her bare pussy had nearly unhinged him. He promised his cock he'd jerk off as soon as Ellen left.

"Excellent." Ellen beamed at his cock and raised the camera. "So handsome and eager. He's really full. That makes for an even better picture."

Aaron swallowed, trying to keep his mind blank as Ellen oohed and aahed over his cock.

"Now I want some shots with his peephole open."

"What?"

Ellen moved in closer. "You know — the slit in his head. I want it open, sort of like it's winking at me in anticipation."

"Jesus, woman." He grabbed his cock and pulled back on it.

"Not like that," she chastised. "That makes him look angry. I'll have to do it. Let me get the tripod set up right."

He whooshed air out his mouth — what the hell did she have in mind? "There," she announced, "this should work."

She returned to where he stood, held the shutter extension bulb in one hand, and with the other hand encircled his cock. Her hand was indeed much softer than his. Gently, she pulled back on his skin. "Yes," she squealed, "that's what I want, he's winking at me. Don't flinch."

He heard the camera clicking away in the quiet of the room.

"He's been so patient with me," Ellen crooned. She knelt at his side and lapped at his cock with her hot tongue.

"Christ." The camera continued clicking. "What are you trying to do?"

She stopped licking and peeked up at him. "I've never had my picture taken while giving head. This is a first. Thought you like firsts."

Before he could blink, she had him in her mouth, suctioning his cock from the tip to the base. He tried his best to breathe and to ignore the camera clicking. Her head was bobbing quickly. She was not only good, but as with most things, she was incredibly efficient. He was on the balls of his feet pumping down her throat before he'd had nearly enough pleasure.

She giggled as his legs wobbled. "Why don't you sit on the couch while I clean up?"

Spent. He collapsed back on the couch. She proceeded to lick him clean. Twice she turned to the camera with come dribbling down her chin.

She caught him gawking. "Sort of like I'm scantily clad with come. Should make for an artsy shot."

As soon as she had him clean, she stood and winked. "There. I think he'll be fine. While you sit there and gather yourself, I'll take care of the gear."

Within a few minutes, Ellen had removed the film from the cameras and stored everything in her bag. She flung the bag over her shoulder and gave him a brilliant smile. "Thanks. There should be some super pics here. See you tomorrow. I can hardly wait for Tina to start on my ass — under your pictorial supervision, of course."

Aaron closed his mouth after the door shut behind her. What the hell was that all about? He rested his head on the back of the couch and closed his eyes. Clearly, she'd orchestrated that entire scene. But why?

She'd planned to blow him from before she entered the room. Damn, she was good! Mike was so right. Though he'd prefer she take a little more time next time.

Next time?

And now she wanted him to do a photo shoot while Tina began to break in her ass? That was supposed to be his job. He gritted his teeth.

He doubted she'd be ready for Mike's cock before they left for Dakota. He curled his lips into a smile. By their return from the prairie, Ellen's ass would not be virgin. That was his solemn vow. She'd already decided she wanted a cock in her ass. She just didn't know she wanted his.

He chuckled. When would he tell her? He shook his head. No way could he tell her anything. He'd have to show her. She'd have to want him as much as he wanted her.

Given what he'd just witnessed, Ellen Jeffers was deluding herself into thinking she was in control of their little game. No way. He lurched to a sitting position.

He had much more experience at this game than she did. It was his game to win or lose. And he wasn't playing to lose. She'd upped the stakes. It was much more fun playing with an equal — what Ellen lacked in experience, she made up for with spirit. Before they were finished, she would be his full equal. He was certain of that.

"Yes, I've talked to your uncle and aunt." Her mother's voice sounded quite clear over the phone. Thankfully, they had a good cell connection, for once. "The old soddy is still there. Jim isn't sure you can get in it without part of the roof collapsing."

"We won't even try that, Mom." Lying on her bed, Ellen grinned at the thought of Aaron getting dirty. She'd known she could count on her mother to get into this prairie woman project. Her mom had shouted for joy when Ellen first told her about it. "All we want is to take pictures of the outside.

How about prairie preservation?"

"Your uncle and aunt have devoted a couple hundred acres of their own land to prairie restoration. They've been involved with some private conservation group for several years. Of course, two hundred acres is only a drop in the bucket when you consider their ranch is nearly two thousand acres."

"True, but that sounds great for what Aaron has in mind."

"I'm cleaning your old room. You and your man can stay there when you visit."

Ellen gasped.

"I'm not so old fashioned that I don't recognize how you young people do things these days."

"But I'd planned on us staying at the motel."

"Nonsense. My daughter is not going to stay at a motel when she comes to visit."

Ellen recognized her mother's familiar tenacity. She looked at the bedroom ceiling and followed a tiny crack. She smiled. Maybe this change of plans could be fun. What would Aaron do about sharing a room with her — and a bed? "We'll work it out, Mom. I appreciate the legwork you're doing for us."

"I've had fun gathering old pioneer stuff from family and friends. I have everything from a butter churn, a flail, lanterns, and so on. Also, I'm fixing some gingham dresses from your cousin over in Redfield. Lacy is about your size and very active in reenacting pioneer days."

"You're doing too much."

"We're looking forward to you and your man coming out here, Ellen. It's not every day we have a celebrity in our midst."

"Celebrity?"

"Aaron Brewster. I've been to his website. He has a knack for bringing simple things to life." There was a slight pause. "He seems to do a lot with nudes."

Ellen remained silent. She hadn't counted on her mother getting on the internet to check out Aaron and his work. She still wondered why she'd never thought of doing that before meeting him.

"So are you posing for him in the nude?"

"Mom." Her throat constricted. "Some."

"While I may be impressed with his tasteful treatment of nudity, I'm not sure your school board will be happy to see one of their teachers in nude photos."

"I haven't signed a release for the nude photos. I doubt that I will."

"I trust you'll use good judgment. You usually do."

"But not always." Ellen snickered.

"No, not always." Ellen heard her mother sigh. "Sometimes, maybe good judgment isn't necessarily the best."

"What do you mean by that?"

"Have you heard from your friend Angie?"

Ellen frowned—what was her mother not saying? When had she made a good judgment that wasn't the best? "We've exchanged a few e-mails. Sounds like she's having a great time."

"Sounds like you both are. Have you been in touch with anyone at the school?"

"No." Ellen hesitated. She'd hardly thought about the school, particularly in the last week. "I wanted to really get away this summer."

"You do seem to be doing that. You may have a difficult time going back."

Ellen felt her body heat. Her throat turned dry. Her mother seemed to have no trouble naming a problem she'd only begun to acknowledge. How could she balance her new persona with her old one? Maybe Tina was right. Maybe she was morphing more significantly than she realized. "It's just a summer thing, Mom." Why didn't she sound convincing?

Her mother laughed. "You're too young for a mid-life crisis. We'll talk more when you get here." After a long pause, she continued, "I haven't heard you sound this happy since you were a little girl. Something must be good for you. Call me when you know when you'll be getting in. I'm looking forward to meeting Mr. Brewster."

"I will. Bye."

Ellen flipped her cell shut. "Good for her," she mumbled. "How about fantastic!"

She was looking forward to the trip to the prairie. She hadn't planned on staying at her mother's house. Her mother already sounded enamored with Aaron. She'd better not be getting the wrong idea. Ellen was bent on wreaking some vengeance on Aaron and maybe having a summer fling—though the summer was already going by too quickly. But any relationship beyond the summer was impossible. She was at heart a realist.

She rolled over and hugged a pillow, wondering what he'd thought of their earlier photo session. From her perspective, it was perfect. She'd gotten exactly what she wanted—the photos, and Aaron's attention.

Her only regret was not taking more time with his cock in her mouth. She looked forward to a rematch when she could linger, but she hadn't wanted Aaron to have time to think and possibly pull away from her. He didn't look displeased when she'd peeked up at him after she'd finished.

She chuckled—she'd already called Tina to discuss plans for tomorrow's session focused on opening her ass. Aaron would be livid, but she had a plan for him, too. He wouldn't be entirely passive, confined to glaring at her through the lens of a camera. She had a role choreographed for him. He'd think she was preparing for Mike's cock.

No way. She wasn't imagining Mike's cock teasing her ass. Aaron would be first. Maybe Mike later, but Aaron first. But not before they were on the prairie.

She looked forward to the prairie wind blowing through her hair. She looked forward to playing in the tall grasses. She looked forward to reconnecting with Clarissa's spirit. Ever since she was a young girl, she'd felt closest to her roots when roaming the prairie or working at the spinning wheel.

Remembering how natural her response was to Tina's initial seduction — and even her inability to say a resounding no to Angie's more subtle overtures — somehow increased her desire to return to the prairie. Maybe the spirit of her great-great-grandmother called her still.

Was she becoming eccentric in her old age? Was her mother right? Was she really happy? Happier than she'd been in a long time? She moaned. For a woman who didn't embrace change easily, that was scary.

She'd lived alone for so long. Now there was Tina and Mike, and Aaron, and even Angie in the wings. None of them fit with who she was.

Ellen swallowed hard and fought back a sob. Did she even know who she was anymore? How could so very much change in a matter of weeks?

She slid a hand over her abs and loins to squeeze her rump. There'd be more change tomorrow. She could hardly wait to witness the surprise on Aaron's face when she and Tina told him what he needed to do to assist with their preparations.

Leaning back against the corner of the love seat with one foot on the arm and the other on the floor, Ellen pulled her bikini panty aside to show off her newly shorn vulva as Aaron had requested. She cast a puzzled glance at Tina, who shrugged in response.

Aaron had taken over as soon as they entered Studio B. He'd wanted her to leave the bikini on for effect.

"Pull the bikini tighter," Aaron ordered from behind the

camera. "That's better. Pinch her nipples a little more, Tina."

Ellen swallowed as Tina rolled her nipples between thumbs and fingers and then tugged on them. Already simmering nicely, Ellen wanted to pull Tina's mouth down to hers.

Tina shook her head. "We'll have him panting in no time," she whispered.

Ellen pursed her lips to blow Tina a kiss.

"Hold that pose," Aaron said. "Step back, Tina. Now blow your kiss. Excellent. I should've thought of that."

Aaron stepped around the camera and looked at her thoughtfully. "Did either of you consider the possibility that I might've liked documenting the shaving of your pussy?"

"I didn't." She caught a glower in his eyes and shook her head.

"Never crossed my mind," Tina chimed in.

"Too bad. That was a lost opportunity."

"There'll be a next time," Tina pointed out.

"But not a first time. There is only one first time for anything, right?"

Ellen smacked her lips as he knelt before her. "What are you doing?"

"Helping set you up for some close-ups. Remember my wall?"

She nodded.

"As you said, I need an updated photo. First, keep the bikini pulled out of the way with your right hand and rest your left hand over your pubic bone, like this."

Her breathing became shallow as he placed her fingers at the top of her clitoral region. He quickly retreated to the camera. She saw no need to give a variety of facial expressions. He was focused entirely on her vulva.

He returned to her, holding the shutter extension in one hand. "Using both hands, part your pussy lips for me."

Swallowing hard, Ellen looked at Tina, who was beaming from ear to ear. Then she nodded at Aaron and did as he'd said. His fervent visual examination fueled a sudden burst of lust deep in her body.

"Not like that," he chastised. "I want the viewer to see your opening. I want it winking at me with anticipation, expecting a finger or maybe a cock."

Goodness, he was using the same words with her as she had with him when she talked about his cock.

"I'll show you what I want." Gently, he squeezed her fingers to encourage them to spread her lips wider.

"Close. Now, expand that portal a little wider with your forefinger. Just open. I want a hint of your finger entering. Just as we have the hint of your asshole puckering at the edge of the bikini."

She hesitated. He guided her finger forward.

"There," he said in triumph. "Open—inviting a finger, a tongue or a cock. We'll let the viewer decide which." He narrowed his eyes at her crotch. "Keep your hands where they are. To maximize the effect of this pic, we need to coax your girl out into the open."

"What?" she gulped. Before she could utter another word. Aaron was dragging a finger along the side of her hooded clitoris.

"This won't take long," he whispered, beginning to stroke her clit between thumb and forefinger.

"Jesus," she mumbled, trying not to react.

"Here she comes out for a peek," Aaron murmured. He immediately stopped massaging her clit.

The camera clicked, and Ellen blinked. She fumed at him for not bringing her off—at herself for wanting him to. She sighed, gathering her body back together. He'd get his soon enough.

"That should complete the pussy series, for now." Aaron

grinned at her and then over at Tina. "So what did you two have in mind for us?"

"Actually," Tina said, stepping forward and smiling at her, "this will work out quite fine. It looks to me like we can forego any more preliminaries. Aaron seems to have taken care of that. Are you okay, girl?"

"I'm fine," Ellen said, purposely glowering at Aaron. "Let's get on with it. How do you want me?"

"First, why don't you get rid of the bikini," Tina said, pulling her tank top over her head.

Ellen quickly slid the panties down her legs. "Your nipples are about as extended as I've ever seen them."

"Watching you two was quite a treat." Tina let her skirt drop to the floor.

"I see you've shaved recently, too," Aaron commented.

Tina smirked. "It was the only way to convince our girl that I had a steady hand. Okay, Ellen, let's move to the bed and have you lie on the end with your feet on the floor. I'll put a pillow under your butt to give me a better angle and the camera a better view."

Ellen walked to the bed and let Tina position her the way she wanted. She turned to see Aaron move the tripod into the center of the room, facing the bed. She inhaled deeply. Was she more thrilled by what Tina was about to do, or by knowing that Aaron was watching? Her lips curved. He wouldn't be watching for long.

"How's that?" Tina asked Aaron. "If I kneel to the side, you ought to have a clear shot."

"Looks good from here. I'm ready whenever you two are."

Tina winked at her. "Sorry if this sounds too clinical. Using plenty of lube is important for anal play."

Ellen nodded, not convinced she felt very playful at the moment.

"You look like you could use a little more priming, girl. We lost something getting everything set up."

"Oh!" Ellen moaned as Tina slid a finger along her vulva.

"I'm going to caress one of the most sensitive spots of the human body. The ridge between your pussy and your anus."

"Oh my. That tickles." Ellen smacked her lips. "A nice tickle."

"Thought so. I'm going to spread some lube over your anus."

Ellen giggled. "That's cold."

"It'll warm up, trust me. Here's just the tip of my finger."

Flinching, Ellen caught her breath.

"You okay?"

She nodded. The camera clicked.

"A little more. There, I'm at the outer ring. You'll open more in a few moments."

Ellen nodded. Tina had explained all this earlier. She knew about the ring. And she knew she'd passed much larger things through that ring than Tina's finger. Still, this had her on edge.

"Relax," Tina coaxed. "I feel you opening. Do you?"

Ellen nodded, but she wasn't exactly sure any more about what was happening down there. Her sensors were in overdrive.

"There. I'm coming in. There. How's that?"

"I hardly feel you." That had been the line she'd been coached to say, but it was true. Amazingly, she hardly felt Tina's finger.

"We'll have to try something larger in a bit. My fingers are long, but quite narrow. How's this?"

Ellen puffed her cheeks and panted, trying to get a feel for the sensations caused by Tina's finger sliding in and out of her ass. "Smooth," she said, "incredibly smooth. Are you getting what you want?" she said to the camera.

"Stunning," Aaron said. "You sure this is your first time?"

"Absolutely."

"You can certainly take something larger," Tina said, slowly withdrawing her finger. "Let me get my vibrators."

"Now my butt feels strangely empty."

"Damn," Tina bellowed. She looked at Ellen with distress and then at Aaron. "I left my bag of vibrators on the kitchen table."

"Oh no," Ellen said, "I'm ready for more. Surely there must be something else we can do. We've built this up over days."

"Don't worry, I'm thinking." Tina glanced over her shoulder and then back to Ellen. "Aaron has much larger fingers and thumbs. What do you think? Will he do?"

Ellen tried her best to look perplexed. "I've got to have something. He'll have to do."

"Come on, Aaron. There's a woman in distress that you have to help out."

"But my pictures?"

"Use the fucking extension, like you did earlier. Hurry, before she changes her mind."

Through half slit eyelids, Ellen watched Aaron nearly stumble over a tripod leg getting to her. Tina handed him the lube.

"You positive about this?" he asked her. His Adam's apple bobbed.

"Certain. Please. Touch me."

He nodded.

When his lubed finger pressed against her anus, Ellen blinked. He must be four times the size of Tina. "Do it."

"Wow," she moaned, staring wildly at Tina.

"That's right, love," Tina said, covering her pussy with the palm of her hand. "He's waiting for you at that ring. You'll open faster this time."

"She's opening," Aaron muttered. "Ready?"

"Yes," Ellen squeaked. "Oh my God." Her jaw went slack.

Even though he was being gentle with her, Aaron's finger stretched her ass. "Are you almost in?" she muttered.

He shook his head. "Half. You want more?"

She nodded vigorously. They'd come this far.

"There," he said at last.

She felt the other fingers of his hand splay out across her butt. She sighed and squirmed, trying to get comfortable. She nodded. "Let's see what happens when you move."

She felt him withdraw partway and slowly reenter. She blew air through pursed lips. He did that a second time. And then a third. And then a fourth. "Oh my God. No one could've told me . . ." He quickened the pace of his finger. Suddenly she lurched forward. "Faster. Now! Don't leave me hanging."

"We won't, girl." Chuckling, Tina wedged a finger into Ellen's vagina and bent over to kiss her engorged clit.

"Oh, hell," Ellen screamed. "I can't feel a thing. I'm crumbling to pieces. Oh my God!" She lurched against the fingers and then collapsed to the bed, thoroughly spent. Her heart pounded in her chest. Air finally reached her lungs. The finger in her vagina slid out easily. As the one in her butt withdrew, tiny frissons of pleasure shot across her rump.

At last it was out, and she gulped in air. She cracked her eyelids open. Tina beamed at her. Even Aaron seemed to have been affected by what had just transpired. Though half dazed, she had no trouble seeing a solid erection tenting his trousers.

Remembering her next line, Ellen struggled to get it out. "It may take a while before I'm ready for Mike's cock in my ass."

Aaron growled something inaudible and his face darkened.

"There's plenty of juices here that I'm not going to let go to waste," Tina said, slipping around Ellen's knee. Once in position, Tina wiggled her butt and looked over her shoulder at Aaron, who continued to glower. "You look like your guy needs a home." Laughing, Tina slapped her butt. "Pick your spot. Both are quite open and ready for you."

Ellen tried not to look shocked. Tina hadn't told her about this part of the plan. Maybe she was improvising.

Aaron gave her a crooked grin. "Maybe he would like a home." He unhooked his belt and kicked his pants and shorts aside. He didn't bother with shucking the dark tee. Smiling devilishly, he slowly lubed his cock before dropping on his knees behind Tina.

Ellen wet her lips as both she and Tina waited for Aaron.

"You can probably figure which home I'm selecting."

She saw him grip his cock to guide it. That was all she could see, but she had no doubt where he was headed.

"Oh, it's been too long," Tina cooed. "Fill my ass. I'm so ready for you."

Ellen saw Aaron suck his lower lip into his mouth as he eased forward. She could hardly breathe, imagining his breadth stretching her own anus.

At last he straightened, inhaled, and grasped Tina's buttocks with both hands. He waggled a little, and Tina moaned.

Ellen winced as he glared at her.

"Are you imagining my cock in your asshole?"

Ellen held her tongue.

"Enough talk," Tina said, flicking her tongue at Ellen's vulva. "As I thought, it's a creamy dessert."

Ellen breathed through her nose as Tina's tongue laved one side of her vulva and Aaron began to flex in and out of Tina. He kept his gaze locked on hers as if he was fucking her. He maintained a steady pace while Tina licked her clean. And then Aaron's eyes closed. She knew he must be close.

"Go for it," Tina wailed. Tina lifted her head and arched back against him. "Fuck me. Oh God, fuck my ass."

"Son of a bitch," Aaron bellowed, his chest quaking and heaving. He laid his forehead on Tina's back and continued jerking in and out of her.

Ellen's heart started up again when Aaron raised his head and, gasping, withdrew from Tina. Tina remained lying with her cheek on Ellen's belly. Ellen combed Tina's long hair between her fingers. "That was powerful, majestic." She grinned at Aaron, who was still catching his breath. "But I don't think we got any pictures."

A corner of his mouth turned up. "Sometimes, even a photo can't do justice to a scene."

"This scene I have emblazoned on my brain."

He nodded. "Me, too. I've got to go get cleaned up." He patted Tina's rump. "I expect we're done for the day."

"Happily so." Tina sat back on her haunches. "Would you two do me a favor?"

Aaron scowled at Tina.

"What?" Ellen asked.

"Work out whatever is keeping you two apart. I love being between you, but I don't want to be in the middle. Understand?"

Aaron grunted, and Tina nodded.

Ellen stood dumfounded as Aaron left the studio. He'd be by later to take care of the equipment. She didn't plan on being there when he got back.

Work things out with him? Maybe. Maybe on the prairie. At least she had no nagging questions about whether he was gay.

He made nearly as much noise when he came as one of the range bulls on her uncle's ranch.

CHAPTER EIGHT

Puzzled, Aaron reread the handwritten note he'd found on his desk when he came into his office. The penmanship was perfectly rounded and curved, the way he remembered from his own grade-school teachers. Another skill he'd failed to achieve.

Ellen wanted him to come to Studio B when he got in. Now what was she up to? He'd hardly seen her for three days. Each of them had been quite involved in darkroom work, and he'd had to make a quick trip up north to take care of some personal business.

Ellen probably hadn't missed him. Given Tina's most recent update, the two of them had been quite diligent in continuing their anal work. With more than a little pride, Tina had announced that Ellen was probably ready for whatever came her way. Aaron set the note back on the desk. Tina had also told him Mike had honored their agreement. She made it clear that she and her husband were enjoying Ellen in most every way imaginable, but Mike had stayed away from her ass.

That was something. He didn't want to dwell long on the image of the three of them intertwined. He much preferred remembering coming in Tina's ass while Ellen looked on inches from his face, her eyes wide and filled with wonder. She hadn't been particularly bothered or surprised that he'd joined in. And she'd seemed quite pleased that he brought her relief with his finger in her ass. That was a precious moment — one he'd remember forever.

Tina had never answered his question of whether she'd purposely forgotten her bag of vibrators and butt plugs. As to her warning, he'd hardly seen Ellen since that day. They'd have time together on the prairie. If they didn't have something worked out by the time they got back to the cities, then he'd probably have to look around to see who else might be available. The summer was flying by.

Aaron closed the studio door softly behind him and leaned against it, drinking in the view of Ellen Jeffers on the couch. Completely nude, she lay on her back with her left arm across her brow and her right knee raised, resting against the back of the couch. Fingers of her right hand toyed with her left breast and nipple. It was Caillebotte's *Nude on a Couch* in the flesh.

Wordlessly, Aaron moved softly across the room to pick up a camera.

It wasn't clear that she ever looked at him. She had to know he was there, but she never flinched at the sound of the camera. Her nipple began to extend under her ministrations. She twirled it slowly between thumb and forefinger.

Aaron swallowed, trying not to let her arouse him. He failed. Miserably.

Her hand moved glacially from her breast to her navel. She circled it with a finger and then moved lower still. Without looking at him directly, without speaking, she let her fingers graze her hidden clitoris and then caress her labia.

Remember to focus! He took full-length shots and close-ups. He might not be breathing, but the camera sang Ellen's praises. How far would she take this? And what did she think she was doing? Satisfying herself, or seducing him? Maybe she was seducing herself.

Her pussy folds had engorged since he'd come into the room. She drew her fingers to her mouth to wet them and leisurely returned them to her vulva. Aaron squinted as she parted her labia. A finger slid up and down her wet slit. And then it disappeared. It traveled inward so surely that he'd hardly noticed it happen. Soft whimpers told him the finger was engaged in its own mission.

Her hips barely moved. Ellen's thumb grazed her clit and she sighed a prolonged ahhh.

Aaron's thighs burned from the intensity of being the voyeur—a role he valued, but one he didn't particularly relish at the moment. She withdrew her finger from her vagina and brought it to her mouth, where she briefly suckled it clean.

She dropped her arm from her brow and looked at him through soft eyes. "A little one. Hi, good morning. You get some good pics?"

He nodded. "Of course I did. What were you doing?"

She gave him a whimsical smile but did not move to sit up. "What did it look like?"

"Like you were pleasuring yourself."

"And?" She arched an eyebrow.

"That you were seducing? Me. Maybe both of us."

"Ah, you are a perceptive man." She sat up and reached for a top and skirt he hadn't noticed.

He set his camera aside. Ellen was done posing for him. Was she done seducing him?

Buttoning her top, she explained, "I wanted you to know that I'm no better or worse than Caillebotte's mistress. And that my passion for our art matches yours, at least some of the time."

"I've noticed that. And what else are you saying?"

"Isn't that obvious? I'm making myself available to you as she did for Caillebotte." She stood and pulled the short skirt up over her thighs, then tucked her top in at the waist. She stepped close to him and dragged a finger down his chest. "I want you to fuck me. I want to fuck you. I've even saved my ass for you. Do you want me?"

He grabbed her by the wrist and lowered her fingers to his crotch. "Is that an answer?"

She squeezed his bulge. "I believe it is." She eyed him. "But not here. I don't want our first time here in the studio. Can we wait for the prairie?"

He nodded. "That's what I've been waiting for. A few more days shouldn't kill me."

"You know" — she stood on her toes and slid her lips across his chin — "I've blown you, you've had your finger in my ass, but we haven't even kissed."

"Would you like to change that? Or do we have to wait?"

"Change. I'm done waiting."

She tipped her head back, and he lowered his, slanting his lips across hers. Their lips blended easily. There was no rush. They'd already agreed what wouldn't happen. She deepened the kiss, and he responded. His tongue parted her lips and she chuckled, sucking him into her mouth. His hands roamed her back. He gathered her bare bottom in his hands.

She broke the kiss and pecked at his lips before smoothing out her skirt. Giving him the look of the disciplinarian, she said, "We've got a date set? Don't make me slap your hands."

"I won't, teach." He chuckled. "You can be mercurial."

"I hope that's not a complaint."

"It's not. Can you answer one question for me?"

"I'll try."

"For a girl who obviously lived a fairly straight and narrow life, how did you ever learn to blow a guy like you do? You could waste a guy in a matter of a minute or two if you wanted to."

Ellen's eyes clouded and then just as quickly sparkled. "I'll take that as a compliment. Next time I won't be in such a hurry." She shrugged. "I developed that talent out of necessity. My husband saw sex as a way to get off. The quicker I got him off, the better we both liked it. Saved a lot of wear and tear on my body. I wasn't into rutting."

"Sorry." Aaron grimaced. "I'll not treat you that way."

She reached out and grazed his arm. "I know you won't. You're a sensitive man." She scowled. "But that doesn't mean I only want gentle and slow." She stuck her tongue out at him, giving him her best sassy look. "I'm growing to like fast and hard, too. Even a little spanking makes me go bonkers."

"Tina has been busy."

"Tina and Mike," Ellen corrected. "You know Tina sings such high praises of taking you two guys on at the same time."

He arched an eyebrow. "That's what you want?"

She didn't shy away. "Probably." She grazed his chin with a forefinger. "If that's what I decide I want, will you help me get it?

He pecked at the tip of her nose. "Where did that simple, naïve prairie schoolteacher go?"

"She may have been a figment of your imagination — or mine." She kissed him one more time before walking to the door. Then she stopped to look at the couch and back at him. "Who knew how much of an inspiration Caillebotte and his mistress would become?"

His erection began to subside at the sound of the door closing. The chase would soon be over. He sighed deeply. Fun and games on the prairie and for the rest of the summer. Why wasn't it enough to leave it there? Seldom had he tried to think of any woman beyond a series of photo shoots or a weekend or two. So why was he already worrying about losing Ellen Jeffers?

"Tell me about your family. I've been so focused on the prairie woman series I've hardly thought about meeting your parents. I don't even know if you have brothers and sisters."

Ellen looked away from Aaron's inquisitive glance. She stared at the approaching South Dakota welcoming sign. She'd napped a little after they'd changed drivers. Actually, she'd merely closed her eyes. Unlike him, she'd hardly been able to think of anything else for the last few days but him meeting her family.

Would her dad freak? Her mother must've prepared him by now. Would her mother give her breathing space? She'd want to know as many details as she could wrench out of her.

She turned to face Aaron. He had such a strong profile, particularly when he was on alert. And he was definitely on alert. "I have an older brother and a younger sister. I doubt either will be around. Jack lives near Tucson with his wife and two kids. He teaches history at the university. Kim lives in Rapid City with her husband. They have a three-year-old. Both of them teach school there."

"You really come from a family of teachers. How about your parents?"

She snickered. "Teachers, too. Dad teaches high school history and Mom teaches high school English. They married right out of college. They're both sixty-three and are trying to sort out when to retire."

"Then you were the wild middle child?"

"Not as wild as you might think. I did get married shortly after high school, which really angered my dad. Both my folks thought I must be pregnant. I wasn't, though we'd been screwing around since we were juniors. Guess that was my rebellion. It's not easy when your parents are teachers and wind up chaperoning dances and everything else in your life."

"But you managed. Apparently."

"I wasn't promiscuous." She winced. "I was only with one boy. We had a commitment, of sorts, before I let him in my panties."

"I see. And your mother expects us to share a bed in your old room?"

"That's right. She thinks we're lovers. I never told her that."

"I'm sure you didn't. So we get to sleep together at last."

She reached over and squeezed his thigh. "Sleeping only."

He gave her a sharp glare.

"If you think we're going to be screwing with my folks listening in, you're crazy."

"Jesus. You must believe torture propels one to a higher level of personal growth. Can't we just go to a motel?"

"No. My mother won't hear of that. We'd cause a big scene that'd take weeks for me to smooth over." She reached over and dragged a fingernail along his thigh. "We'll work something out. We have several days. Didn't you tell me photographers have to have patience?"

"Maybe not as much as third grade teachers." He gave her a hopeful look. "Perhaps we should pull off at the next rest area and take care of things. Or we could stop at a motel on the way. We could always say we had two flat tires."

"Funny, funny." Ellen shook her head. "When we do consummate this quirky relationship of ours, I want it to be done right. I don't want a quickie in the back seat or at a fleabag hotel."

He turned to give her a quick smile and then stared back at the wide-open road. "We have a quirky relationship. That sounds about right." He peeked at her again. "And I agree. When we finally get around to making love, I intend on making it last."

She swallowed quickly. "Maybe we should find something else to talk about. We'll be there in less than an hour and a half." She peeked over at the erection pressing against his jeans. "You'll want to be able to walk by then."

He nodded. "And your uncle and aunt live another hour and a half west."

"Northwest. We'll drive out there tomorrow, if the weather holds. I am looking forward to this photo shoot."

"Me, too. I've been planning this for years. Now that the right woman came along, it's finally time."

"My mother has been gathering lots of possible props. I really think she sees your work as a vindication of her great grandmother Clarissa."

"*Our* work," he corrected. "Clarissa — the fallen woman."

Ellen scowled but didn't look at Aaron. "That's such an odd combination of words. It's as if the woman is solely responsible for her state. Like everyone else, Clarissa could only play the cards she was dealt."

"Like Caillebotte's mistress."

"Exactly."

"And you?"

She laughed, then slowly turned to look at Aaron before answering. "Perhaps I've been given a fresh deck to play with." She glanced out at the expansive prairie. "And maybe that's the real secret of *Nude on a Couch* — maybe she was also playing with a fresh deck of cards."

"You are quite imaginative."

"That surprises you? You expected third-grade teachers to be dull?"

He cleared his throat and reached for her hand.

She intertwined their fingers.

"Let's just say you're not at all what I expected when I first saw your resume."

"I surprised you?"

"Over and over."

She leaned across to kiss his cheek. "I like surprising you. I'll see if I can come up with a few more surprises."

"I'm counting on that."

"And you've surprised me, too."

"As it should be." He smirked. Without taking his attention from the road, he asked, "Did you really think I was gay?"

She folded her hands in her lap. "What was I supposed to think? You gave no sign of reacting to me."

"Wasn't Tina blowing me a clue?"

"I couldn't explain that. And then Tina and Mike kept me so occupied I didn't have much time to think about you."

"Wish I could say the same," he grumbled.

"Oh, wow." He had her full attention. "Were you thinking about us that weekend?"

He glowered quickly at her. "How could I not? You guys were fucking your brains out, and I spent most of the weekend working in the darkroom. So when did you know for sure I wasn't gay?"

"Tina and Mike told me, but I knew for sure when you entered Tina's ass. Your face was pure lust for her."

He smacked his lips. "You're wrong about that. I was lusting for both of you."

"Jesus. Maybe we *should* find a hotel." She exhaled softly. "I was hoping you wanted me, too. I even thought you did. It was amazing feeling you screwing Tina while she ate my pussy. I wanted you to come in both of us. You seemed so consumed with both of us. I hoped you weren't faking."

"I don't fake." He left one hand on the steering wheel and straightened his erection with the other. "Now, if you can't find something less tantalizing to talk about, maybe you should keep your thoughts to yourself. I don't want to embarrass myself as soon as I meet your parents."

"Okay." She giggled. "We're only about twenty miles from our exit."

Aaron pushed his chair back from the dining room table. "I

may not eat for a week," he quipped, winking at Ellen's mother. "I can't ever recall having a better cherry pie."

Mrs. Jeffers preened, as he knew she would. She was an older version of Ellen and he'd liked her immediately. He expected the feeling was mutual. He glanced at Ellen's father, who had been a bit more reserved than his wife. Had Mr. Jeffers been to his web page also? "And that steak was awesome."

"Glad you liked it." Mr. Jeffers nodded. "I always like having an excuse to fire up the grill. Having Ellen come home for a visit is more than reason enough. From what Helen tells me, you're planning on heading over to the prairie project tomorrow."

"We hope to. I'd like to get a feel for the place. It may take a few days to get what we want. Of course, that depends on the weather." Aaron turned his smile on Mrs. Jeffers. "I do appreciate all the things you've been gathering for this project, including the stories. Stories always help shape what I see."

"I've enjoyed getting the word out. It's amazing what people still have in their attics and basements. Bruce has already stowed some of the stuff under the rig."

"The rig?" Ellen frowned. "Why the rig?"

Aaron looked from mother to daughter. Were they speaking in a foreign language?

Mrs. Jeffers laughed. "The rig is our motor home."

"Oh."

"Your father" — Mrs. Jeffers gave Ellen a knowing look — "suggested we loan you the motor home for your stay with us. That'll give you some privacy, and you can also take it out to the prairie. If you don't feel like driving back every night, you'll have what you need with you."

"The rig!" Ellen couldn't conceal her glee. "I love it. What a fantastic idea!" She blew her dad a kiss. "Thank you. We'll take good care of it."

Aaron couldn't deny looking forward to the privacy factor, but if *the rig* was that humongous vehicle they'd parked next to when they arrived, he wasn't convinced they could get it out of the driveway. "Can you drive it?"

Ellen leaned away from him as if he'd just asked the stupidest question she'd ever heard. "Of course I can. I've borrowed it for two-week-long vacations. It's perfect. Haven't you ever been in a motor home?"

He shook his head slowly. Everyone at the table laughed at his expense.

"Don't worry," Mrs. Jeffers said. "Ellen is an excellent driver, or we wouldn't be letting her have it."

Mr. Jeffers cleared his throat. "No offense, but it's probably best if you let Ellen do all the driving."

Aaron shrugged. "I'm not about to try driving that thing." He winked at Ellen. "I'll try to navigate, if need be."

Ellen ignored his comment. "What a great idea. We'll run out to the store tonight and begin stocking it."

"I've changed the bed," Mrs. Jeffers pointed out with a pleasant smile. "The basic staple foods are there. I didn't know what you'd prefer to eat, so I didn't try to stock the fridge."

"No problem. We'll take care of that." Ellen reached across to squeeze her dad's fingers. "This is very thoughtful of you."

He grimaced. "Yeah, well, you're thirty-three years old. Guess you know what you're doing."

"I hope I do." Her lips turned up into a smile. "And you both taught me how to pick myself up off the floor when I need to."

Aaron's breath caught in his windpipe as the drift of the conversation penetrated his brain. He wasn't accustomed to being talked about.

Ellen reached over to take his hand in hers. "I'll be okay," she said softly to her parents. "Don't worry."

"That's what parents do," Mrs. Jeffers quipped. "But we wish you both well with this prairie woman project . . . and whatever else you're working on."

Ellen winked at him. "Let's clear the table. Once we get the dishes in the dishwasher, I'll give you a quick tour of our new home away from home. And then we can run to the store."

"Plan on coming into the house for breakfast in the morning," Ellen's mother said, pushing away from the table. "There's no need to get the rig heated up until you have to."

Aaron glanced at Ellen's rosy cheeks. He didn't doubt she was thinking of heating up the motor home, but not by turning on the stove.

"I initially thought I was walking into a cave," Aaron said, stretching out beside Ellen on the queen-size bed, "but this rig, as you call it, is quite spacious." The grin stretching across his face nearly glowed.

Ellen nodded and handed him a glass of Chardonnay. "I'm glad you like it. This is absolutely perfect for us. For our entire venture. I'm so pleased Dad thought of this."

She scraped a fingernail across his bare chest and smiled on seeing the bulge gathering in his sweatpants. It pleased her that neither one of them was bent on charging forward. They seemed content to nibble on the moment. She liked that. A lot.

Aaron brought her finger to his lips and kissed it. "You're incredibly sexy in satin. Baby blue accentuates your blue eyes. Did you wear this special for the occasion?"

Ellen swallowed as Aaron traced the line of her baby doll across the rise of her breasts. His fingers came within inches of her aching nipples. "I did. I like a touch of romantic now and then. Tina helped pick it out."

"Ah. Were the choker pearls her idea?"

Ellen shook her head. "Mine. They came to me as the oldest daughter. They were originally my great-great-grandmother's. The story is they came to her from Clarissa's lover. That may or may not be true."

"So, a touch of risqué along with the romantic. I like the way the soft light of the rig backlights you."

"Always the photographer," Ellen said, reaching for her wine glass.

"It's an occupational hazard. I'll want to work with you and the mirrors on the closet at the foot of the bed. I like to play with reflections — double images."

"You imagine double when you look at me?"

His laughter was quick and deep. "Dealing with one of you may be about all I can handle."

She narrowed her eyes. "No photography tonight?"

He shook his head. "I plan on feasting on you in the flesh. I don't even want a lens between us."

"Me either. Surprisingly, I have a voracious appetite." She dragged a finger along his strong jaw line. "Perhaps yours will match mine."

She didn't wait for Aaron's response. She flicked her tongue at his chin and pushed him back on the pillows, then pecked at his nose and the corners of his mouth.

He chuckled and wrapped his arms around her, opening his mouth for her to explore.

Without hesitating, she scraped the roof of his mouth with the tip of her tongue. Slowly, she eased her tongue in and out. At last he responded by clamping down on her tongue and gently sucking it, to her delight.

He could do slow. Until now, she hadn't been sure. His tongue pushed against hers, sparking a lover's duel. She moaned as his tongue pressed its way until she opened her mouth wider, giving it more room. She suckled as if she'd never suckled a tongue before. His exquisitely filled her, yet gave her space.

At the same moment, their hands began searching. His roamed across her back until they settled on her bare rump. The silk had worked its way up to her waist. She couldn't recall whether he'd assisted or not—she was too busy teasing his nipples. She pulled gently on one with her teeth and then the other before sliding lower. Her tongue rimmed his navel.

He tilted his pelvis and arched up to greet her as she approached. Together they helped her pivot on her knees until he cupped her mound with a palm and she was able to slide his sweatpants down over his thighs and legs. He kicked them off, and she reveled in the object of her search swaying before her in its fullness.

She flicked her tongue out at the soft head of Aaron's cock and was immediately rewarded by the groan of its master. "You like," she murmured.

"You know I do. Be careful. We don't want a short night."

She chuckled. "I'll try."

With his help, she cast one leg across his chest. His lips immediately began wetting her inner thigh as his mouth struck out on its own quest. She waggled against his open mouth as it settled over her pussy lips, then took the tip of his shaft in her mouth. Determined not to hurry, she backed off and laved the full length of his cock. She cupped his testicles, bouncing them gently.

Ellen tried to breathe while he chewed on her labia. His fingers kneaded her buttocks. She took him back into her mouth as two of his fingers gently but determinedly corkscrewed their way into her vagina. Aaron's cock muffled the sounds of her first orgasm of the evening. Sighing, she knew it would not be her last.

His tongue replaced his fingers, and she began sliding her hands slowly up and down his shaft. They played in unison for long minutes. Her vision blurred as he drove her closer and closer. She dug her fingernails into his thighs and clamped down on his cock as another wave of pleasure swept across her body.

She blinked and renewed her journey up and down his shaft. She heard his lips smacking as he swallowed her juices. His tongue resumed its search for more. Ten fingers raked across her lower back and ass. She smiled as fingers slid down the crevice of her buttocks. She'd wondered how long it would take him to zero in on another of his favorite targets.

She popped off his cock quickly to wet her index finger and then drew him back into her warmth. Two could play this game.

No sooner had she resettled than she felt a finger rimming her anus. She smiled around Aaron's cock and slid her finger down to rim his anus.

His groan caused her to chortle. She knew she had to be careful. She wanted him close, but she didn't want to push him over the edge. Not for the first time, she celebrated being a woman. Men had some physical limitations that she was glad she didn't share. She expected that he could come more than once, but maybe not more than two or three times. And she wanted more than that. Maybe she was greedy. Hell, she'd already gotten more than that.

She worked her finger in up to the knuckle until she met with resistance. She'd only done this with Tina and Mike, yet she knew what to expect. Aaron grunted as she waited and then she gasped as his finger stretched her own portal. "Oh my," she managed to say around his cock.

"Such a beautiful ass," Aaron grunted.

She responded by easing her finger though his opening ring. His gasp of warm breath covered pussy and ass before his finger pushed inward. Impaled. They were both impaled. She dropped his cock from her mouth and wiggled her finger in his butt.

"Easy, girl," Aaron warned, beginning to drive his finger in and out of her ass.

She didn't try to match his pace. And then she couldn't think of anything. His mouth on her vulva. His finger in her ass. And then he flicked his tongue at her clit and she was gone. She rocked back against him, helping him wedge his finger deeper. She clenched and relaxed, clenched and relaxed, until she felt her flow trickling down to him. She laid her cheek on his pelvis and eased her finger out of his butt. She giggled. "Do you think we're ever going to get your cock in my pussy?"

Aaron growled something unintelligible.

She puffed air through her lips as he gingerly pulled his finger from her ass, then turned around to face him.

He smiled ear to ear. "Did you have something in mind?"

She rolled onto her back. "Why don't you come on top? I don't need fancy. I just want you."

Nodding, he shifted to kneel between her wide-open thighs. "You deserve fancy, but I can't wait any longer, either. Not another minute."

She watched him quickly skim his cock and then felt its head being dragged up and down her vulva. "So good." She fought back tears. "But hurry. In me." She raised her knees, bringing the soles of her feet to the mattress.

He groaned. "Amazing." He leaned forward, and the head of his cock penetrated her opening. He paused.

"More," she squealed. "No need to wait." She wrapped her legs around his butt and pulled him forward. "Oh, yes. All of him. Oh my God. So full." She raked her fingernails across his back and lurched against him. "Fuck me."

"Ellen," he grunted. And then he began to slowly work his way in and out of her. It was nearly surreal. So smooth. So sensuous.

He beamed a smile at her. She blew a kiss. And then his

mouth settled over hers. His hips never slowed. Their tongues began matching the pace of his cock. Too much. She slid off his mouth. She had to fight for breath. Her loins were so open. She tried to swallow him up, to draw him into her building climax.

He kept his weight on his hands and knees, reared back, and drove into her as if he was rushing to catch up with her. The entire rig shook. He glided in and out of her as she nursed a medium-sized orgasm. He wasn't finished.

When she was ready again, she nodded. She brushed a hand across his cheek and squeezed his cock with her inner muscles. "Join me this time."

He rammed into her and she dug her fingernails into his shoulders. She thrust hard, meeting him stroke for stroke. His face contorted and his eyes glazed in concentration. She felt him expanding inside her. "Yes." She giggled. "Come with me."

He nodded and bellowed her name. And then she felt his cock jerking, sharing his essence. She hoisted her hips off the bed, kissing his groin with her pussy lips. She tried to remain glued to him as he continued pumping, and then from out of nowhere, she shattered. She fell back to the bed.

Minutes later, she opened her eyes to see Aaron resting his head on one elbow, waiting patiently for her to rejoin him. His grin was one of sheer satisfaction. "You were gone for a while."

She stuck her tongue out at him. "We're lucky I made it back." She stretched and yawned, delighting in the feel of his semi-hard staff still inside her. "The French speak of orgasm as a petite death." She sighed. "This time, I had so many, I nearly died."

Aaron chuckled. "I trust that's poetic license, but you are so lovely to watch when you come."

"You seemed to be doing all right yourself."

"Very." He scowled. "I hope your folks weren't watching. This rig was rocking back and forth."

Ellen giggled and kissed his lips. "Don't worry about it. It's dark out. Besides, there's a saying in the RV world — if the rig is rocking, don't come a knocking."

Laughing, Aaron rolled them over so she was on top. "You are such a breath of fresh air."

Ellen bent down and kissed the tip of his nose. "Guess you've just never been with a woman of the prairie before. Do you want to fuck my ass yet tonight?"

He scowled at her. "We'll get around to that. Why don't we just settle in and get some sleep?"

She rested her cheek on her shoulder. "I'm not too heavy for you?"

"Never."

Sighing softly, Ellen luxuriated in the strong fingers stroking her back, lulling her to sleep. Aaron had surprised her. She'd expected caring but demanding. He'd nearly turned her to mush with gentle and romantic.

She smirked. But they had gotten the rig rocking pretty good. His breathing steadied beneath her. What would Tina say if she could see them now? Aaron *could* be a romantic.

CHAPTER NINE

"Stunning," Aaron said, not attempting to conceal the awe in his voice. "I've read about it. I've even seen pictures, but nothing prepared me for seeing those tall grasses bending in the wind. Incredible."

Ellen held his hand as she led him across the majestic prairie. "It's not hard to imagine getting lost among the big bluestem grasses. What must it have been like to see these grasses stretching for miles any direction from the seat of a covered wagon?"

She squeezed his fingers and smiled radiantly. "I'm glad you like the prairie. As for the wind, she's your constant companion out here. The prairie changes constantly. We've already missed most of the flowering season. Fall comes early to this land. In a few more weeks, this'll be a rich cover of browns and tans."

Ellen looked quickly to their right. "Did you hear that? A rooster pheasant."

"I'm not deaf." He admired the sight of Ellen, dressed in gingham and shading her eyes to peer across the shorter grasses. They stood at the edge of the tall grasses, which dwarfed both of them. "Do you suppose the rooster was calling to his mate?"

Ellen grinned at him. "If so, she didn't respond."

"Did he get stood up?"

"Maybe she's still getting herself ready for her day."

"Probably preening and trying to figure out how best to torture her guy."

She poked him in the side. "I didn't know you were an expert on the mating habits of pheasants."

"Just a guess. Are females any different across the species?"

"Before you get any more amorous ideas, maybe we should start the photo shoot. It did take quite a while for you to get out of bed this morning."

He planted a kiss on the top of her head. "I didn't know I'd enjoy listening to you squeal so early in the morning. Those birds must've begun chirping before the sun even came up."

"I don't squeal," Ellen protested. "And they do start early. Maybe they think the sun comes up because of them." She covered his bulging penis. "Did he come up because of me?"

"He did. And you do squeal, thankfully without restraint. Given the way your mother grinned at us and your dad glowered when we went in for breakfast, I expect you may have wakened them."

"Oh well." Ellen shrugged her shoulders. "Maybe we inspired them."

"Them?" Aaron took a step backward. "Your parents? You said they're in their sixties."

"So?" She scowled. "Certainly you don't think they're too old for sex?"

Feeling his cheeks warm, Aaron glanced across the prairie.

She squeezed his arm. "You may want to do a photo series on sex over fifty. According to my mother, they've never had better sex than they're having now."

He blinked. "Your mother talks sex with you?"

"Of course. There isn't much we don't talk about. She doesn't give me details, but she definitely wants me to know that sex isn't the prerogative of the young. Fewer worries, children gone, and willingness to experiment goes a long way. She was the first person to suggest lube to me."

"Damn. But your father doesn't talk about sex with you."

"He either tries to switch the subject or leaves the room when my mother won't stop."

"No wonder she smiles so much."

Ellen grinned broadly and quickly sobered. "It's pretty bad when you're envious of your own mother's love life."

He nodded and lifted her chin. "You haven't been envious lately, have you?"

She shook her head. Her eyes rounded as his lips lowered to her mouth.

He kissed her softly, then winked. "We'll need to continue working on that. But we'd better get some pics before we lose the light. Why don't you kick off your sandals and stand here at the edge of the tall grasses? Leave the bonnet on for now. We'll begin with you fully clothed.

Minutes later, he said, "Give me that determined look which comes so naturally to you — that's right. Put one hand on your hip and shade your eyes with the other as if you're looking out across the endless prairie. Beautiful. Now some profile shots."

He kept the camera humming as Ellen moved easily from one position to another and from one expression to another. He'd never seen her looking so at one with her environment. It had been a splendid idea to get her out of the studio. The subtle beauty she'd projected under the lights came into full bloom on the prairie.

"Let's remember our audience. Turn away from the camera and lift your skirts to your waist as if you're trying not to drag them across the grasses."

He gulped at the sight of her bare ass. He'd hadn't known she wasn't wearing underwear. Maybe it was the combination of her nakedness and the fresh air, but he was immediately hard. Achingly hard.

"Bend over as if you're picking a flower. Damn. Have I told you how fond I'm becoming of your bare pussy?"

"I believe you have." She peeked over her shoulder. "But I doubt I'll tire of hearing you say it."

"Turn around and keep your dress raised up. Oh yeah. Damn. Damn. Give me a pout. Now that wide-open smile."

He set the camera on the ground, then snapped off several long grass-stems and handed them to her. She'd let her dress fall when he stopped taking pictures. He lifted her dress. "Hold the hem in one hand and the grasses in the other. Now let's let the stems frame your labia like this. Let's get one tit out from under cover. Very nice. Now let the seedpods brush against the nipple. Perfect. You look like the maid of the harvest."

He stepped back and grabbed the camera. "Incredible. Use your judgment. Give me a series of expressions. That's right. Keep it going."

He stepped forward and grinned at her unspoken question. "Hold that pose. We need to get your labia a little more puffed up."

"Thought we might," she murmured. "I suppose you're going to take care of that."

"Thought I'd give it a try." He dragged a finger up either side of her vulva and repeated that action.

Ellen's eyes narrowed and a whimper escaped her thinned lips.

He smiled. "I believe you're getting there quickly."

She nodded.

"It must be the fresh air."

"Or being out in the open like this."

She gasped but did nothing to stop him. "Anyone could come by."

He chuckled. "I doubt that. There's no one within miles of us. If anyone is going to come, it will be you." He brushed the seedpod across her nipple. "It'll make for a better photo if your clit is visible."

She arched an eyebrow at him.

"I'll take care of it." He dragged a finger across her shrouded clit.

"Jesus," she murmured. "Are you going to make me come?"

He shook his head and stepped back to focus the camera. "Superb. She's out looking about. Looking for more. Do you want more?"

She nodded.

"I wonder who will get more turned on looking at you standing before the tall grasses anticipating your orgasm — men or women."

"You think women look at these photos?"

"I know they do. Does it turn you on knowing that men and women will be fantasizing about you? Imagining themselves bringing you off as they bring themselves off."

Ellen swallowed and nodded. "At first, I didn't think it would, but it does."

"I thought so. You like to watch, but you also like to be watched. Go ahead. Put the grasses aside and stroke your clit. Do what you need to. I'll watch through the lens. Imagine how you'll inspire your fans."

She didn't hesitate. The grasses fell softly to the ground. Keeping the dress out of the way with one hand, she palmed her pussy with the other. She gave the camera a daring look and strummed her clit with a thumb.

Aaron did his best to hold the camera steady while taking a quick string of pictures of Ellen's finger disappearing in and out of her channel. She tilted her pelvis and rocked against the probing finger. And then her mouth slackened. Somehow, she managed to keep her eyelids half open, maintaining contact with anyone watching, encouraging any and all to join her. Once again, Aaron delighted in capturing her ability to appeal to others while pleasing herself.

He knew the orgasm had been a small one, but it had been genuine. And it was the first he'd taken of his prairie woman climaxing in her prairie habitat. It would make a stunning photo.

"Delicious," she murmured, wetting her lips. "Are we done?"

"No. Stay right there. Let the hem fall. That's right. Now direct your attention to your breast."

"It's too sensitive to the touch right after I orgasm."

"I'm not asking you to touch it. Just hold the gingham away and look at it."

"Like this?" She tucked the fabric under her right breast.

"No. That's too provocative. I want something more subtle. You just came. Hold the top of the dress aside with your left hand like this. Excellent. Your left breast isn't quite in view and the right nipple is peeking out. I'm going to take this pose from several angles."

He focused the camera. "Ellen, look at the nipple as if you're still marveling over that delicious orgasm."

"That's easy." She chuckled. "I still am."

"Gorgeous. Smile softly. Behold the future. Damn, you're looking like earth mother embodied. Think of a lover's lips on that nipple."

"That's easy. Your lips. Mike's lips. Tina's lips."

He clicked the camera, fighting the urge to tell her to only focus on his lips. "Now imagine a baby's mouth tugging on that nipple."

She looked at him in near panic. "That's not fair, Aaron. I've never had a baby. And I doubt that I will."

"Pretend. Please. Stay with that emotion. I see longing. You want a baby?"

She gulped, and he knew she was holding back tears. His heart nearly shattered as she closed her eyes and then partially lifted her eyelids to embrace the nipple with a soft stare.

Aaron gasped. Had he ever been present when a woman fantasized about motherhood?

He took several more shots before setting the camera aside. Ellen never stirred. He walked to her and gathered her in his arms. "Sorry," he whispered. "I didn't realize how difficult that'd be for you."

She sobbed into his shoulder and shook her head. Struggling for air, she raised her head to give him a crooked smile. "It's okay. I rarely allow myself to experience those emotions." She laid her cheek on his shirt. "Another bone of contention with my ex. We were going to try to have children when we got settled in our marriage. We were never settled enough."

"I'm sorry," Aaron said softly into her hair. "I know you'll make a superb mother."

Ellen stepped away and squared her shoulders. "I probably have some students that disagree with that notion. But thank you. Who knows? Maybe I'll find a guy yet who wants to play house with me. There's time." She winced. "But my biological clock is ticking a little louder each year."

Aaron tucked an arm around her waist and led her back to the RV. She hadn't asked if he ever thought of being a father. His prairie woman probably couldn't imagine him being a father. She might be surprised by how often he wondered about that himself.

He shook his head, trying to clear it. It was going to take some time to get the image of Ellen Jeffers giving her breast such a motherly stare out of his head. He knew he had another photo for his bedroom wall.

Ellen sat across the small RV table and grinned at Aaron's satisfied smile. It had been ages since she'd cooked for a man. The empty dishes attested to the fact that she could still cook.

"Your mother must've taught her daughters to cook." Aaron rubbed his tummy. "I'm amazed you could cook up such a scrumptious meal out in the middle of nowhere."

"We have all the comforts of home. I'm glad you like my cooking," she said softly.

"Do you get to cook often during the school year?"

She shook her head. "The microwave is my primary stove, I'm afraid. In case you're curious, I don't make a habit of cooking for men."

"That's a shame. Guess I'm a lucky bastard."

"You may be very lucky before this night is done."

"I wonder if all prairie women looked so lovely in gingham."

"I expect many of them had hard lives. This prairie isn't very forgiving. Did you know that the root systems of many of these plants are longer than the grasses themselves?"

"Deeply rooted." He reached across the small space and brushed a finger across the back of her hand. "So are you deeply rooted in the prairie?"

She withdrew her hand. His touch suddenly seemed too intimate. She shrugged. "Rooted. Maybe. Some days I feel trapped. Angie — my best friend — and I kid about looking for teaching positions in the Twin Cities."

"Really." Aaron sat up straighter.

"We've never looked."

"Maybe you'd prefer to work at the academy."

She scowled. "Right."

"I'm not kidding. I'm serious. You have a feel and an eye for photography that's rare. You understand it as art. Most people don't. Tell me, how do you usually spend your summers, when you're not exploring your art?"

"Teach. I'm usually involved with summer school for juniors and seniors."

"Not third graders."

"Nope. I teach a creative writing seminar and an introductory French class."

"You really have a range of teaching subjects and levels."

"My folks always counseled us to keep as many options open as possible. Next summer I may offer a photography class. I'm working with the upper school to set up a darkroom. Even if we can't get photography in the schoolroom, it should be a relatively inexpensive after-school project."

"You really do plan on using this experience."

"Of course I do. This isn't merely a summer lark."

"But you see yourself going back and picking up your life where you left it at the beginning of summer."

"Of course I do." She blanched. "Why wouldn't I?"

"What about Tina?" he growled.

"Tina? What about her?" She smacked her lips. "Oh. That's a summer fling," she stammered.

Aaron darkened.

"I guess I haven't thought that far ahead. I'm just trying to live day by day." She arched an eyebrow. "Which is very rare for me to do. Maybe I'll have to drive over for a visit." She shook her head. "That'd probably be harder. I hate goodbyes."

"I take it you and Angie aren't involved — in that way."

"Not yet," she blurted out. She had found herself thinking more and more about Angie. She tipped her head to the side. "She wanted me to come with her to Europe."

"She wanted more than a travel companion?"

"Yes. She made that clear. I was shocked."

"Interesting. Maybe she primed you for Tina."

"I admit I've wondered about that. It doesn't matter. The town we live in is so small that we'd never be able to carry on an affair without someone getting wind of it. And that would be that."

"You'd be booted out of the school?"

136

"Quickly and efficiently. No fuss for the papers. We'd just be out on our silly asses." She stood to clear the last of their plates. He immediately slid off the bench seat to help.

"Speaking of asses," she quipped. "You've learned a lot about me in the last several weeks, and I hardly know a thing about you. Why don't you enlighten me while I do up these dishes quick? I hate to have to look at dirty dishes in the morning."

"There's not much to tell. And what does that have to do with asses?"

She grazed his chin with the back of a sudsy hand. "I need to know more about the man who claims my ass than I know about you."

"Son of a bitch." He grinned broadly. "Then think of me as an open book. You've been giving this a lot of thought."

"I have at that," she said, soaking the dishes. "I know exactly the place, the position and the time." She made a point of glancing at the wall clock. "The time is rapidly approaching. But before filling my ass, why don't you try filling my ears? Who are you? Where did you come from? What are your hopes and dreams? Why was it so important to get Mike and Tina to pledge they'd save my ass for you? And what led you to believe I'd go along with that?" She grabbed the dishrag. "That should be enough questions for starters. You might want to begin talking."

"Damn, woman," he grumbled, reaching under the gingham dress she still wore to squeeze her bare bottom. "You drive some hard bargains."

She giggled and squirmed away from his hand. "Don't try to divert me with talk about hardness. I expect you'll be justly rewarded with this bargain. Are you a native of the Twin Cities area?"

"Yep. Born and raised there—in one of the posh suburbs, on a lake, of course."

"Of course." She grinned at him. "So your parents were wealthy. Go on."

"Filthy rich. I went to the best schools. I had choices of Ivy League schools and settled on Brown."

"But you came back to Minnesota."

"I've never loved a place more than the Twin Cities. It's where I belong. There's a freshness about the place that I didn't see in the east."

"Maybe it's the influence of the prairie."

"I wondered about that earlier today."

"You're close to your family? Do you have brothers and sisters?"

"Nope. I expect if my parents had it to do over again, they wouldn't have had me."

"Aaron!" She scowled and scrubbed a pot.

"It's okay. They never approved of me. I was raised primarily by a nanny. My folks traveled and still travel a lot. Maybe that's why I seldom do. I like what I do. They detest it. Maybe that's part of why I love it so."

"Is it the photography, or that you do so many nudes?"

"Both. Any form of art would've been beneath them, but photography is despicable because any Joe Blow can snap a picture."

"That's sad."

"As for the nudity, I expect my mother hasn't let my dad get close to her since she conceived me. They seem to have reached an accommodation. Isn't that what marriage is about?"

Ellen sighed and began drying the dishes. "You may be right. But then I never got there." She winced at him. "But I do hope marriage is about more than accommodation."

He nodded and smiled softly. "Your folks seem to have much more than that. What really sticks in my folks' craw is that my grandfather left me a trust fund that they couldn't touch and which became mine when I turned twenty-one."

"Wow."

"Yeah. I won't deny that I'm able to do some of what I do because my grandfather turned out to be my benefactor."

"Isn't that the way it's always been with art? In order to push the envelope, the artist needs a benefactor of some sort."

"Too often, yes."

"I imagine they frown at you screwing all your models."

Aaron's eyes sparkled, matching his laughter. "Are you wondering about my parents, or asking a question of your own?"

His stare suddenly became too intense and she quickly glanced away.

He grabbed her shoulders and glared at her, then his eyes softened.

She swallowed.

"You deserve a spanking for making assumptions about me like that."

She grew warm. "Why?" she squeaked.

"Occasionally, I help prepare a female model, but I usually leave that up to my assistants. I try to keep my love life and professional life separate."

"But Tina?"

"I've been fucking Tina for years, before she and Mike hooked up."

"And you still do."

"That's right. Sometimes with Mike and sometimes without."

"I admit, I still don't understand that."

"But you seem to enjoy it."

She wet her lips and nodded.

"And you've fantasized about me and Mike fucking Tina."

She nodded.

"And you've fantasized about me and Mike fucking you."

Ellen puffed air from her lips and nodded again. She saw no need to deny the obvious.

Aaron leaned closer to brush his lips across hers. "And I'm here to breathe life into your fantasies."

"Why me? If you avoid your models."

He shook his head. "Some questions don't have answers. I tried to stay away from you."

"But you couldn't?"

"It may have been your innocence. The way you embrace new ventures. And you didn't start out being a model."

"And my ass. Why did we need to save it for you?"

"I wanted it," he ground out. "I'm not sure I've ever wanted anything more. Don't ask me why. I don't know why."

"I accept that," she said softly. "Not everything can be easily explained, particularly emotions." She rose on her toes and kissed him gently. "I don't even know how old you are."

"Thirty in April."

"Oh my," she whispered huskily. "I'm older than you are."

"By three years. Does that matter?"

"Not for what I want you to do." She held his stare. "I agree. I believe I do deserve a spanking for making such erroneous assumptions about you. And then I want you to fuck my ass."

"I hoped that might be what you've been leading up to. Here, or in the bedroom?"

"In the bedroom. I want to be on my hands and knees facing the closet mirrors at the foot of the bed. I want to see your face when you enter me. You looked so glorious when you entered Tina's ass while she nibbled on my pussy."

He looked like he couldn't think of a comeback.

She smiled, then took him by the hand. "If you're ready to let an old lady lead you to her boudoir, I'm ready for a young stud to claim my ass."

"Christ," Aaron grunted, "I've been ready since I first saw your tight ass through the camera lens."

CHAPTER TEN

"You had enough?"

Ellen grinned at their reflection in the closet mirror. Aaron knelt behind her with his open hand raised in the air. She shook her head and waggled her raised butt. "No way. Don't be a wimp, Aaron. Tina spanks me harder than that." She winked and goaded, "You have a long way to go to match the sting Mike gives me."

Aaron colored. "Dammit, woman, don't push me too hard."

Watching his hand descend to slap her flesh, Ellen flinched. "Oh, now you're starting to cook."

He glowered at her as his palm connected once more with her butt, knocking her a little off balance.

"Much better. Is my ass starting to glow for you?"

"Yes, both cheeks are turning pink. Are you stinging now?"

She nodded.

He didn't wait for an answer before slapping a butt cheek again. His lips curled rakishly. "More than when Mike spanks you?"

She grinned broadly and shook her head.

"Damn," he grumbled, popping her butt three times in rapid succession, each more intense than the last.

"Almost." She pouted. "Can you fondle my clit, too? I like to come while being spanked."

She giggled when Aaron's nostrils flared as he moved to meet her request. Her giggles quickly turned to groans and then to whimpers. She tossed her head from side to side while Aaron paddled her relentlessly with one hand and strummed her clit with the other as if she were a banjo. "So good. Oh wow. Stop. Wait!"

He sat back immediately and watched her rock back and forth on her knees as if riding a balloon.

She shuddered. Catching her breath, she smiled at his reflection. "Wonderful. Now you can take the sting away by kissing my bottom."

"I'll do better than that," he said, moving directly behind her to plant a kiss on her butt. "I'm going to kiss your ass, lick your ass, and fuck your ass, in that order." He raised his head to stare at her in the mirror. "Unless you have a better idea."

She shook her head. "If you manage all of that, you'll earn an A plus in my grade book for sure. I'm already lubed."

"I can tell. And I always aimed to please the teacher."

Ellen inhaled deeply as Aaron's lips caressed her burning buttocks. He *had* stung her harder than Tina or Mike. She couldn't explain why it was important for him to be the lover who spanked her the hardest.

Relishing his cooling lips, she realized she'd begun to think of him as a lover. She frowned at her reflection. Why wouldn't she? That was what they were. Just like Tina and Mike. They were all lovers. They just hadn't been all together at the same place — yet.

"Jesus," she murmured as his rough tongue laved one butt cheek and then the other. He peered over her rump, giving her a devilish grin and teasing her with his tongue. She wiggled her butt, issuing her own invitation. He'd been there before.

He separated her butt cheeks between his large hands and ducked his head.

"Oh my God!" She groaned as his tongue burrowed into her anus. There'd be no preliminary rimming this time. He was showing her what his attention was focused on — probing her ass. She pushed back against him. His breath warmed her ass as he sank in deep. He wrapped an arm around her hips and began again to stroke her clit. "Not again," she muttered.

He laughed without giving her a moment's reprieve. His tongue and fingers drove her beyond reasoning, beyond thinking. He steadied her weight to keep her from collapsing. Only after filling and emptying and filling her lungs did she open her eyes to look at his triumphant smile. "You better give me your cock while I still have enough strength to kneel."

He nodded, concern flashing across his face. "Why don't you rest on your elbows rather than your hands? That'll be easier on you, and" — he winked — "it'll give me an even better view of the target."

"I hadn't noticed you'd misplaced it," she said, lowering to her elbows. "This is better," she admitted. "I trust you found what was lost."

"I never said it was lost. Give me a moment to lube my cock, and I'll add a little for you, too."

She wet her lips as his finger spread lube on her anus and dipped seductively inside.

He bit his lower lip and eyed her in the mirror. "Okay, Ellen, here we go. Say goodbye to your virgin ass."

She nodded at his image. His lust surpassed what she'd remembered when he'd entered Tina in Studio B. She couldn't think of any appropriate words.

"Damn, look at you. You're opening without my help. You're as eager as I am."

"Hurry," she whispered hoarsely.

She swallowed hard as the head of his cock banged against her anus.

"Damn, you're so ready. All the foreplay helped."

She nodded. He held her buttocks apart and slipped the crown of his shaft in. She tried her best not to clench.

"Good girl," he said softly, apparently sensing her effort to relax. "Be patient. We'll get there."

She waited, but she wasn't overly patient. She puffed out her cheeks. "I'm softening. Try some more."

He nodded and pressed slightly forward, stretching her. She tried not to wince. He stopped. She shook her head and pushed back against him. "Oh my God," she whimpered. "I'm doing it. We're doing it."

"Wait."

"No." She pushed hard back against his thighs. And then she started to giggle. "I've got him. Jesus, you're big. I've never tried anything this big. But I've got him. All of him. Right?"

Aaron laughed and nodded. "To my balls. You didn't leave anything out. You could've waited a little longer."

"Why?" She smiled impishly. "I believe you were going to fuck my ass. I don't feel anything happening. Other than maybe having a big log up my ass." She shifted forward a little and then back.

"Christ, woman. You want it—you're going to get it." He grabbed her hips, holding her like a vice, and then he slowly pulled partway out.

She saw her eyes bulge in the mirror as he impaled her again.

He did it three more times, catching a rhythm.

"Oh, wow. Incredible. Do it. I love it."

The beads on his brow matched her own, and his breathing became audibly labored. He never slowed, thank God. Her eyelids fluttered shut. She opened them quickly—she didn't want to miss anything of this first time.

She saw his mouth open. He gulped in air and stared at his cock, which was moving fluidly in and out of her ass. She remained still, not wanting to disrupt his concentration or their tableaux. Ever so briefly, she wished they had a picture of this moment.

And then she began to shatter. "What's happening?" She couldn't distinguish what was taking place back there. Everything was falling apart at the same time. She fought for consciousness.

"Oh, hell," Aaron bellowed. "I'm filling your ass."

Ellen closed her eyes. She wanted to watch him emptying into her, but she couldn't hold her eyelids open any longer. She wanted to cheer him on, but she could only whimper. She wanted to thank him for being so thorough with her, but only half-baked words of love flitted across her lips. Shuddering, she gave up to the silence, vaguely aware of his trembling body covering hers.

At least he hadn't been totally unaffected. He helped her move from her knees so they lay side by side. He made no effort to withdraw from her. She wasn't ready for him to leave her.

Why couldn't she turn her brain off? She wasn't ready to talk with him about what had just transpired. She wasn't sure she ever could, because she couldn't tell what had happened — certainly more than taking a cock in her ass. She knew it wouldn't have been the same with Mike, even if he'd been first. That awareness thrilled her and scared her. She might not be able to look at Aaron until the morning.

Gulping in air, Aaron couldn't discern which of them was shaking more. He'd shared plenty of powerful lovemaking moments, but this one was right up there. The mirrors had made it such a total sensory experience. He'd never had a woman flirt so while being spanked. She was right, he'd looked like a lust-filled animal when he entered her ass, and so had she. She'd wanted him to be first in her ass — not because he'd ordered it, but because she desired it.

He kissed the back of her neck. It might take several lifetimes to figure out his prairie woman. But it was Ellen's soft glowing look as she treasured her last orgasm that he'd remember most. That look had nearly unhinged him.

For a moment, he thought it was more than pleasure, more than satisfaction, more than gratitude. For a moment, it had been a look of love.

He shook his head, dragging his nose across her shoulders as she slept. He tried to draw her closer. It had been a fleeting look. Perhaps he'd only been projecting his feelings of the moment.

He'd never thought much about love. It hadn't been a problem or a goal. Was that what he'd just experienced?

It wouldn't last, but it was nice to have been totally in tune with another human being like that, wanting to give them the world, wanting to fulfill their every fantasy. He thought he'd had such transitory moments with Tina on occasion. But this was different. More profound. More wrenching.

He clutched Ellen tight to his body. He couldn't make it last. Would they even talk about this night beyond how they'd taken each other to fantastic sexual plateaus? Would they dare talk about the emotional bonding?

He didn't want to sleep, because he knew those feelings wouldn't be there in the morning. With trembling fingers, he cupped Ellen's breast. What if they were there in the morning?

"Son of a bitch," he murmured softly before kissing Ellen's neck one last time as he drifted in her wake.

"Uncle Jim asked that we not try to go in," Ellen said, walking around the old soddy. "I can understand why. He's looking into how he can shore it up without damaging the walls more."

"It's an amazing structure," Aaron said. "Baked by wind and sun, I guess. I've seen adobe of the southwest, but I've never seen anything like this. Looks like caked mud, grasses, and I don't know what else."

"Anything that might stick together. I know the roof has undergone repair, probably several times. I don't know about the walls. They're very thick."

"You've been in the house?"

"When I was a little girl, and then my mother brought me out here when I was fourteen to explain Clarissa to me."

"That must've been fascinating."

"It was. I already knew much of the story, but not all of it."

"And this is her place."

"The original soddy. The wood house she and Hazel built didn't last, but this structure did. Ironic, huh?"

"Amazing. And she would've used most of these things your mother collected for the shoot."

"That's right. These, or others like them." Ellen ran fingers over the spinning wheel. "This wheel was hers. The flail comes down from her. The hurricane lamps probably don't. There's an old butter churn. I don't know its history. But they're all authentic pieces. None of them are replicas."

"Very good."

"You do have a passion for authenticity." She stepped across the baked ground to squeeze his arm. "That must go along with trying to be original and wanting to be first." She studied him thoughtfully.

He held her gaze.

"Neither one of us seems eager to talk about last night."

He shrugged. "Maybe we're afraid if we do, it will evaporate like a mirage."

She nodded. "I think I know what you mean, but I am glad you were my first." She smirked. "Incredibly authentic"—she took a deep breath—"but I don't think I have anything else

148

virginal to give you."

He tried to mask the flicker of emotion on his face, but he caught her frown and knew he hadn't succeeded.

She stood on her toes to kiss him. "I hope you won't be put off by seconds, thirds, and so on."

He grinned broadly and kissed her soundly. "I believe I'm developing quite a yearning for *so on*. I doubt that making love with you could be anything other than authentic."

"Goodness," she said, hugging him tight. "I will treasure those words. I hope you're right." She pulled away from him. "We'd better get back to picture-taking before this yearning for more authenticity becomes overpowering."

An hour and a half later, Aaron changed lenses one more time. This would likely be their only trip to the sod house. He wanted to make sure he hadn't left anything out. They'd done a long series with Ellen at the spinning wheel. He'd had her holding the flail, an object he'd never heard of before. They'd even taken a clump of prairie grasses to show how it had been used to separated stalks and seeds. They'd used the lamps and several baskets. And, of course, he had plenty of Ellen in front of the sod house itself. As was his custom, he'd begun with her fully dressed in gingham, and then they'd shot pictures of her partially clad and totally nude.

He studied Ellen back in her gingham dress. They should probably wrap up, but something didn't feel finished. He spied the butter churn again. They'd already used it as a prop, but he'd thought of an alternative pose. "If you're not too tired, why don't we try a couple more with you and the churn?"

"I'm not too tired. And we probably won't be back here anytime soon."

He nodded. "Sit on that three-legged stool as if you're

churning butter."

"Like this," Ellen said after she was in position.

"That's right. Pull the dress up over your knees. Nothing too risqué. This is going to be a study of breasts."

She eyed him cautiously. "Why not?" She started to reach for the buttons on her dress.

"Let me." She folded her hands in her lap and let him undo the buttons. When he had them undone to her waist, he lowered the left side of the dress off her shoulder to expose one breast. "Perfect start. I'm going to take profile and frontal shots."

He clicked the shutter. "Look down at the churn. Now at the camera. Give me innocence. Now sultry. Beautiful."

Without leaving the camera, he said, "Ellen, pull your arms out of the dress and lay the top in your lap. Lovely. Your full tits add promise to the picture. The churn coupled with this view of your breasts will speak to the observer subliminally of nurturing. You are the prairie mother abounding with milk and honey."

Ellen winced and struggled to clear her throat. "You have the oddest imagination—clearly an artist's imagination."

"Or a lover's," he said softly. "Let the churn be and pull on your nipples. Pinch them." He clicked the camera. "More. Think of me coming in your ass last night. Yes, now they're lengthening."

"They get any tighter, I'm going to scream."

"And you scream nicely, too. Okay, grab the churn again and I'll get more shots of you working. Fantastic." He knelt in front of Ellen to take some shots of her face framed by her boobs.

She stuck her tongue out at him.

"Do that again. Can you lift your breast to your mouth and lick your nipple?"

"Of course."

"Jesus." He clicked off shots. She'd done one better. She was sucking her nipple and rounding her eyes. He stood and disentangled his arousal.

She giggled and sat on the stool, looking incredibly innocent. "An occupational hazard, I suppose."

"Every job has its difficulties."

"Are we done?"

"Yes."

"Good." Ellen stood and poked her arms back through the armholes of the dress but made no attempt to button back up. She grabbed his hand and tugged at him.

He frowned.

"Put the camera down. This series, for me, is, in part, about honoring Clarissa. I have one more thing I've wanted to do to honor her."

"What's that?" he asked, setting the camera on the churn.

She led him around the back of the sod house and entered the edge of what must have been acres of Indian grass. Not nearly as tall as the big bluestem, but quite tall.

"Deer are fond of making beds in here. I believe we can, too. I'm going to make love with you in the sweetgrass. I've wanted to do this since I was in my teens, but I never found a man who could appreciate the prairie enough."

Taken back, Aaron knew he must look dumbfounded. "Not even your husband."

"Not even my husband. Will you help me honor Clarissa?"

"You know I will. It's an honor to be asked."

Aaron let Ellen lead the way deeper into the sweetgrass. With the sod house still in view, Ellen stopped their progress and began matting down the surrounding tall grasses. He waited for her to arrange things the way she wanted them.

She dropped to her knees and grinned up at him. "Join me."

He knelt down, letting his gaze roam over her, from her

sparkling eyes, to her slightly bowed lips, to her nipples standing erect. She shrugged out of the top of the dress, kissed him, and pressed her palms against his chest. "Lie down on your back for me.

He lay down, surprised by the springy bed she'd prepared for them. The scent of the newly crushed sweetgrass filled his nostrils. Without haste, Ellen undid his belt buckle and worked his trousers down until she could pull them off. His shorts were next.

His heart skipped a bit as she paused long enough to admire his full cock before curling her fingers around it and bending down to wet it with her tongue. Ellen eyed him out of the corner of an eye as she guided him into her mouth. He raked his fingers through her hair. Languidly, she inched him deep into her throat until her lips pressed against his groin. She cupped his balls and backed halfway off his shaft before sinking back down again.

"Ellen, Ellen," he moaned. He knew she wouldn't finish him this way, but his entire body was warmed by her attention.

Without speaking, she eased him from her mouth and placed one leg across him so she knelt above his cock. She tugged the gingham dress over her head and tossed it aside onto his trousers.

His lungs filled with anticipation. Ellen's eyes glazed. He wasn't sure she was even with him. Had she been transported back to Clarissa's century?

Ellen grabbed his cock, and he watched as she guided it between her raised legs. Her heat encased its head, then much of its shaft, and then all of it. She sat there for a long moment, as if pondering her options.

He lay still, listening. Was it his heart or hers he heard pounding? Birds chirped in the distance. A soft prairie breeze caused a ripple among the grasses and blew Ellen's hair across her face. And then the calm returned.

Ellen placed her palms on her hips and rose up his shaft. She wet her lips and dropped and rose again. She appeared to be in a trance.

He resisted reaching out to her.

She began a slow ride, maintaining a steady tempo. She closed her eyes and lifted her arms high above her head, then picked up the pace. His cock appeared and disappeared over and over. He waited.

She dropped a hand to her clit and teased it into coming out from hiding. Rising and falling, Ellen keened to the prairie, announcing her climax. Slowly she continued riding him.

Aaron knew she was focusing, gathering herself for more. Clarissa would want more — would demand more.

At last she settled on his groin and opened her eyes. She grinned softly and inhaled deeply. "Thanks for waiting. I needed that first one to be just me and Clarissa." She flicked her tongue at him. "Not that you weren't essential. I hope you enjoyed the ride."

"Immensely. Now what?"

"You show me. How does my prairie man want to love his prairie woman?" She pouted. "That is, if you do."

"Watch me," he grunted, easily flipping the squealing Ellen onto her back. He knelt between her thighs, fully impaled in her tight sheath.

"This will work fine," she said, running her fingernails down his backside. "Sweetgrass makes a soft bed, doesn't it?"

He tested their joining by shifting from side to side. He leaned over to kiss her lips and then each of her nipples.

"Wonderful," she intoned. "Love me."

Aaron slipped his hands under her buttocks and lifted. He seated himself firmly, and then he began to love her the best he could. He flexed in and out of her steadily. A dreamy smile formed on her lips.

He never stopped. He never paused. Her tongue parted her lips. To his delight, she was building for another petite death. "Play with yourself. I want to watch you come again."

She cranked an eyelid up. "Don't you ever tire of watching me come?"

"Never." She surprised him by reaching over her mound to encircle the base of his cock as he continued diving in and out of her. "Don't mind me. Do your clit."

She pouted and withdrew to cover her clitoris. He backed nearly out of her, and her eyes sprang wide. He chuckled and directed his cock toward her G spot.

"Oh Christ," she squealed, pawing at her clit. "You know every button to push. I'm falling over the edge."

"Again," he grunted, pulling her hips tighter as he drove his cock deep.

She threw her arms back and tilted her pelvis, then lifted her legs high in the air and spread them wide, causing her channel to grip him tighter still.

He watched her orgasms rolling across her body. He glanced quickly to the sky, then back at Ellen—her eyes were open, but he didn't think she could see him. Her mouth gaped. Never before had they sent her climbing that pinnacle of continuing orgasms as she was doing now. She had become one with the prairie wind.

And he had helped her get there. And he was on autopilot. He could keep this up as long as his strength held up.

"Come with me," Ellen pleaded. "Don't let me come alone." Her heels pounded his backside.

His response was a roar. He slammed into her. "Hold on."

She clasped him with her arms and legs, and he hurtled forward, propelling both of them into oblivion. His climax shot through him and into her as if it was nitro. He couldn't stop jerking.

He lost track of Ellen. He nearly lost track of himself. The world had gone dark. Then he heard his own ragged breathing. He settled her rump on the grass and flexed his fingers.

At last he opened his eyes to see Ellen glowing at him.

"My prairie man," she whispered. "Get down here so I can hug you."

He shook his head and crashed, rolling them onto their sides.

She brushed perspiration from his forehead. "I'd heard of long, rolling orgasms. I thought they were somebody's fantasy. Whew." She kissed the tip of his nose. "You okay?"

He nodded.

"I think we did fine honoring Clarissa." She winked. "Hopefully, she was loved so well."

He wet his lips. "Sounds like she was, later on."

Ellen ran fingernails across his pecs. "I hope Caillebotte's mistress was loved so well."

He brushed the back of his hand across her cheek. "I hope Caillebotte was loved so well." He arched an eyebrow. "After all, if she was a woman of the night, she was more experienced with having sex while maintaining her distance."

Ellen rolled to her back and looked pensively at the cloudless sky. "I don't think it's possible to maintain distance while making love on the prairie."

"I know what you mean," he mused. "It's been that way ever since we started the photo shoot yesterday."

"I wish we could stay out here," she added wistfully.

"Even the prairie would probably get old."

"Probably."

Ellen's sigh nearly burst his heart. "Perhaps we'll find a way to keep the prairie spirit with us."

She took a long time before she responded. "Maybe," she replied in hushed tones, "we should just cherish what we have in the moment."

Ellen rose to her knees and then to her feet. Without

embarrassment, she grabbed him by the hand and pulled him up. "We need to get dressed. Mom is expecting us for dinner." She kissed his chin. "I'll never, ever forget this adventure on the prairie."

"Me, either."

She reached for the dress and donned it quickly. He put on his shorts and pants as she buttoned up. Their trip to the prairie was about over. He was already missing the place. He knew she was, too.

CHAPTER ELEVEN

Pursing her lips, Ellen waited patiently for her mother to change the topic of conversation. She'd taken longer than usual to catch her up on the latest local and family gossip. Ellen peered out the dining room window to the deck, where her dad was entertaining Aaron, no doubt at her mother's request. Aaron was showing appropriate interest. They were probably discussing the prospects for the Twins. Baseball might have been one of the few interests they shared — other than her, of course. But she doubted either man was likely to be talking about her.

She glanced back at her mother, who she was sure was about to broach the topic the men shied away from.

"Aaron certainly sounds pleased with the prairie woman photo shoot," her mother commented with a gleam in her eyes. "I like the fact that he seems so convinced that you fill his image of the prairie woman. Clarissa would be pleased."

"Strange, isn't it?" Ellen said. "We all speak of Clarissa as if we knew her, but we never saw her in the flesh."

"Does it really matter? She's come to stand for so much of what we're about. Independent. Rooted. Bold. Daring. Adventurous. Determined."

"I wish." Ellen again glanced out the window at the men. "But I imagine Clarissa had her weak moments, too."

"I'm sure she did. We all do. But she knew how to be decisive when she needed to. We've all had potential life-changing moments." Her mother sobered and pushed the hair back away from her face. "I imagine you see your father and me as very stuck-in-the-mud old folks. I suspect most children don't regard their parents as particularly adventurous."

Ellen shook her head. "You're just you. You seem to be doing what you want to do. You enjoy doing things together."

"We do, and I can honestly say we love each other."

"Of course you do."

"You looked so radiant when you stepped out of the rig when you got back from the prairie." Her mother gulped. "I was immediately envious."

"Mom."

"Shh. I'm trying to say something here. You both smelled of sweetgrass, as if you'd been rolling in it."

"Mom."

"Don't. Please. I know what it feels like to be loved on the open prairie. Every woman should. The question is, what now? Will you be moving to the Cities? Will you live with Aaron? Will Angie go with you?"

"Angie?"

Her mother covered her hand and squeezed her fingers. "I have to ask you a very personal question."

Ellen nodded, trying not to hold her breath.

"Have you been with a woman? Slept with a woman? Remember, I've been to Aaron's web pages. There are several wonderfully tasteful photos of women with women."

Ellen gulped. "Yes. This summer. Tina."

"I knew it." Her mother smiled sadly. "There's something about a woman who's been with a woman. I can't quite explain it."

"Mom. Why is it so important for you to know? How do you know what it's like to be with a woman?" Ellen's eyebrows shot up, then she gasped and covered her mouth.

"It's in your blood, girl." Her mother's eye took on a distant look. "Jill came into my life after your brother was born. I was happy before Jill. At least, I thought I was. We met at a convention." She heaved a sigh. "It happened. We kept seeing each other for about six months. She was from a neighboring town."

"Dad?"

"He knew. I didn't try to keep Jill a secret—it was the sixties. Free love, at least some places . . ." Her mother wet her lips. "The three of us got along fine." Her mouth pinched. "Real fine. And it wasn't just sex. It was love. But we were ahead of our time. If we'd had more courage, we might've all picked up and moved, maybe to San Francisco, which was certainly more open by then.

"But no. Instead, Jill moved out there. We still exchanged Christmas cards, but we never saw her after she left. She married and had her own family. Tragically, she died two years ago."

"And why are you telling me all of this now?"

Her mother brushed back a tear. "You seem so intent on living your life as we lived ours. We're happy. Don't get me wrong. But there could've been more. Much more." She paused. "There should've been more. You didn't have to become a teacher. You don't have to stay in South Dakota. You can value the land and its spirit without being a slave to it. At least you divorced that creep of a husband."

Ellen's mother leaned back in her chair. "I thought maybe you'd get together with Angie, but I never saw that glow until this trip. You are finding yourself as a woman, Ellen. My advice is, do everything possible not to lose it. You don't have to fit into a box. You can have it all."

Ellen shook her head. "I'm not exactly sure what you're saying, but I know I have a lot to sort out. I didn't know that until we were out on the prairie. I haven't seriously thought about what this means for my career, for living in South Dakota, for anything. I'm not even sure what I'm trying to sort out." She glanced out at Aaron. "And I'm not at all certain he's feeling any of the things I'm feeling."

"Whether he knows it or not, I believe he is. You're both glowing. All I hope for you is that you don't run from yourself. I don't know what that means for you. Does the future involve Aaron, Angie, or this Tina you mentioned, or maybe somebody you haven't even met? I don't have a clue. Just don't deny who you are."

"I'll try. Clarissa — she refused to deny herself."

"She must've been a pistol in her time."

"I expect she would've been in any time." Ellen compressed her lips. "I'm glad you told me. If nothing else, you've made me think."

"Think all you want, but don't forget to feel. And listen with your heart. Your dad said that, in the midst of everything back then. We did okay by each other and our kids. We opted for security and the known. But we wonder now if we might've listened better to our hearts."

"You want me to drop you at the studio?"

Aaron glanced quickly at Ellen as she turned off the interstate. They'd hardly spoken the entire trip back to the Cities. They hadn't said much to each other since they'd returned from the soddy.

She'd been so exuberant even during dinner, but then he'd gone outside with her father and left her alone with her mother. Ellen hadn't been the same since. It wasn't his place to pry, but he really did want his prairie woman back. It was as if she'd been an apparition of the tall grasses. "Why don't you drop me at my place? I want to work in my home darkroom."

She scowled at the traffic. "I don't even know where you live."

"Maybe it's time you did. I'll give you directions. It's not far from where you're staying."

She gave him a withering glare.

"Your address is on your employee data forms."

She nodded without further comment.

Within minutes he was directing her into his sweeping driveway and up to the portico of his large brick home.

Her eyes rounded.

It was far more than he needed, but his grandfather had always told him real estate was an important investment.

"And you live alone?" she said, helping him haul the equipment into the house.

He chuckled. "My grandfather lived here with me until his death three years ago. Now it's an investment. I only use about half the space. When the price is right, I may sell and pick up something smaller. Let me show you around."

Ellen stood in the foyer. Her mouth fell open as she took in the winding staircase leading to the second floor. "I'd better be going," she stammered. She gave him a startled look. "I've got lots to do."

He stepped in front of her, blocking her exit. "So what happens now? To us?"

"Us?" she squeaked.

"I thought we had something going on the prairie — something worth further exploration. I thought you did, too."

Her eyes took on a wild look. "Don't push me." She glanced around the portion of the house that was visible from where they stood. She gulped. "This is too domestic. I'm sorry. I've got so much to sort through. I can't do it here. I can't do it with you."

"Okay." He stepped aside. "I'm not about to hold a woman captive."

"Don't get bent out of shape. Please. I had a great time." She heaved a sigh. "A fantastic time. Maybe even life changing. But I have to slow down, take a step backward."

"You don't want to be alone with me?"

"Maybe I don't trust myself being alone with you, particularly here. This is too much."

"You can be mysterious. I'll give you that. I thought we'd get together with Tina and Mike when we got back."

Streaks of color rose up her neck.

He cocked his head. "You still want us all to get together?"

She wet her lips. "Yes. Does that sound crazy?"

"Sounds like being alone with me is more scary than losing yourself in four-way sex."

She said nothing.

"Okay. I may be the crazy one, but as we know, I'm a guy with a lot of patience." He cupped her chin and brushed his lips across hers, pleased that she did not back away. "I'll set something up." He narrowed his eyes. "I'll invite them over for dinner."

"Here?"

"Here. This is where we will initiate you to the pleasures of four-way sex. Don't let this house spook you. It's only a house."

She nodded. Her lips curled into a tiny smile. "It should be a light meal."

"Will you help me with the meal?"

"Yes, you know I like to cook."

He smiled. "I was counting on that. Tomorrow is Friday. Why don't we shoot for Saturday night? Who knows — dessert could stretch well into Sunday."

She smacked her lips. "That sounds like fun. Thanks for understanding." She turned to leave.

"I didn't say I understood." He patted her butt lightly. "See you in the morning. I'm not about to give up on my prairie woman anytime soon. You might want to add that fact to everything you're sorting out."

The following morning, Ellen stepped out of the shower and hurriedly toweled herself off. She'd nearly overslept. After spending much of the night tossing and turning, she'd finally fallen asleep.

Her brain had turned to mush. Her future remained murky. How could she have a future? She didn't know who she was. She never had. Why hadn't her mother told her earlier about Jill? Cripes, what if her parents had worked out something different with Jill? According to her mother, Jill had been in the picture before Ellen's birth, which wasn't until 1969. Did Ellen owe her existence to a failed love? To her parents being unwilling to follow their hearts?

She sighed and strolled into the bedroom. She'd been grinding this over and over. There was no reason to believe the three of them wouldn't have decided to have more children.

She pulled on a pair of panties and stepped into a skirt. Being attracted to Tina hadn't been a fluke after all. Her emotional connection with Angie wasn't a fluke. She'd thought Clarissa was the eccentric fluke.

But being bi was in her blood. That was what her mother had said. And she had no reason to discount that conclusion. Until her conversation with her mother, she'd sort of written off her affair with Tina as an experimental summer fling. The entire summer was supposed to be a fling.

Now she wasn't so sure. She wasn't dense. Aaron had made it clear he didn't see her as a summer fling. She shivered and shrugged into her top. Her fingers trembled, fumbling with the buttons. How could she deal with him if she wasn't sure about herself? She had to decide what to do about being bi. She could make the same decision her mother had — deny it and hide it.

If she didn't choose that route, then how could she

realistically expect to keep her job? If she decided to embrace her bisexuality, she'd want to live in a place where she could be who she was.

She touched up her lipstick. Perhaps the most surprising part of her mother's disclosure was that her dad had known and had supported her mother. She shook her head. Children probably had a hard enough time imagining their parents as sexual beings — imagining them involved in a three-way relationship was mind blowing.

And what about Aaron? She'd witnessed a possessive streak in him on more than one occasion. If she allowed the two of them to get closer, would he be as willing for her to express her sexuality with others?

She headed downstairs. How could any two people ever get closer than they'd been on the sweetgrass behind the soddy? She still hadn't fully integrated that experience into her psyche. In the long run, that moment might have been more threatening than the conversation with her mother.

All of that would have to wait. She had a schedule to keep. She squared her shoulders, ready to take on Aaron and the rest of the world.

Frustrated, Ellen stared through the lens at the partially clad women. All she'd asked them to do was kiss.

She backed away from the camera and glared at Aaron, who stood behind a second tripod. He'd given her directing control of this photo shoot because, he explained, it involved two women, and she understood women better than he did. His only response was to turn up his palms.

He should've brought in an established lesbian couple for this series rather than relying on these two models. They claimed to be into women, but they had yet to demonstrate much proof of that claim. They were painfully tentative with each other.

Ellen glanced at Tina, who was also frowning at the two women. Stepping in front of the camera, Ellen said, "Ladies, enough. I don't know what the problem is, but you're not getting at what I'm looking for. This is a study that begins with lips and tongues. Seduction. I want seduction. And then more."

Raking her hair with steady fingers, she nodded at Tina. "Come here. Let's show them what I want. You two watch carefully."

Ellen held out a hand to Tina.

Grinning softly, Tina stepped into her arms. "Hi, I've missed you."

"I've missed you, too." Ellen placed a finger across Tina's parted lips. They held each other's gaze in anticipation. Ellen practically purred as Tina ran a thumb over the corner of her mouth. She placed her hands behind Tina's head and drew her close. Tina intertwined her fingers in Ellen's hair and pulled her even closer.

Ellen grinned and flicked her tongue out, teasing. Tina did the same. Their tongues neared. They touched. Ellen heard a camera clicking. Out of the corner of her eye, she saw the two models mimicking what she and Tina were doing. She tapped Tina's tongue playfully. Suddenly it didn't matter what the models were doing. It didn't matter what Aaron was doing. The only thing that mattered was giving and receiving pleasure with the woman in her arms.

She fingered Tina's choke collar and drew her tongue into her mouth. Tina moaned, letting Ellen suckle unimpeded. Ellen tried to breathe through her nose. Giving up, she backed away to gulp in air. Tina's eyes filled with want.

Ellen didn't protest when Tina's fingers began unfastening her blouse buttons. She shrugged out of it and worked Tina's tank top over her head. Smiling, she again covered Tina's mouth with hers and pushed her tongue through her lover's parted lips. Tina suckled thoroughly as Ellen let her hands roam over Tina's naked back.

When Tina had to break away for breath, Ellen used the opportunity to lick her way down Tina's throat across the choke collar to the rise of a breast. Tina moaned and rose on her toes. Chuckling softly, Ellen laved the underside of a breast before taking it into her mouth. Tina laced her fingers behind her head as if fearful Ellen might leave prematurely.

Tina needn't worry. There was no hurry. Aaron wouldn't run out of film anytime soon. She peeked across at the models and grinned against the breast. She'd never considered herself a role model in matters of sex and lovemaking.

Ellen dropped Tina's breast from her mouth and straightened to offer a breast to Tina, who quickly engulfed the proffered tit. Tina licked, chewed, and suckled. Ellen whimpered, digging her fingernails into Tina's shoulders.

Reluctantly, Ellen drew Tina up. She pecked at her nose and the corners of her mouth and stared deeply into her dark eyes. She glanced away quickly to Aaron. "Are we getting some good shots?"

"Incredible."

She'd been vaguely aware that he'd been stepping quietly around them with a free-held camera. "Good." She pursed her lips at him, then grinned at Tina. "Ladies," she said, pulling on the zipper of Tina's short skirt, "as I said, this is a study of lips and tongues."

Tina grinned broadly but didn't move to help.

This was Ellen's call. She pushed Tina's skirt down until Tina could step out of it. Nodding, Ellen clasped her hands and brought them to the buttons holding up her own skirt.

Tina smiled, then unfastened the buttons and slid the skirt and panties downward until Ellen was able to kick them aside.

Dropping to her knees, Ellen tongued Tina's vulva as Tina

guided her head with fingers intertwined in her hair.

"You might want to try something else," Aaron said softly from behind them. "I'm only getting the back of your head."

Ellen blinked. She'd nearly forgotten the shoot. She turned around on her knees to face the camera and then leaned back against Tina, encouraging her to widen her stance. "Smile at the camera," she chirped, tipping her head between Tina's thighs to drive her tongue into Tina's parted labia.

"Good God," Tina groaned, settling over Ellen's tongue.

Ellen paused long enough to ask, "Is this better, Aaron?"

"Spectacular."

Nodding, Ellen returned to her task. She reached behind to clutch Tina's buttocks. Tina's moans told her she was closing in on a good one.

"That's good, Tina," Aaron said. "Pull on your nipples. She's driving you over the top, isn't she?"

"Yes," Tina gasped. "I can't move."

"Too bad. Ellen's pussy is so engorged. Her nipples are so erect. You'll have to take care of her later."

"I will." Tina's voice was two octaves higher than normal.

Relentlessly, Ellen dove her tongue in and out of Tina, delighting in her initial flow.

"Here I come," Tina whimpered. "Don't stop."

Ellen held back a chuckle. No way she'd stop until she'd swallowed Tina's entire flow. She heard squeals coming from beside them. She didn't have to look to know what the two models were up to. Liking her new role model image, Ellen took her time licking Tina clean.

She didn't realize how much strain had been on her neck until she straightened. Tina sighed heavily and dropped to her knees beside her. Ellen smiled when Tina flicked out her tongue to lick a remaining drop or two from the corner of her mouth.

Tina spoke first. "Will you come home with me so I can

return the favor without so many eyes?"

Ellen glanced around the room at Aaron and the two models before responding to Tina. She shook her head, then kissed Tina's open mouth. "Will you come back to my place? I don't want to share you."

"I'd love that," Tina purred. She glanced at Aaron. "The guys can wait until tomorrow night. Let's get dressed. Aaron can take care of what's left to do here."

"Welcome to my world," Tina said gleefully after Ellen shared her conversation with her mother. Tina paused to stir the tea sitting on Ellen's kitchen counter. "I'm not hurt. I understand why you didn't think your involvement with me meant you were bi. I know about flings and experimentation. You didn't expect loving me would involve discovering and loving yourself differently. Thank God your mother talked with you."

Nodding, Ellen grazed her lips across Tina's cheek. They stood side by side in the kitchen, watching the tea steep. After Tina had delightfully returned the favor in the upstairs bedroom, they'd slipped on tank tops to come downstairs and brew tea. Ellen shivered, admiring Tina's bare pussy. Neither of them had bothered with panties. Her body still hummed from Tina's loving touches. "You're a good listener. I'm so glad you came back here with me. I needed to talk with you. I don't know anyone else who might understand. Angie might, but she's still in Europe. Do you know if any of your relatives were bi?"

Tina shook her head. "If they were, they more than likely repressed any such revolting feelings. I'm so pleased your mother shared her story with you. That had to take a lot of guts."

"I wish she'd told me earlier, but you're right. I'm glad she did. I've known about Clarissa for much of my life, but my mother . . ." Her voice trailed off. "And Mike is okay with you taking on female lovers?"

"He's wonderful about it. Of course, he knew I was bi before we married. The important thing for us is for me not to keep secrets. Even partners I don't bring home for him to share, he wants to hear about. Some of our best sex happens after I return from a night of loving." Tina arched an eyebrow. "It's like he wants to make sure I'm still wearing his brand."

"Maybe he's jealous."

"I don't believe so. It just intensifies things. Some of my married female friends tell me their best sex with their husbands comes after church choir practice. They can't explain that any more than I can explain Mike and me on a night I've been with a woman."

Ellen grinned. "You'll have intense sex later tonight?"

"Yes, but I hadn't planned on going home tonight, unless you're kicking me out."

Ellen patted Tina's bare pussy lightly. "I hoped you might stay, but I don't want to make Mike angry."

"Umm. I'll call him. He won't be angry. He'll understand. He likes you—a lot. Speaking of angry, Aaron didn't look totally pleased when you invited me here."

Ellen shrugged. She wasn't particularly ready to discuss Aaron.

"Isn't that interesting?" Tina reached over to brush a finger across a nipple pressing against the tank top. "Your nipple just grew taut at the mention of Aaron's name. You haven't said anything about the prairie shoot."

"It was fine," Ellen replied evenly. "Our tea is ready. Why don't we take these into the living room?"

Ellen led the way through the dining room to the living room.

Following behind, Tina patted her bare butt.

Ellen giggled and waggled her bottom suggestively. With

any luck and a little distraction, maybe she'd ducked Tina's curiosity about Aaron.

"No secrets, girl." Tina curled on the couch to face her. She covered Ellen's exposed mound with a palm. "I suppose you and Aaron got better acquainted."

Ellen nodded as Tina slid finger pads up both sides of her vulva. "Much." Tina wasn't going to be distracted, even by sex. Ellen chewed on her lower lip as Tina alternately caressed and palmed her.

"He's good, isn't he?"

Trying not to flinch, Ellen looked down at Tina's fingers working their magic. "You know he is, better than I do."

"Touché." Tina chuckled. "I assume your ass isn't virgin any longer?"

Ellen shook her head as Tina scraped a fingertip along the ridge between her pussy and anus. "That was incredible," she gasped. "I hadn't expected it to be that spectacular."

"Mike will be happy to learn your ass is no longer off limits. I trust Aaron isn't trying to keep it to himself."

Ellen squared her chin. "Aaron doesn't own my ass. I'm looking forward to sharing it with Mike, if that's okay with you."

"Of course it is. One of these days we'll try my strap-on. You seem to be a natural when it comes to anal play."

"I never considered myself a natural with sex at all until I met you." She pushed Tina's fingers lower. "Perhaps you should help me stay open for your husband."

"Hold that thought," Tina said between giggles. "Didn't I see strawberry jam in the fridge?"

"Yes." Ellen narrowed her eyes at Tina's bare butt as she scurried toward the kitchen.

Quickly Tina returned, holding up the jar. "One of my favorites." Tina winked at her and uncapped the jar.

"My goodness, what are you doing?"

"Preparing a snack." Tina dipped a finger into the jar and pulled out a hunk of jam. She beamed. "Why don't you get on the floor on your knees and lie across the couch for me? After all, you are the hostess."

Trying not to laugh too hard, Ellen slid off the couch and turned to face away from her lover. "That's sticky," she squealed, as Tina began spreading the jam liberally across her ass and pussy.

"But it will be tasty." Tina spread more jam on the ridge between pussy and anus. "We'll take a long soapy bath later. You'll be squeaky clean before we give you over to the guys tomorrow."

The guys. Ellen rotated her neck, trying not to think too much about the guys. She had enough difficulty keeping track of what Tina was doing. She heard Tina putting the cap back on the jar.

"Jam today. Sandwich tomorrow," Tina quipped. "You will want a sandwich with the guys tomorrow, right?"

Ellen swallowed hard before nodding. "If they're willing."

Tina chuckled as she squeezed Ellen's butt cheeks. "I don't think that will be a problem."

Ellen winced when she felt Tina's tongue gliding along the curve of her butt.

"Um, very nice. Now I have to concentrate on my craving for strawberry jam. I do love a hostess who serves liberal portions."

Ellen couldn't restrain her whimpers as Tina's tongue focused on her vulva. There were many advantages to having a shaved pussy—this had to be near the top of the list. She wanted to purr. Instead, she whimpered more loudly.

"Tasty. Very tasty," Tina crooned. "I do love pussy à la jam."

Ellen held herself rigid as Tina licked at the trail of jam leading from her pussy to her anus. She reached under her belly for her clit.

Tina slapped her butt. "Not yet. We're not nearly ready for that. Be still. Let me gobble you up."

Tina's tongue rimmed her anus, and Ellen arched her neck back and wailed.

"You do love this, don't you?"

"Yes."

She nearly went limp went Tina's furled tongue pushed into her butt. She lurched back each time Tina dove in.

Tina backed away, breathing heavily. "Am I as good as Aaron?"

"Yes."

Tina rose to her feet and began dragging her pussy over and around Ellen's rump. "Nice," Tina whispered. "Amazing what a little friction can do." Tina grabbed Ellen's hips and began humping her.

"What?"

"If I had my strap-on, you wouldn't be asking. Don't move," Tina ordered in a strained voice. "Let me fuck you. I'm so ready."

Ellen's jaw dropped and her ears filled with the sounds of flesh slapping flesh. Tina's nails dug into her shoulders.

"Jesus, I'm coming," Tina wailed.

Ellen ground back against Tina. She hadn't done a thing to help Tina, but she could feel the woman's juices sliding down a butt cheek. She laughed softly. Maybe she'd begin to believe she was a natural after all.

"Sorry about that," Tina apologized. "I sort of got carried away. We were supposed to be preparing your asshole."

Ellen laughed aloud. "Don't ever apologize for coming. I don't want the focus to be solely on me."

Sighing, Tina said, "You have such a beautiful ass. No wonder Aaron wanted to be first. Let's see what we can do for you. You should be quite turned on by now."

"Everywhere," Ellen admitted.

"Good."

Ellen puffed her cheeks out as she felt Tina's thumb tapping on her anus.

"I wish my thumb was bigger."

"Try two fingers," Ellen said before she thought about what she was saying.

"All right! Here's one. You are quite open. Here's a second. You okay?"

Ellen exhaled and nodded. "Oh wow," she groaned when Tina rotated her fingers while sinking them farther in.

"That's it. You'll have to wait for tomorrow night if you want deeper."

"Tina. Can you do my pussy, too?"

Chuckling softly, Tina worked fingers from her other hand into Ellen's channel.

Ellen rocked back and forth and from side to side, getting a better feel for Tina's fingers.

"You really are practicing for the guys, aren't you? You're going to take them at the same time."

"Yes. I hope to."

"This is good, but a male sandwich is much, much better."

"This is damn good." Ellen squirmed against the fingers impaling her.

Tina bent over and bit her butt cheek, and Ellen yelped. And then Tina's fingers began sliding in and out of her as if they'd been waiting overly long.

Ellen sank her head into a cushion and let Tina guide her up a ladder toward the inevitable conclusion of jam on pussy and ass.

"I gotcha, girl."

Ellen nodded furiously.

"Both holes filled by one lover. Tomorrow night . . . both filled by two lovers. Welcome to one of the delights of being bi."

"Oh, I'm done," Ellen wailed, crashing her torso onto the couch. Moments later, she grinned into the cushion as she felt Tina cleaning her vulva with her tongue.

At last Tina leaned back.

Ellen struggled to turn around to sit on the floor, then grinned broadly at her friend. "Hope you enjoyed your snack."

"I hope you enjoyed it half as much as I did. Why don't you catch your breath before we start the bath?"

She nodded. "I'll get there, but I'm not ready."

"So why didn't you want to come to my house with me?"

Ellen twined her fingers with Tina's. "I wanted to talk with you alone. I wanted you to myself like this — without cameras or watching eyes. I didn't want Aaron to think I was excluding him by spending time with you and Mike."

"I figured that was part of it. You really do have some feelings that are running deep for Aaron."

Ellen felt her shoulders sag. She wasn't going to be able to escape his shadow easily. "Yes, maybe too deep."

"That doesn't surprise me either. Aaron is a fantastic guy in my book. He's needed to find the right woman for some time now."

Ellen scowled. "That doesn't make me the right woman."

"At least you didn't say you're not the right woman." Tina held up a palm to forestall interruption. "You look pretty right to me, but that's not my decision to make. So how are you integrating this newly discovered bi identity with teaching third grade in a Plains small town?"

Ellen couldn't hold back a large sigh. "Maybe we should do that bath before I try to answer that one." She saw the sparkle in Tina's eyes — the bath could easily take much of the night. "I can't. I don't know what to do. I haven't decided. But I can't reconcile my identity very easily. There's no way my lifestyle could be tolerated at the school or in the community if it were to become known."

"Ah." Tina nodded knowingly. "And like Clarissa, you're not good at hiding who you are."

"Something like that, I suppose. My mother must've been, but I can't imagine how she managed that."

"Sounds like she wound up having to make a choice."

Ellen nodded. "I suppose we all do."

"And yours?"

"If I had the guts, I'd call my principal first and then a realtor. How can I go back to how things were before listening to my mother, before you, before Aaron?" She moved easily into Tina's open arms and sobbed.

To her credit, Tina did nothing to stop the tears. She held her and rubbed her back — definitely what Ellen needed.

Regaining her equilibrium, Ellen leaned back against the couch. "I don't even have a job. It's probably too late in the summer to get a teaching job here."

"I can help you with that if you want. I work at the academy and for Aaron part-time. I'm sure he'd have a job for you."

"He's said as much, but I wouldn't want to be dependent on him" — she smacked her lips — "if I'm exploring a relationship with him."

"Hmm. I also get work through a high-powered temp agency."

Ellen frowned.

"You'd be surprised how much money many corporations, universities, and businesses are willing to pay folks to avoid bringing them on long term. The pay is quite good. The benefits package through the agency sucks, but it's better than nothing. Let me know if you want contacts and referrals. Aaron also has excellent connections at the art museums. Most anything is possible if you're willing to try."

"I am discovering that." Ellen smiled. "Slowly, but surely. I think I'm ready for that bubble bath." She reached out and let Tina help her to her feet. "I get to scrub you first."

"We'd better take it slow. The guys are going to be pissed if we don't save something for them."

Ellen dipped a hand down between them to massage Tina's mound. "I believe we are inexhaustible. Having you squirt over my ass was something. I'm so happy to be a woman."

Tina chortled. "Especially a bi woman."

Ellen kissed Tina quickly. "Race you to the bath."

Chapter Twelve

"This is going to be delicious," Ellen said, tentatively tasting the shrimp and spinach soup before stirring it again. She smiled brightly at Aaron as he put the final touches on four salads. He'd told her it was a spiced seafood and noodle salad. He was about to put them in the fridge so they could chill before the meal. Kabobs of chicken and a variety of vegetables were ready for grilling and were the main course for their Japanese meal.

This was a kitchen to die for. She'd never seen so many conveniences in one place. Clearly, Aaron wasn't shy when it came to cooking. This made her kitchen look as ancient as the sod house.

"I'm glad you approve," Aaron said, closing the stainless-steel fridge. "Dessert, sticky rice with mangoes, is already chilling. We'll get it out later so it will be at room temperature when we serve it."

"You seem to have thought of everything. I thought I was supposed to help with the cooking."

"You are," he said cheerfully. "You're stirring the pot."

"Ummm." She decided not to go after a possible double meaning. She inhaled the strong aromas of the room, not for the first time admiring Aaron in his striking black kimono. He'd had her change into a red kimono decorated with an array of colorful flower designs. Two kimonos lay on the living room couch, awaiting Mike and Tina.

He moved closer and took the ladle from her to taste the soup. "Perfect," he said, grinning. "I had to start preparing the meal early this morning." He arched an eyebrow knowingly. "I didn't want to disturb you and Tina. I assume you two had an enjoyable evening and morning."

"Very."

"You had a good start before you left the studio." He put the ladle down on the counter. "That was a brilliant move to save the photo shoot. Deidre and Lisa didn't have any sense for finesse. But they did follow your lead quite nicely. I loved that trick with the tongues, hardly touching, and then ever so lightly."

"You mean like this?" She stuck out her tongue, inviting him to join her.

"Yeah." Chuckling, he slipped his tongue between her lips to caress the tip of hers.

She withdrew. "I trust you got some good pics."

"I sure did. I'm afraid you and Tina stole the show. After you left, Deidre and Lisa seemed to get lost."

She stepped closer and slid a hand inside his kimono to finger a nipple. "Well, did you have to show them the way?"

"No. To their disappointment, I soon ushered them out of the studio so I could start working in the darkroom."

"And did you think of Tina and me last night?"

He slid a hand inside her kimono and teased a breast before responding.

She warmed immediately. How could such a simple gesture after a night and morning of lovemaking rev her up so quickly?

"How could I not? The two women I love the most were exploring each other intimately. You were sharing with each other things that I had done with each of you. Of course I thought about you."

Trying to ignore his use of the *L* word, she plunged ahead. "Were you jealous?" She needed to know.

He shook his head. "Would I prefer to be with you? Of

course. Jealous? How can I be jealous of you and Tina? I spent much of the time planning for tonight. I like to think of your time with Tina as a prelude for the present."

"For you and Mike."

"Exactly."

"You guys are amazing."

"Hold that thought. I hope you're in for much amazement before you leave me again."

She opened her mouth to tell him that she hadn't left him when the doorbell rang.

He patted her breast and tightened her kimono sash. "I believe our foursome is complete." He kissed her quickly and left the kitchen to welcome Tina and Mike.

Stunned by his confidence as much as by his words, Ellen rubbed her throat and remained in the kitchen, trying to collect her wits. Did he mean the foursome was complete for the evening — or was he implying more than that? His eyes sparkled with devilment. He probably wasn't thinking merely about the evening.

She stirred the soup to stay busy. The man was moving far faster than she was prepared for. Moving! Tina had talked about her moving to the Cities and finding a job as though it was as simple as getting out of bed. Didn't they know she couldn't just pick up and leave? She had too much to lose.

What if there was too much to lose if she didn't follow her destiny? Where had that word come from? Was that her mother's doing? Was her destiny really a matter of blood?

"I'm glad Aaron waited to show you the downstairs until we got here," Tina said, clutching Ellen by the hand. "He's done so much with it. It's absolutely one of my favorite places."

Ellen let Tina lead her down the stairs as Aaron and Mike followed behind. Tina looked stunning in a lavender kimono with a dainty yellow flower pattern. Mike looked totally masculine in his dark blue kimono robe. Trying not to get ahead of herself, Ellen let her eyes adjust to the dimly lit space they were entering.

"Oh my God," she squealed. "It's another world. How did you manage all of this?"

She didn't wait for Aaron to answer before hurrying to the center of the room, to the large open space. Three-quarters of the downstairs had been turned into some sort of shrine to oriental erotic art. Lithographs in color as well as black and white depicting men and women in all sorts of combinations and coital positions were tastefully arranged on the walls. A huge wide-screen TV in the middle of the outside wall displayed a stunning piece of art of one woman helping another woman settle on top of a man's cock. Ellen caught her breath as the picture changed before her, transforming into a geisha being mounted from behind by a man with an enormous cock. She tore her gaze away, realizing that Aaron had set up a *PowerPoint* program to fuel their desires. As if she needed any more fueling.

Background music throbbed with the beat of a belly dancer, then switched to something more subtle — softer, but no less sensual. This was a room designed to celebrate and stimulate the senses.

She inhaled the light aroma of candles and walked to the end of the room, which was partially hidden by paper screens like those she'd seen in Japanese restaurants. These were decorated with geisha girls, butterflies, and cranes. Beyond the screens was a sleeping area of futons from wall to wall, strewn with blue and cream pillows and a matching comforter decorated in scenes of a pagoda and women carrying parasols.

"This is lovely," she said, softly squeezing Tina's fingers. "Did you help with this?"

"Some, but most of the credit goes to Aaron. He's traveled

to parts of the orient."

"A few of these pieces are originals," Aaron pointed out. "Most are replicas. I still add to the collection now and then. Are you aware that the Impressionists were fascinated with oriental art? Some were particularly taken with erotic art."

"Yes, I remember. It inspired some of their work. Many of them did garden paintings like the Japanese gardens. And as we all know, some were fascinated with the female body."

"Can't blame them for that," Mike said. "Have you noticed the sculptures? It's not only amazing to me that someone could carve such eroticism in stone—but that it survived weather and war and intolerance boggles the mind."

"This one is my favorite," Tina said, pointing at a small stone statue of a nude woman with one arm raised behind her head, adorned only with strands of some sort of jewelry. She represented a full-bodied woman. "Look at her pussy." Tina giggled.

"Oh my!" Ellen laughed. "Did they shave back then?"

"I don't know, but she's as bald as you and me. Look." Tina stood beside the statue, parted her robe, and struck a similar pose. "Stand on her other side. Let the guys compare the similarities."

Ellen widened her eyes.

"This isn't a time to get modest on us, girl," Tina said softly. "You're not showing us anything we all haven't seen and"—Tina flicked out her tongue—"tasted."

Ellen shrugged. It did seem like she should be way past modesty, especially given where they all knew she wanted things to proceed. She tried to smile as she stepped beside the statue and parted her robe.

Aaron gave a low whistle. "They do look amazingly similar. I wonder how those women accomplished that. I doubt the sculptor thought of that on his own."

Mike ran his palm over the statue's vulva. "Rather rough

and worn with time."

Ellen tried not to flinch as his dark fingers trailed over her own vulva.

"Smooth," he announced, grinning rakishly. "And ripe for the plucking."

"Same goes for this one," Aaron said, grinning as he palmed Tina's vulva. Chuckling, Aaron pulled Tina's robe back around her and tied the sash. "Tempting. But we don't want to get ahead of ourselves. I've worked hard in the kitchen most of the day." He pecked at Tina's nose. "While you and Ellen played. Tie her back up, Mike. Ellen's not the first course."

"I see you have the meal carefully choreographed." Mike knotted Ellen's sash.

"No one will go away hungry. I can guarantee that." Aaron took Ellen's hand. "I don't believe you paid much attention to the other end of the room."

"How could I? My eyes were immediately drawn to the big screen and then to the lounge area. But this is equally stunning," she said as he guided her to the opposite end of the room. A large stone fireplace set off the end wall, but what was equally attractive was a dark table in an inset. There were no chairs around the low, narrow bench table. It might as well be an altar. Pillows were arranged along the sides of the table for sitting, while the inset provided convenient back support. In oriental style, the table would provide space for serving a meal. Guests would sit on the pillows and eat from hand-held bowls.

The table explained why she'd seen no table settings in the dining room or kitchen. "This is where we'll eat?"

"Uh, huh."

"There's plenty of room on the table to bring everything down and spread the meal out. What a wonderful use of space! Did you design this?"

"Yes. But we won't be bringing all the meal down here at once." His lips curved into a small smile. "As you said, we need to keep the meal light. We will begin with soup. We'll clear the table, and you will be the second course. After which we'll have more tea and continue with the salad."

"Whoa," Ellen tilted her head and arched an eyebrow. "I'm the second course." She smacked her lips and stared at the alcove. "On the table."

"It's made of rosewood. It'll hold you."

"And you're all going to . . ."

"As I said, you're the second course," Aaron said patiently. "It's our way of honoring and celebrating you, of welcoming you to our foursome."

She glanced from one smiling face to another and then back at Aaron. "And you wanted me to know this now? You didn't want to spring it on me?"

"Sometimes I want to surprise you." He held her stare and parted her robe until he comfortably cupped a breast. He bent down and flicked his tongue at a straining nipple. Raising his head, he smiled broadly. "Sometimes I want you to anticipate. This is a time for anticipation."

"Okay." She parted his robe and encircled his rigid cock. "As long as I'm not the only one anticipating." She arched an eyebrow. "I believe the soup is ready for serving."

Satisfied with his culinary efforts, Aaron glanced around their table.

"Scrumptious," Tina practically purred, ripping a shrimp apart with her teeth. She sipped more of the hot soup before adding, "You two have cooked up quite a concoction for all of us."

"Aaron did all the preparation and cooking," Ellen quickly interjected. "I just helped with some of the final prep."

If Ellen was anxious about the next course, she wasn't letting anyone know it. She struck him as quite cool and confident — like a woman who knew exactly what she wanted and was determined to get it.

He glanced quickly at Mike, whose attention seemed glued to the two women. Did he know what Ellen expected from them? Surely Tina must've told him Ellen's wish for a male sandwich, if Ellen hadn't told him herself. That wouldn't pose a problem for him or Mike. They'd satisfied Tina's similar desire countless times. It might take them a little longer to find a satisfactory rhythm with Ellen because it would be her first sandwich, but they'd get there.

Ellen would get her wish, but not soon. He'd planned her sandwich for the sixth course — between the main course and dessert.

A slight blush rose on Ellen's neck.

He smiled — maybe she was wondering about how many courses this meal had and how often she was expected to be part of the serving. He smacked his lips. Dessert might have to wait until morning.

"Aaron. Aaron!"

"What?" He looked sharply at Tina.

"If you'd listen up instead of trying to figure out how to get Ellen to fall in love with you . . ."

Aaron stiffened and glowered at his long-time lover. Beside him, Ellen gasped.

"I have something important to tell you."

"It'd better be important, given that lead-in," he grumbled, seeing no need to try to convince everyone Tina had him pegged wrong.

Tina rose from the pillows and walked over to a nearby shelf that held some of his prized jade pieces. She rubbed a palm over the extended belly of a figure depicting a pregnant woman and then parted her robe to graze her flat tummy. She gave Mike a wicked smile before directing her gaze to him.

Aaron had seen that look on her several times before. She had a secret to share.

"This may be one of your last chances to be in my pussy for a while." She paused, and he slowly began to comprehend her meaning.

Sitting beside him, Ellen covered her mouth.

"That's right. Mike and I have agreed that I should go off birth control after my next period, which should be soon. We're going to make a baby."

Ellen leaped to her feet and ran to hug Tina.

Aaron glanced at Mike, who gave him a shrug and a sheepish grin. Making a baby? Of course he wouldn't go near Tina if she wasn't protected. There'd been times when he'd wondered when this day would arrive. Still, he wasn't prepared. He was excited — but also a little bereft.

"Are you happy for us?" Tina asked, coming back to the table area. "You'll be Uncle Aaron and godfather wrapped into one," she said, settling down on his lap. She squirmed across his semi-hard cock. "I'll still have a couple special orifices available to this guy. What do you think?"

"I think you're adorable," he said, kissing her hair. He winked at Mike. "Maybe I can photograph the moment of conception."

Mike roared. Ellen tried not to laugh but failed, and Tina punched his arm.

"I won't have green lights popping on to tell you when that happens. And what about you, Ellen?" Tina continued. "What do you think about our little news?"

"I think it's wonderful. You and Mike are going to make such fine parents." Her eyes gleamed. "I don't know about your selection of godfather, but I guess he'll do."

"Mike and I are hoping you'll be the baby's aunt and godmother."

"Me?" Taken back, Ellen gulped. "But you hardly know me."

"That's not true, and you know it. And you're the only one here who has experience with kids. But we don't want to rush you." Tina slid over onto Ellen's lap.

Ellen wrapped an arm tightly around her.

"And Mike and I will need your help when I'm late in pregnancy."

Ellen leaned back and scowled.

"That's right. You'll have to do double duty taking care of our men. We're not expecting Mike to go without a little pussy for three months or so."

"Aren't you assuming a lot?" Ellen's voice rose as if she was about to argue, and then her lips curved up into a smile. She pecked at Tina's nose. "If that's what you want, I guess I could drive over for a weekend once a month to take care of Mike."

What about me, Aaron wanted to shout, but he remained silent—the byplay between the women might be much more revealing than any outburst from him.

"I'm betting you won't have to drive very far by then. I expect I'll be needing lots of attention, too. Maybe just cuddling, and you are a fantastic cuddler."

Ellen's eyes softened—Tina's words seemed to have a soothing effect.

Aaron wished his words could be equally soothing. He hung on every hushed word, feeling a bit like an intruder listening in on an exchange between lovers. The announcement of wanting a baby had jumpstarted whatever had been building between Tina and Ellen.

"I love cuddling with you," Ellen said just above a whisper, "but I haven't decided I'm moving."

"You will." Tina parted Ellen's kimono and caressed a breast. Aaron saw the nipple jut forward. "I need you, and I think you need me. You won't deny that?"

Ellen shook her head, parting Tina's robe in turn to cradle Tina's breast.

Tina ran her tongue across Ellen's throat. "I told you I'd help you find a job."

Aaron resisted pointing out that he had a job for Ellen.

"I'd have to find a place to live." Ellen gulped, continuing to pet Tina's breast. "It must be very expensive living in the Cities."

"You can stay with us as long as you want." Tina looked to Mike for agreement, and he nodded without speaking. "Of course, Aaron has plenty of room here, too."

"I don't even use half this house," Aaron said, trying to sound calm and unaffected.

Ellen didn't even look at him. She shook her head at Tina. "I won't be rushed."

"No one's trying to rush you, girl." Tina pressed her lips against Ellen's and Ellen responded cautiously. "We just want you to consider your options. Life is too short not to think outside the ordinary."

"You are extraordinary." Ellen giggled, kissing Tina soundly. "I'll think about it. I would certainly miss our cuddles."

Tina glanced back at Aaron while pulling on Ellen's nipple. She winked and then eyed Ellen. "We must be about ready for our second course, don't you think?"

Ellen nodded, covering Tina's fingers.

"Why don't you two spread our second course out on the table," Aaron said, "and I'll clear these soup bowls."

Glancing quickly over his shoulder at Tina and Mike as they laid Ellen down on the table, Aaron hurried to the kitchen. He tried not to be jealous or envious of Tina. Clearly, the relationship between the women had advanced further than his relationship with Ellen. Or at the very least, they were able to talk about it.

He didn't mind sharing with Tina and Mike—that had been part of his scenario from the beginning. But he didn't want to be the afterthought, either. He rinsed out the bowls, trying to collect his wits. Maybe Ellen couldn't really be available and open to him until she came to grips with being in love with a woman.

He'd bide his time. What choice did he have? He loved two women. Thankfully they'd fallen in love with each other. Now if Ellen could fall in love with him, their foursome really would be complete.

Blindfolded, Ellen lay comfortably on the table. Tina had left Ellen's kimono on to provide a little cushion. Hands roamed over her body—across her cheekbones and down her throat, across her abs and down her legs and ankles. The blindfold intensified the sensations, but she knew who was where. Tina, kneeling on her left, was intent on massaging her face, neck and shoulders. On her right, Aaron was kneading her belly and working around her breasts without touching either one. Mike knelt at the end of the table between her legs, which were draped over the table.

Her entire body had come to life, threatening to divert her thoughts from the conversation with Tina. Such fantastic news for Tina and Mike. She hoped they wouldn't have difficulty getting pregnant. The rest of the conversation was more unsettling. Tina had made it clear in front of everyone that she wanted and expected this love affair to continue. Ellen blew air through compressed lips. She didn't have a problem naming it for what it was. It was a love affair. But how could this affair have any realistic future?

And was it only a love affair with Tina? Or did it emotionally include Mike and Aaron? She smiled to herself as hands settled over her breasts and mound.

And what if . . ."Oh," Ellen murmured. "My tits . . ." No one else spoke aloud. But each person spoke volumes with lips and tongues. Both breasts were being lovingly suckled. There was no urgency. No sense that this was only a waystation to something else. Her lovers transmitted feelings that couldn't be ignored.

Mike draped her legs over his shoulders and zig-zagged his tongue across her now throbbing pussy lips. She'd been ready for this since Aaron had announced she would be the second course. She'd been ready for this since Mike had fondled her mound beside the statue. She'd been ready for this moment since Aaron had asked her to change into the kimono. She sighed, letting sensations wash over her. Maybe she'd been ready for this from the beginning of time.

Tina and Aaron tugged gently on her nipples with their teeth, and Mike's tongue began wedging its way into her pussy. Ellen wrapped one arm around Tina's head and the other around Aaron's. She locked her ankles behind Mike. If she was the second course, then she was about to serve.

Three sets of fingers toyed with her clit, and she nearly shot off the table. She lurched forward, gulping for air. Whimpering, she settled back against the table and tilted her pelvis, wanting, demanding.

Mike drove a finger in beside his tongue. She bucked against tongue and finger until she rewarded both with her flow. And then she collapsed.

She heard Mike's chuckles among slurping sounds as he lapped at her juices.

"Next," Tina said softly.

Ellen hugged Tina with her thighs as she replaced her husband and sipped at juices still ebbing from Ellen's depths. She nearly drifted under the spell of Tina's familiar tongue.

"Last," Aaron said, hoarsely.

Ellen nodded. Of course, he'd be last. He was the host. She raised her legs high as he took his place. She felt his tongue dip inside as if searching for a little extra. And then his tongue cleaned her bare labia of any stickiness that might still cling to it. Seemingly satisfied, he patted her mound and left.

Tina untied her blindfold, and Ellen slowly opened her eyes to adjust again to the dimly lighted room. "I love you all," she blurted out. She gulped — Mike and Tina were beaming at her. Aaron looked somewhat shocked.

She held her hand out to him. "I'm sorry. Don't take too seriously what a woman says after she's been loved so thoroughly by three tongues."

He shrugged, failing to look nonplussed. "I won't forget," he said, pulling her kimono about her and retying her sash. "But maybe a little wine in addition to tea is in order — and of course, our salads."

"I'd like that, as soon as I can move again." She gave him a tiny smile. At least he hadn't tried to take advantage of the moment. She knew he wouldn't forget her words, but then she doubted she would, either.

CHAPTER THIRTEEN

A aron sipped his tea and settled back against the pillows. There'd been little conversation while they'd eaten their salads. Tina and Ellen had done some whispering back and forth. Ellen seemed revived.

He smiled. He could take a nap, but she probably wouldn't vote for that, if she had a vote. When had she become such a voracious fan of sex? Maybe she needed to be part of a ménage to be satisfied.

She'd tried to take back her declaration of love. That still hurt a little. Had she only meant those words for Tina, or maybe for Tina and Mike? Clearly, she hadn't monitored her words in the rush of sexual bliss. He knew about such moments. He grinned. Maybe in this case, sex was a truth serum.

Ellen was obviously smitten by Tina, and he had no doubt that Tina was equally smitten. He'd never seen his long-term lover so deeply engaged with another woman. And this notion of having a baby only seemed to cement their bonding.

Where did that leave him — in the middle, or on the outside looking in? He didn't like that Ellen was more comfortable with her feelings for Tina than for him. He glanced at Mike, who seemed to be basking in the women's love. Hell, Ellen might have stronger feelings even for Mike than for him. If nothing else, her feelings for Mike were likely less conflicted.

"Now, what's the fourth course?" Mike asked. He rubbed his stomach. "I think my salad has settled."

Aaron smiled at his long-time buddy. "It's your choice. Your wife and Ellen were together all last night and much of the morning. I think it's only fair that you have the next selection."

"That's simple," Mike said, rising to his feet and pulling Ellen up by the hand. "It's been too long since you visited. Would you like to join me at the other end of the room, away from prying eyes? We might be able to figure out the fourth course for ourselves."

"I'd love that," Ellen said, grinning at Mike. "It has been too long."

"I'm sure you and Tina can come up with something to do," Mike said, slapping Aaron on the shoulder as he walked by.

Aaron nodded silently, unable to take his gaze away as the two ducked behind the screens at the other end of the room. Mike flipped on a light near the futons. So much for being hidden from prying eyes. He and Ellen were backlit and clearly visible as dark shadows through the paper-thin screens.

Aaron's shoulders slumped as he watched Ellen take the lead, pushing Mike's kimono off his shoulders. Without removing her own, she dropped to her knees and took his cock into her mouth where he stood. She seemed in such a hurry they hadn't even bothered getting on the futons. Once she had Mike in her mouth, she slowed. Apparently, she wasn't going to bring him off quickly.

"Are you jealous?" Tina asked, untying his sash. She wrapped her fingers around his shaft and skimmed it lightly.

He looked at her.

"They're enjoying themselves. We might as well, too. You didn't answer my question. Are you jealous?"

"Of Mike? I'm trying not to be." He drew her kimono up over her back so he could cup her bare bottom.

She leaned over to kiss his cock, then swirled her tongue around its crown and winked at him. "And what about me,

Aaron? Are you jealous of me?"

He shrugged and watched her take his cock into her mouth. He glanced across the room to see Ellen still working on Mike's cock in a similar fashion. "She loves you," he said without criticism. "That's evident."

"Umm." Tina left his cock in her hand long enough to say, "As much as I love her. So does that make you jealous?" She popped him in back into her mouth and eased him into her throat.

He saw Mike flexing in and out of Ellen's mouth before pulling away from her and drawing her up to stand in front of him with her back against his chest. He undid her robe, and it fell to the floor.

Aaron groaned as Tina bobbed up and down his cock. He riffled his fingers lovingly through her hair. "How can I be jealous of you? I love you, too."

She dropped him from her mouth. "Good. I hoped you might say something like that. Ellen is an important addition for us. I don't want the feelings she and I share to come between us."

He followed her gaze down to the silk screens. Ellen stood crouched over, her feet on the floor and her hands on the futons. Mike was entering her from behind.

Tina chuckled. "That's one of Mike's favorite positions. Incredibly powerful. Deep penetration. He won't last long that way, but Ellen will be well-fucked." She kissed his cheek. "If you can pull your eyes away from them long enough, I'd like this guy in my pussy."

He gave Tina a crooked smile. "Whatever works for you."

Tina stood and shrugged out of her kimono, then knelt on the pillows in the inset facing Mike and Ellen's direction. "I love watching the two of them almost as much as you do. Being backlit gives them a shadowy, other-worldly ambiance."

He grunted and removed his robe before positioning

himself behind Tina's raised butt. She waggled it provocatively, and he brought his cockhead to her soaking channel. He eased into her without hurry and didn't halt until fully encased.

"I love how you fill me. I'll miss this—for a while."

"Sounds like you won't be lonely."

"She's falling in love with you, you know?"

Aaron glanced down the room to where Mike was clearly picking up his tempo driving in and out of Ellen. "It's hard to tell," he muttered.

"Well, she is. Don't be stupid. Oh!" Tina pushed back hard against him. "Mike already has her squealing. I love to listen to her come. Fuck me, Aaron. Fill me."

"Sounds like there isn't much you don't love about her," he said, pulling nearly out of Tina only to slam back in. Repeatedly, he drove in and out, to Tina's giggles and encouragement.

He tapped her asshole with a thumb, and she went ballistic. He looked up at the sounds of Mike's howls and Ellen's screams. Ellen remained crouched over as Mike pounded in and out of her. Well-fucked, as Tina had said. Their silhouettes blurred. Was it them or him?

"Oh shit!" He began to erupt inside Tina.

"Yes," Tina shouted joyfully. "Keeping coming. Don't stop."

Aaron tossed his head from side to side as he emptied into her. Eventually, he slowed and stopped. He hung over her back, planting kisses on her neck. "You're real special."

"As are you—and as are they." Tina nodded toward Mike and Ellen as they approached hand in hand. Neither had bothered donning the kimonos.

"I'm afraid we need showers between courses," Ellen said, seemingly relaxed and at ease. "That was a workout."

"Looked like," Aaron said, easing out of Tina. "Showers

sound like an excellent idea while I'm grilling." He patted Tina's butt. "No joint showers."

"Damn!" Tina turned her head to grin at him. "Yes, master. We can wait if we must."

"I expect the wait will be worth it. Ellen will choose the next course after this one. I expect we all know what that choice will be."

Ellen blushed only slightly. "Maybe I should surprise you."

"But you won't."

"Not a chance," she said quickly. "Given the trip I just had with one cock, I can hardly wait to try two at once."

"I have to take sufficient time between courses," he pointed out like a concerned parent.

"Don't tease her, Aaron," Tina chided. "You're looking forward to the sandwich as much as the rest of us."

Shrugging his robe back on, Aaron nodded and headed for the kitchen. He was looking forward to the sixth course, but maybe not quite as much as everyone else.

As the evening wore on, Ellen found herself ducking away from the furtive glances of her partners. The moment she'd been anticipating for days was finally approaching. She was excited — was some of that excitement simply misplaced bravado? She wasn't at all sure she could take Aaron and Mike at the same time. They were both large men.

And she was on edge. She'd been in some state of arousal ever since she entered Aaron's house hours earlier, and that didn't count the time she'd spent with Tina. Was she becoming a sexual connoisseur or a sexual glutton?

They'd eaten the kabobs, toured Aaron's lawn and gardens attractively lit with Japanese lanterns, and now lounged again on the pillows around the table where she so recently had lain and been feasted on. Her skin warmed with the memory.

"Second thoughts?" Tina asked, interlacing their fingers.

Ellen glanced quickly at her and then away. "No. Not really."

"You'll be fine. Our guys are quite experienced. They'll be careful with you."

Ellen nodded, trying not to yawn. How could she be tired now?

"So, what are you and Aaron going to do next?"

Confused, Ellen blinked at Tina. She felt Aaron tense on the other side of her.

"I don't mean in the next hour or two," Tina continued. "What happens after the prairie woman series? Do you have plans for more photo shoots beyond the usual?"

Ellen looked to Aaron for help. She didn't have plans beyond her current work.

"We haven't talked about plans," Aaron said noncommittally. "You seem to have gotten further talking with her about the future than I have."

Ellen felt the air go out of Aaron.

Looking somewhat unsteady, he asked, "What would you want to work on if we had the opportunity?" He must've seen her draw back. "Leave aside the practical matters."

Chuckling softly, Ellen tried to breathe. "It's not easy setting aside practical matters."

"Humor us," Mike interjected. "What stirs you?"

"Okay." She gave Tina a shy smile. "I'm sure it's been done before, but I'd probably want to do a photo documentary of a woman during pregnancy."

"How sweet." Tina beamed. "That'd be so cool."

"Just because something has been done before doesn't mean it's not a worthy undertaking." Aaron covered her knee with his hand.

She didn't flinch away.

"If everyone took that tack, there probably wouldn't be more paintings, more books, more much of anything." He squeezed her knee and removed his hand. "A pregnant woman series crossed my mind as soon as Tina shared her hopes."

"What about you, Aaron?" Tina insisted. "What happens after you're done with Ellen?"

"I never said I planned on being done with Ellen."

Ellen's throat clenched.

"I didn't mean that," Tina replied. "When you're done with the prairie woman series? What next?"

Aaron shrugged. "I've been thinking of spending some concentrated time studying the Dutch Masters."

"Really?" Ellen blurted out. "They're among my favorites."

"That's not surprising. That group of painters had as much influence on art as any group, and much earlier than the French. Some of their work, I believe, inspired some of the beginning efforts with photography. If I pursue that study, then I'll want to spend some extended time in Holland."

"Oh my." Ellen stopped herself before saying traveling to the Netherlands had been a longstanding dream of hers.

"But I've also been giving the prairie woman series more thought."

She frowned. "I thought we were just about finished with that, other than darkroom work."

"I've been thinking about the final product," Aaron explained. "Initially, I had thought only of a pictorial display in galleries. After being to the prairie with you, I've begun to wonder about doing a book with pictures and stories."

"Stories?" Ellen's heart fluttered.

"You and your mother have plenty of stories. You can write. You do teach high school English some summers."

"Of course I do, but . . . could we tell Clarissa's story?"

Aaron cracked a smile. "Why not?"

"Goodness. Would we use some of the nude photos of me on the prairie?"

"That'd be up to you. You'd have to sign the releases."

"I can't consider that if I'm still teaching at the school."

"You do have a lot of choices to make before long," Tina said. "But before we turn this little gathering into a production meeting, maybe you should decide how you want to manage two cocks."

"So much for subtlety," Mike chided, elbowing his wife.

"This isn't a time for subtle. We'd better get on with it before one of us falls asleep." Tina arched an eyebrow at Aaron. "I hope you were planning on us spending the night."

"I was. I don't have a big breakfast planned, but I did expect this would be a long night." He chuckled. "We may save dessert for breakfast."

"I hope you're talking about the dessert in the fridge. I'm not sure I'll be lifting much more than a finger come morning." Tina smiled at Ellen. "And I'll be surprised if you're awake before noon."

Tina stood and grabbed Ellen's hand. "Come on—let me escort you to the futons. I expect the guys will follow."

Tina directed Aaron to lie down on his back. "Get settled," she told him. His cock stood straight up. "See anything you want?" she asked, looking at Ellen.

"Yes," she managed to squeak.

"Well, come on," Tina said. "Don't want this hard rod to get cold. It's weaving about like a heat sensor. Let me help." Tina clasped Aaron's erect cock.

Ellen smiled, took a deep breath, and straddled Aaron on her knees. Finally she lowered her torso, letting Tina guide Aaron's cockhead into her channel. Aaron's eyes glazed as he stared at her sliding down his shaft. She squirmed, seating him soundly. Tentatively, she bounced up and down, testing his length and their fit.

"Enough of that," Tina chastised. "Don't get ahead of me." Tina kissed her cheek and placed a hand on her back. "Now stretch out prone on Aaron's chest. You're going to love this. Excellent."

Ellen smiled at Aaron and nibbled on his chin. "Tina is quite the choreographer. Maybe we should let her do more of the studio setups."

"Maybe," he grunted. "You sure you're going to be okay with this?"

"You'll be the first to know if I'm not." She turned her head to look at Tina, then gulped at the sight of Tina using both hands to lube her husband's cock. For the first time, Ellen seriously doubted she had enough room for him and Aaron.

"Don't worry." Tina winked. "He'll fit. I'm going to add a little more lube to you while Mike gets into position. Okay?"

Ellen nodded and tried not to clench her buttocks as Tina worked more lube into her anus. When she saw Aaron peering at her intently, she closed her eyes tight — she didn't want him to see into her soul.

Tina's hands skimmed over her lower back and butt cheeks.

Ellen didn't know if she could tingle more than she already was.

"Just as I did with Aaron, I'm going to hold Mike's cock and help him enter your ass. Okay?" Tina's lips caressed a butt cheek when Ellen nodded. "Someday I'll wear my strap-on, and then you can try three cocks."

Ellen's eyes popped wide open to see Aaron's face filled with a mixture of mirth and concern. There wasn't time to think about three cocks as she felt the crown of Mike's pole press against her anus. *Oh my God.* It was happening. She was stretching — no, she was being split in two.

She covered Aaron's open mouth with hers, letting him swallow her whimpers. She lifted her head and breathed when Mike's progress stopped.

"You've got his head in," Tina informed her, as if she didn't know. "You okay?"

Nodding, she murmured, "I think so."

"Let me know," Mike said, "if you need me to back out."

"No, don't. I'll be fine. Really." She gulped in air, trying to steady herself. "There. Try a little more."

"Okay."

Her eyes bulged. She felt him inching in bit by bit, forcing her wider and wider.

"One-third in," Tina announced in her cheerleading role. "Half."

"Oh my God!" Ellen moaned, her heart pounding. "So full. I can't. He's in," she yelped, feeling his thighs nestle against her butt. "Don't move." She sucked in air, filling her lungs.

"You've got him." Tina clapped her hands. "You're impaled on both cocks, girl. Careful, don't move. Let yourself adjust. Let them adjust. This is tight for the guys, too."

"Oh." Ellen winced. She hadn't thought about what it must be like for them. She remained frozen in place, waiting for Tina or someone to provide more instruction.

Tina scooted down to face her. "You still okay?"

Ellen nodded. "I think so. I think I'm relaxing a little."

"Good." Tina giggled.

"What's so funny?"

"You look good in a sandwich squeezed between one light piece of bread and one dark. You're so tan, you're almost a blend. I hadn't noticed that before." Tina knelt beside them and palmed her own pussy with one hand, then dipped the other hand lower, toward her anus, and easily inserted a finger.

Ellen gulped.

Tina smiled at her. "There. I'm ready. Why don't you begin, Mike? Careful."

The only response Mike made was a grunt.

Ellen couldn't keep her mouth shut when he pulled part-way out of her ass and slid back in. He did that several times, as if testing this new fit.

"Still okay?" Tina arched an eyebrow.

Ellen nodded. "Tight."

"Okay. Let Aaron give it a try."

Ellen blinked at Tina, then nodded at Aaron. She'd nearly forgotten he was there. She puffed air from her hollowed cheeks as he squeezed in and out. She gave both him and Tina another nod before Tina could ask how she was doing.

"Now alternate, guys," Tina coached. "Mike, then Aaron."

"Oh my God," Ellen wailed. There wasn't a moment to adjust the unfurling sense of fullness and tightness — her ass and then her vagina. She gulped and grinned a little at Tina as she began to respond to the rhythm the guys had set.

"Fuck her, boys," Tina shouted gleefully. "Enjoy your sandwich, girl. This is what you've been waiting for."

Ellen arched her neck and pressed back against both cocks. She was so open, so full. She giggled and laughed. They'd established a rhythm that threatened to send her to the moon. She closed her eyes, letting Tina tend to her own needs. Mike's strong fingers dug into her shoulders as his cock probed deeper and deeper. His heaving breaths warmed her neck.

She caught her breath as Aaron stilled beneath her, giving over to Mike's roaring that he was close. She tried not to scream, and then she screamed anyway. Mike's cock pulsated in her ass. Aaron pulled her head down so he could cover her mouth with his. She moaned and groaned into Aaron's mouth as Mike continued pumping into her ass.

At last, Mike pulled out of her. "What an incredible ass," he mumbled, collapsing on the futons beside his wife.

Ellen had hardly adjusted to Mike pulling out before Aaron

began churning in and out of her other channel. She wailed, curling her fingers into his chest hair. Hanging on tight, Ellen couldn't remember when she'd started to come. Before Mike left her. But she'd lost track of what was happening. Now Aaron was reminding her with a ferocity she'd seldom experienced from him.

He held her tight, keeping her from bouncing off him. And he drove his hips rapidly, almost violently. His cock ravaged her vagina. He gripped her buttocks firmly, and then he howled, and again she laughed nearly hysterically as she felt him emptying into her.

She was beyond orgasm. There must be a word to describe beyond orgasm, but she couldn't think of it. She panted as Aaron heaved beneath her. His grip on her butt relaxed. His legs settled on the futon. She found that she could breathe again. She felt his heart pounding. No doubt, he could feel hers, too.

He skimmed his hands lightly over her shoulders and gave her a crooked smile, then raked his fingers through her hair. "So how is my prairie woman?"

"She's fine," Ellen said, grinning. "Amazingly fine. Tired, but fine."

"Your first sandwich met your expectations? You should be quite full."

"Surpassed, by far." She peeked at Mike and Tina, who were cuddled next to them. "Thanks."

"Looks like the sixth course is complete." Aaron yawned. "Unless you have to go to the bathroom, we might just stay like this for a while. Dessert can wait for morning."

"I can wait a bit. But I will have to clean up. It feels like I'm dripping come from both of you." She arched an eyebrow. "Imagine that." She dragged a finger along Aaron's nose. "You've done such a fantastic job with this entire meal. We've all made some selections. Don't you have one?"

He took her finger and sucked on it. "I do. The eighth course. Will you stay with me tomorrow after Tina and Mike leave? Will you spend the night with me?"

She smiled softly, remembering how she'd rejected that idea once before. "Seems like that's where we were just a few days ago." She nodded. "I look forward to spending the day and night with you. I'm not sure if I'm going to be very athletic, but maybe we can talk more about the prairie woman book."

"I like talking about anything that has to do with my prairie woman. How about a nap?"

She kissed his chin and rested her head on his shoulder. His hand caressed her back. She peeked over at Mike and Tina again — they were already asleep. She hadn't realized how exhausting a sandwich would be. Although depleted, she couldn't help but think about other combinations. The future held lots of possibilities she'd never considered.

She kissed Aaron's shoulder. It looked like he was going to be part of her short-term future. How long would it take to do a book? And how much would she have to give up to pursue that project? Would that be her excuse to make some major changes?

She smiled at the zinging aftershocks still cutting across her loins — she'd already made several major changes in her lifestyle.

CHAPTER FOURTEEN

"I didn't know you could be so carefree," Ellen teased, curling her fingers around his, which rested on her bare thigh. Her other hand gripped the bar of the Ferris Wheel tightly as she stared off over the rolling hills of southern Minnesota.

Aaron had taken her to a theme park south of the Cities for a change of pace. Tina and Mike had gone home mid-morning. "I haven't been on a Ferris Wheel for years," he admitted.

"Why now?" she asked, facing him.

"A whim, I guess. I wanted to see your hair being blown by the wind. I knew you'd embrace carnival rides like a young girl. I love to watch you lose yourself in the moment." He leaned over and brushed his lips across hers. "It's not what I expect of elementary school teachers."

"Shows what you know," she huffed. "Working with kids requires you to be in the moment, to engage fantasy"—she elbowed him—"and to play. And if you're wanting to fantasize about making love with young women, I'm sure there are numerous co-eds going in and out of the studio fantasizing about having sex with an avant-garde artist."

"But I'm not fantasizing about them. I only fantasize about you."

"And Tina?"

The giant wheel jerked to a stop, leaving them on top swaying gently to and fro. "I wouldn't call that a fantasy. But you seem to enjoy watching her love me."

"Oh, I do. Why shouldn't I? You and Tina make music. Watching you and Mike with Tina is like watching a small symphony. You three are so in sync. I feel clumsy in comparison."

"Comparisons aren't required. And you did enjoy being in the middle."

"Immensely. Last night and this morning." She glanced down as the ride began to move again. "I wish it didn't have to end," she muttered, more to herself than to him.

Before he could respond, they'd stopped at the bottom, and the assistant was helping Ellen out of the seat. He smiled as she walked out ahead of him through the ropes. Maybe she was dreaming at least a little bit about what would happen next. He'd worried that only he, Tina, and Mike were thinking about the future.

He caught up with her and grabbed her hand. "Want a hotdog or something?"

She wrinkled her nose and gave a huge grin. "Or something. Let's get hotdogs and then hop on the carousel. That's a ride I haven't been on since I was a little girl — no teen would get caught dead on one of those wooden horses."

"This is wonderful," Ellen said above the sing-song music of the carousel. Aaron must feel like Ichabod Crane astride the pony next to hers, but he humored her. He was so good to her. She sighed — but was he good *for* her? Tina and Mike certainly thought so. Even her mother and dad had liked him.

She bit into the hotdog and chewed cautiously. Peeking out of the corner of her eye, she tried her best to assess him. He'd been so eager to show her this fantasyland, and he'd even left his camera in the car, though she expected he was imagining taking pictures of her riding the carousel — probably fully clothed, scantily clad, and naked. Too bad they had to share the place with scores of others. She smirked. She wouldn't put it past Aaron to rent the place on a day or time when it was closed.

She looked up quickly at a mother sitting two horses in front of her, comforting her daughter, who had begun to slip off the slippery saddle. The little girl in pigtails dropped the reins and threw her arms around her mother's neck. Ellen couldn't hear what the mother was saying, but gradually the girl settled back down on the saddle and nodded. She clutched the reins tight and chortled at her mother as she bounced up and down, encouraging the wooden pony to go faster. Another crisis settled with patience and understanding.

Ellen glanced quickly at Aaron, who was also watching the mother-daughter scene unfold in front of them. Trying to breathe normally, she blinked her eyes. Making love with Aaron was the least complicated aspect of their relationship. That was true whether it was just the two of them, or three, or all four. Lovemaking had a cocoon element to it. It was of this world, but not completely. The only decision that had to be made involved how best to ride the waves of pleasure.

The carousel slowed to a halt. The little girl in front of them screamed her dismay at having to leave the ride, but the mother simply held her and comforted her. Ellen gave an involuntary shudder — was motherhood in her future? Where had that question come from?

Ellen tucked her arm in the crook of Aaron's as they stepped off the carousel. "Can we go back? I don't think I can handle any more rides."

"Sure." Aaron chuckled. "The thirty-year-old stomach isn't as resilient as the thirteen-year-old's?"

She nodded her agreement. "The thirteen-year-old isn't hamstrung by reality."

Aaron frowned.

To her relief, he did not pursue the topic further.

"It's very pleasant out here in your back yard," Ellen oohed against Aaron's throat. "Was your grandfather into privacy, or were the privacy fences your idea?"

"They were in long before I moved here. You're a tease," he moaned, grasping her hips so she'd stopped squirming across his stiff arousal. She'd been sitting on his lap sipping wine since they'd finished dinner and retreated to the back yard. The evening was a little cool for mid-summer. Maybe it would be an early fall. He slid a hand along her inner thigh until he cupped her panty-clad mound.

She tipped her head back, draining the last of the wine. Setting the empty glass down on the end table, she kissed his chin and reached under her skirt to pull aside the panty, giving him free access to her sex. "I thought teases were girls who promised but didn't deliver."

Grinning, he worked fingers up both sides of her moist, puffy labia, over and across ridges he'd memorized by sight and feel. She purred into his neck and swayed gently against his hand, encouraging more exploration.

"Is this what you want?" He eased a finger into her heat, and she squeezed.

"Ummm. Very nice. Tell me more about your plans for the prairie woman book." She ran her wet lips across his throat. "Do you really think I can write stories for it?"

Not moving his finger, he let it soak up her heat. "You know you can."

"If we do a book together, I'd have to sign picture releases."

"That's right. Are you ready to do that? I know that's a leap for you — but you are the prairie woman. There is no other."

"I like that," she murmured, shifting her weight and the angle of his impaled finger.

He wasn't sure if she was talking about being the prairie woman or the sensations the friction of finger against tender flesh yielded.

"Would we have to include nude photos?"

"Probably. It's hard to imagine the series without at least some nude shots."

"I know," she whispered softly into his neck. "I want them to be tasteful."

"Of course. And we'll only use what you approve."

"Would I have to use my name in the credits?"

"I'd want both of our names on the book as co-authors, but the model could be given a different name. We wouldn't have to include our own pictures on the jacket. So only people who know you well would recognize you. Assuming they'd buy the book."

"It's a huge step. I'm not ready to say yes." She smiled and rocked against his finger. "Sort of like your continuum notions, I suppose. I'm at the definite maybe point."

"That's progress."

"I know. If we do use nudes, I want the model credit to read Clarissa."

"Super. Why didn't I think of that?"

"Because you're not me." She gave him one of her shy looks. "You must've wondered why I was so quiet on the way back from the prairie."

"It did cross my mind to wonder, but I didn't want to pry." He wiggled his finger deep in her channel.

"Good God, is that what you're doing down there? Prying?"

He kissed her softly. "Unlocking your secrets. So why were you so thoughtful on the way back? Were you thinking about us?"

She shook her head. "Some, but mostly about what my mother shared with me the night before we left."

"And?"

"She thinks I'm quite naturally bi."

He scowled and chuckled. "And that was a surprise? You've known about Clarissa for years. That's what had you going for hours on end?"

She shook her head. "Nope. Mom is convinced because she's bi, too."

Startled, he nearly pulled out of her vagina. "Your mother?"

She nodded. "She took on a female lover before I was born, but after she had Jack.

"Damn. That must've been a shock."

"It was."

"Did your dad know?'

Ellen gave him a crooked grin. "He was part of it."

Now he knew his jaw had dropped. "Your dad . . . a three-way relationship?"

Ellen nodded. "Apparently it lasted for six months before Jill moved to the west coast. They all chose security over the unknown. Mom and Dad now look back and wonder what life might've been like if they'd chosen differently."

"And she thought you now needed to know about that?"

Ellen shrugged. "Mom claims that a woman glows differently once she's been with another woman. She thought I glowed and wanted me to know that I'm quite normal, living out my own blood and destiny."

"Wow. She blessed your sexuality."

"Yeah. I guess that's one way of putting it. Amazing, isn't it?"

"Stunning. My folks would disown me if they could." Light bulbs began to flash in his brain. "And you've talked with Tina about this already?"

"That's right. I knew she'd understand."

"But you weren't sure about me?"

She shook her head.

"So, that's why she's felt so free to encourage you to give

up your teaching position and move here." He tried not to look deflated. None of that discussion had had anything to do with him.

She squirmed against his finger getting his attention. "You're not jealous, are you? Tina's bisexual. It seemed natural to talk with her first. To gain her perspective. So does it bother you that I'm bi?"

He shook his head vigorously, not liking the feel of his cheeks burning. "Why should it? I've been involved with Tina for years. With Tina and Mike," he corrected.

She kissed the tip of his nose. "Maybe you have a possessive streak you're not aware of. Sometimes I see a strange look come over your face when Mike is fucking me or when Tina has me gushing over her mouth. I know I must be wrong, but . . ."

He slanted a finger across her lips. "I know you're wrong. Were you thinking that when Mike's cock was in your ass and mine in your pussy?" He wiggled her finger.

"No," she said, wetting her lips. She gave him a half smile. "Of course, you could've been railing against me and I would never have noticed. That was overwhelming. Perfectly overwhelming. Hmmm. Are we going to make love out here?"

She'd just smoothly shifted the subject back to a more appealing topic than whether he was jealous. He'd roll with it. "Do you want to make love here or upstairs in my bedroom?"

"Your bedroom? You've never taken me there." She eased off his finger, then stood, reaching for his hand. "I'd love to see your bedroom."

"My goodness, it's an erotic photo gallery," Ellen gasped, leaving Aaron at the bedroom door to enter the room. The spacious room dwarfed a king-sized bed, easy chairs and sofa. She'd never been in a bedroom so huge. Wall mirrors provided a sense of almost endless space. A ceiling mirror hung over the bed, which was covered in a tasteful soft blue comforter. A marble jacuzzi took up one corner of the room. A door opened onto a large bathroom and another into a walk-in closet.

But all of that paled compared to the black and white photos on the walls. She kicked off her sandals, and her toes dug into the carpet. Swallowing, she walked closer to scan first one wall and then another. Her mouth gaped when she recognized an enlarged photo of her bare pussy hanging next to Tina's. There was also a photo of Mike's cock and another of Aaron's. She reached out and ran a finger over a glass-covered photo of her and Tina coupled in a classic sixty-nine pose. The picture of her and Tina teasing each other's tongues hung close to the bed. Another photo showed her on her knees with her back to the camera, sucking on Mike's cock. She could hardly believe what she was seeing.

Her hand came to her throat. There was a photo of Tina sandwiched between Mike and Aaron. Ellen's nipples ached as she followed a series of the three of them engaged in various love acts. There was even one of her astride Aaron on the prairie grasses. She'd forgotten that he'd taken a few timed pictures of them together.

She stepped closer to the bed to look at a half dozen others from the prairie. She was fully clothed in the gingham dress except for bare feet. In another, she sat naked from the waist up, with the butter churn between her thighs. There was a nude shot of her at the spinning wheel, but the most stunning picture was the one where she stared softly down at a bared breast, with the other partially hidden by gingham. It was the only titled picture — Expectant Mother.

Her heart clutched. She couldn't deny the meaning of the picture, even if it wasn't true. She did look like an expectant mother. She folded her arms under her breasts and stared at

Aaron. "How could you? I didn't give permission for any of these photos to be shown. Why? What are you doing?"

Aaron stepped across the room and curled an arm around her waist.

She didn't move.

"This is my private collection," he explained.

"But others will see them. Your lovers," she stammered.

He shook his head. "Only Mike and Tina come to this room. And now you."

"And now me," she repeated. "But why?" She scowled as his comment sank in. "No others. But why me?"

"You're one of us. You didn't balk when Tina made that clear. You're part of the foursome."

"But . . . I don't know what I'm going to do."

He shook his head. "Doesn't matter. You're part of the foursome until you tell us you're not. Hasn't Tina made that clear?"

She frowned at the pictures of her and Tina. "Sort of. I guess. But I didn't think that meant . . ."

Aaron stepped behind her and hugged her. "It doesn't matter where you are. You're one of us until you say you're not."

"But what if I don't want . . ." She couldn't complete the thought, because she did want.

He must've sensed what she was thinking. While still behind her, he began unbuttoning her blouse and she let him. "But what if . . ."

"Save the what-ifs until later," he whispered in her ear. He nuzzled her buttocks with his firm erection.

She sighed and pushed back against him. She pushed her skirt down over her thighs. "There's not one of me and you and Mike," she said mockingly.

"There will be." He hooked an arm around her waist to cover her vulva with a palm. "You probably didn't even

212

notice. Tina took a couple shots while you were so pleasantly distracted."

"She didn't." She quickly twisted her head around.

"She most definitely did. She's not as good with a camera as you are, but I trust she did well enough. I'll take a shot of the four of us at another time. Thought that might be too intrusive."

"Intrusive?" She turned in his arms and grappled with his belt. "Intrusive. Why should that stop you? You've been intrusive since the day I met you." She dipped a hand into his shorts. "Right now, I'm gripping my favorite intruder. If you don't mind, these damn pictures are making me terribly horny. Do you think this guy can do something about that?"

"I'm sure of it," Aaron grunted, shucking his pants.

Folding his body comfortably around Ellen's backside, Aaron felt his cock hardening again inside her warm channel. He studied their image in the mirror opposite the bed. She had that dreamy well-loved look. Their lovemaking had been slow and gentle. It had been as if they were holding hands skipping up a hill of ecstasy together, each helping the other to a wide range of pleasure. Their breathing had steadied. Each was now lost in post-orgasmic bliss.

He wished he could read her mind. Her eyes closed as if she was concealing her soul from him.

Taking Ellen to the amusement park had been whimsy at its finest. She had been as excited as he'd expected. He loved surprising her. He loved watching her respond instinctively. For a woman so accustomed to planning details, she could be enthusiastically spontaneous.

Bringing her to his bedroom had been a risk he knew he had to take. His gallery had thrown her at first, but she'd adjusted to it. His heart did a stutter step. She'd accepted its message — she was indeed part of their foursome.

He wanted to shout for joy, but he silently kissed her shoulder. She'd toyed with where the picture Tina had taken of Ellen's first male sandwich should hang. And she'd suggested they needed a timed shot of the four of them making love to fill out the series.

His fears of rejection had been unfounded. She was his, and he was hers. They could get on with their lives.

He nibbled on Ellen's shoulder.

Her eyelids parted, and she gave him a lazy smile in the mirror.

If he had to label that reflection, he'd call it pure satisfaction. "Would you prefer a fall wedding? Or maybe a Christmas wedding?"

"Wedding?" Her eyelids flew open. Her brow furrowed. "Wedding!"

She pulled out of his embrace before he could stop her and glowered at him "Are you crazy? I didn't say anything about a wedding."

"But . . ." he grunted. "You agreed you're part of the foursome."

"Oh, hell," Ellen yelled, her focus on the ceiling. Then she gave him a look of sheer terror and scrambled for her clothes.

He sat up — what the hell was happening?

"Don't you come near me," she shouted. "Wedding. Christ!"

She yanked panties up her thighs. The skirt quickly followed. She was buttoning her blouse before Aaron realized he'd made a mistake. A huge one. "I'm sorry. I didn't mean to spook you."

"Spook me!" Ellen's finger paused on a button. "Spook me? I never said I wanted to get married. I don't even know that I'm moving. I've been married," she rattled on. "It's the pits." She reached for her sandals. "And you never asked me to marry you. You just assumed."

"Oh shit!" She was beyond reasoning, not that he had a lot of logic to offer her, either. "I thought we were—"

"We had some good sex," Ellen interrupted. "No, fantastic sex. But marriage requires much more than that. Tina wants me to move here. You want a wedding. Christ. I don't have a clue what I want, but it sure isn't a wedding."

Aaron held his tongue, nor did he get up to try to comfort her. Ellen had a full head of steam, and she wasn't going to be calmed any time soon.

"What a mess!" Ellen looked around at the bedroom photos. "I've never had a better day than today." She glared back at him. "And then you had to go and fuck it up with your assumptions about me, about us." She grabbed her purse. "I doubt I'll be at work tomorrow."

"That's okay. Take as much time as you need."

"I don't know when I'll be able to look at you again." She winced. "Or if I can. Jesus, you really know how to fuck things up."

His skin turned clammy as tears filled her eyes.

Inexplicably she stepped to the bed and kissed the top of his head, then stumbled away as if afraid he'd try to grab her.

He didn't.

"Thanks for helping me discover who I am. Don't try to find me, Aaron. I've got a lot to sort through. You're only a part of it, if you're even that." She turned and quietly walked out of his bedroom.

He sucked air into his burning lungs. She'd rejected him. Just like that. She didn't have to worry about him trying to find her. Not a chance. There was always another model out there if he wanted one.

He peered at the photos of his prairie woman staring back at him. She was wrong about one thing. He was definitely part of what she had to sort through—a lot larger part than she imagined.

He stood and reached for the first picture. His arms collapsed to his sides. "Damn," he mumbled, heading for the bathroom. He wasn't ready to take her pictures down.

CHAPTER FIFTEEN

"I can't call him—not yet." Ellen stared at a young family climbing out of their car at the I-90 rest area. She switched the cell phone to her other ear and walked over to a picnic table away from the visitor building. "I need to see my folks first. Is he okay?"

"If you call fumbling around like a rejected puppy for nearly two weeks okay, then maybe." Tina chuckled. "You, at least, are able to stay busy. Quitting a job and putting a house on the market must not leave much time for worrying about lovers."

"Don't I wish!"

"When will you be moving in?"

"I'll probably be back in a few days. You sure Mike is okay with me staying with you guys until I find my own place? I won't take long."

"You're kidding. He's looking forward to having you handy. He can't wait to tell Aaron."

"But he won't."

"Don't worry. We won't say anything to Aaron until you do."

"Oh. I forgot to ask. How's the baby project coming?"

"Just fine." Tina giggled. "Don't know how successful we've been, but Mike is very diligent about keeping plenty of his little sperm fellows swimming around down there. Hopefully, an egg is giving some little fellow a proper welcome."

Ellen chewed on her bottom lip. "And is Aaron getting pictures?"

"Of course he is. Not every time, but we try to get over to his place as often as we can. He's managed to take some beautiful photos which he's labeled *Conception* with a question mark."

"And he's fine with his role?"

"It's probably the only photo shoot that's energizing him these days. And your concern for his welfare is noted. I'm finding plenty of ways to keep him satisfied. Though I suspect he's getting hungry for pussy — for a certain pussy in particular."

"Right. I doubt he even has my pictures on the wall anymore." She gasped — she hated being so circumspect with Tina.

"Coy doesn't work, girl. To satisfy your curiosity, I'm pleased to inform you that you still adorn his walls in all your glory. There's even a new picture."

"There is?"

"Uh-huh. One of the shots I took of you sandwiched between the guys."

"Damn." Her loins clenched. "I didn't even know you took any pictures until Aaron told me."

"You did seem to be concentrating on other matters at the time."

"And he has it on the wall?"

"Yep."

The memory of the Japanese meal the four of them had shared sent a shiver down Ellen's spine. "I do miss you. All of you."

"We can pick up where we left off whenever you want."

"But he wants to marry me."

"So? He doesn't have to marry you tomorrow, does he?"

Ellen closed her eyes. "I don't suppose so. But I don't want to lead him on, either."

"And you're certain you'll never want to marry him?"

"No. Of course I don't know that." She frowned. "I didn't let him say when. I assumed . . ."

"You two are always making assumptions. Too often you're wrong. And I miss you, too."

Ellen grinned. "Yeah. I'd love to show you the prairie someday."

"You're more earthy than I am. I'm not at all sure I'd want to make love in the tall grasses like you and Aaron did."

"We could use a blanket."

"Get your head together, girl, and hurry back. I'm creaming just talking to you. Mike and I will be here for you, but you really need to square things with Aaron."

"You won't tell him I called."

"The connection is breaking up. My battery must be low. Talk with you later."

Ellen scowled at the phone in her hand — she'd bet there was no battery problem. Tina just didn't want to make any promises regarding Aaron. Grimacing, Ellen headed back to her car. That was the third time she'd talked to Tina in the past ten days or so. During each previous call, Tina had agreed not to tell Aaron she'd called.

Perhaps Tina was running out of patience with her. Ellen quickened her steps. She knew she was running out of time. She did have to settle on a plan for Aaron. It wasn't that she hadn't considered countless scenarios, but she hadn't decided on one.

She had to talk with her parents first. Once she got South Dakota squared away, she could devote her entire attention to the Twin Cities and the tempest brewing there.

"You don't think I'm a fool?" Ellen asked, glancing at her mom and dad. The three of them were seated on her parents' back deck overlooking a well-cared-for lawn and flower beds. The seasons were turning.

She'd always loved late summer and early fall with the anticipation of the first frost and a crispness that braced one with a hearty good morning. She couldn't shed the feeling that this seasonal shift was laced with more tension than usual.

As she expected, her mother spoke first. "I think you're making the right choice for you." Her mother gave her dad a wistful look. "We can't always go back and change things, but you're not giving up on teaching. If you want to find a teaching job in the Cities, you will. Maybe not this year. You're following your heart, and that's what matters."

She waited for her father, who took his time.

"Your mother's right," he said, nodding. "You're an excellent teacher, Ellen, but you'll do fine at whatever you decide to do. I think you're wise to get a realtor involved with your house. It's challenging being a landlord, and being a distant landlord only makes matters worse." A sadness swept across his face. "And I'm afraid you're right. Once you own your sexuality, it will be very difficult to move back as if nothing is different."

The late evening birds were calling their soft bedding sounds — why did it sound so mournful tonight? "It's been a hectic two weeks. I had to talk to the principal first. She wasn't thrilled, but she understood. The realtor is optimistic, but then I suppose they always are. At least my renter is okay with going month to month and may even try to figure out if she can buy."

"And you have a safe temporary living arrangement?"

"Yes, Mom." Ellen grinned. "Tina and Mike will put me up until I find something more permanent. At least until I find a job, which I'll want to do as soon as possible. I've managed to save over the years, but I don't want to drain my savings, either."

"You've always been rather frugal." Her dad arched an eyebrow. "Wish I could say the same about your brother and sister."

"And what are you going to do about Aaron?" her mother asked. "You've been here four hours and haven't mentioned him. Is he still in the picture? I thought you two had something going."

Ellen shrugged. How could she answer a question she had no answer to? They hadn't communicated at all. She had told him not to try to find her. But he could've called. He did have her cell number.

Tina had told her it was probably good to let him stew for a while. Aaron wasn't used to being rejected by a woman.

But she hadn't rejected him. Not completely. She shivered. At least she hadn't planned on that. She'd simply reacted that night in his bedroom. She'd been a jangle of nerves from nearly nonstop loving for forty-eight hours. And then there'd been the amusement park and then his bedroom lined with pictures of his lovers. Only three.

She kept her eyes focused on a rabbit munching near one of the flower beds. "He wants me to marry him," she squeaked.

"Oh my," her mother gasped. "He is serious. Why didn't you tell us? What did you say?"

"I ran." She turned to stare at her mother. "I'm not ready to marry. Not again."

"But how do you feel about Aaron?"

"I like him a lot. A real lot. He treats me very well. We share so many interests. He says he loves me. How can he?"

"Very easily." Her mother squeezed her arm. "You're a very lovely girl, Ellen. Do you want him to go away?"

"No," she responded sharply. "I'm not sure he knows what love is."

"And you do?"

She scowled at her father. She'd expected that question from her mother, not him. She shrugged. "I thought I did once."

"Ah. Maybe you have as much to learn about love as your photographer does."

She held her dad's steady gaze.

"But you don't want to marry. At least not yet."

"That's right."

"Then don't." He steepled his fingers. "I'm not sure I ever expected to have this conversation with one of my daughters, but my advice is to make sure you can live together before marrying."

Ellen gulped and tried not to look shocked. This was her father. She'd always thought of him as rather traditional. She glanced at her grinning mother. Apparently, he wasn't nearly as traditional as she'd thought.

"If I were young and single today, I'd want to be as positive about the woman I was thinking about marrying as I could be." Her dad darkened. "After watching you go through one divorce, I wouldn't want to see you go through another. If you think this is your guy, give him a try, but don't put yourself in a box."

"Your dad is right, Ellen. Don't hold back on taking a risk just to avoid pain, but don't set yourself up for more pain than necessary. You're both adults. Do what feels right for you. And you know we'll support you no matter what you choose to do."

"You two are something else." Ellen grinned and moved to hug her mother and then her father. "I love you guys. I think I'm going to go for a walk. I still have a lot to sort out."

Recognizing the familiar call of a mourning dove, Ellen walked out of her parents' yard and headed down the sidewalk. Her lungs burned. What would Aaron think if he'd overheard that conversation?

So much had happened in the past two weeks, but nothing

had changed between her and Aaron. Did he even think about her? He must. He hadn't removed her pictures from his bedroom.

Who would blink first? Could a relationship end because of pride? Should she call him? Maybe she should just show up on his doorstep.

She fingered the cell phone she'd slipped into her pocket before leaving the back deck. She pulled her hand out of the pocket. Not tonight. She might try him tomorrow. Maybe she'd check with Tina one more time before calling Aaron. That did seem a safer strategy. Why was it so important to play it safe with Aaron? She hadn't taken one safe action since she'd left the Cities — other than not calling him.

Ellen looked to the East. Was he thinking about her now?

Breathing through pursed lips, Aaron held Tina's head between his hands as she bobbed slowly up and down his shaft. He glanced over her backside at Mike, whose eyes had taken on that glazed look as he pounded incessantly in his wife's pussy.

Aaron gasped and scowled down at Tina, who had pulled off his cock. She gripped him firmly in one hand and rocked back against Mike.

"Sorry," she moaned, "I'll take care of you soon. Maybe this is the moment."

"Maybe," he replied, clicking the remote camera sitting on the tripod across from his bed. They'd probably never know for sure, but at least they'd have some shots of the month leading up to whenever she conceived.

"I'm coming," Mike growled, grabbing his wife's shoulders, holding her tight as he began emptying his seed.

"Wonderful," Tina moaned. She knelt like a holy vessel receiving her daily contribution.

Aaron filled his lungs, moved by being included in this moment. While he wasn't always present for this baby making, he was present often enough to know that he wanted his own child. He glanced over at the photo of Ellen in the gingham dress gazing at her bare breast. She'd be a fantastic mother. And she was the one he wanted to be the mother of his child — of their child. He had no doubt about that now.

"You ready for me?" Tina said softly, skimming his cock through her fingers. "Or do you just want to fantasize about our prairie woman?"

"I'm ready," he grunted, lowering her head to his cock.

Without finesse, Tina set a quick, steady pace, alternating short strokes with long ones.

Aaron gritted his teeth and tried to ignore Mike, who was grinning broadly and still pumping slowly in and out of his wife.

"This could be you and Ellen," Mike taunted. "It's an incredible feeling planting your seed for real."

"Jesus Christ," Aaron grunted, working Tina's head faster over his cock until he began to spew down her throat.

Tina stayed with him, taking everything he could muster.

He stared at the photos on the wall. They blurred.

"There's still one picture missing," Mike pointed out.

Aaron glowered at him as he withdrew from Tina's mouth.

"You need," Mike continued, easing out of Tina's pussy, "a picture of the four of us making love."

"Damn," Aaron mumbled. "Will you two ever let up about her?"

"Probably not," Tina quipped. "Until you stop feeling sorry for yourself and do what's right."

"And that is?"

"Go after her. Romance her." Tina chuckled. "Drag her back if you have to."

"You man enough?" Mike chided.

Aaron shifted to sit on the edge of the bed. He couldn't keep his focus off the photos. "You really think she's the one?"

"We know she's the one," Tina accused. "And you do, too. Do you realize if you don't act fairly soon, you may lose her for all of us?"

Aaron glanced quickly at Tina. "Have you talked to her? Did she tell you that?"

Tina shrugged. "Not in so many words. But a girl will only wait so long."

"But she told me not to try to find her."

"Jesus, Aaron, you must know women don't always mean what they say." Mike gave him a hard look. "I wouldn't be with Tina if I took every word she said as her last word."

"You're probably right about that. So where is she?" He eyed Tina closely. "Don't tell me you don't know."

"I won't break a confidence. She told me not to tell." Tina got off the bed and walked over to the series of pictures he'd taken on the prairie. She turned and grinned. "Where would a prairie woman go to sort out her life?"

Tossing on his bed the following night, Aaron carried on the same internal debate he'd been having off and on since he'd left Tina and Mike the night before. Should he track Ellen down in South Dakota?

She'd been adamant about giving her space and time. That was what she'd said, but he hadn't heard a word from her. Was she waiting for him to take the next step? Or had she simply given up on them?

What did he have to lose if he did go after her? Embarrassment. Hell, she might be with another guy or another woman by now. She'd been gone over two weeks. How long did it take for a woman to get her head together?

But still, he didn't like the idea of not honoring her wishes. He didn't need to force a woman to love him. He threw the sheet and light blanket off and sat up. Switching on the bed-stand light, he got up and went to the bathroom.

When he returned, he admired the photos near the bed. Ellen stared out of the photo at him with a look of contentment as Tina suckled a breast. He'd never had a lover with more sensitive breasts than Ellen's. His throat muscles worked involuntarily, as if he needed another reminder of what he was missing. His bedroom photo gallery was turning the room into a torture chamber.

The ring of his cell phone jerked him alert.

"Son of a bitch," he mumbled, checking caller ID. He'd have a better idea about a trip to South Dakota soon. "Hey. Thought maybe you fell off the face of the earth."

"I couldn't sleep. I'm so keyed up. I hope it's not too late to call."

"You know you can call me any time, Ellen. Day or night. What's up? Where are you?"

"I'm at my parents' house. In my old room. You remember I showed it to you when you were out here?"

"Yeah, I remember. The frilly bed with stuffed animals on it and walls still decorated with rocks stars from your adolescent years."

"That's right. Mom doesn't see a need to change it, I guess. My sister's room is pretty much the same. My brother's room has been redone into a guestroom."

"So . . . you must be in bed?"

"Good guess," she snickered. "I'm wearing my letter sweater. I think I told you I lettered in softball and swimming."

"I do recall." Aaron coughed. "And does the sweater still fit?"

"It's a little snug," she said softly. "My boobs grew more after high school. The sweater doesn't quite reach my waist anymore."

Aaron cleared his throat, and his cock grew to full strength as he imagined the picture Ellen was painting for him. "And the sweater is all you're wearing?"

"Exactly."

"And why are you telling me all of this?" Aaron asked, settling back against the headboard, holding the phone with one hand and encircling his cock with the other.

"I thought maybe you could help me fall asleep. I've been hugging my favorite teddy bear, but she's not helping much."

"Now, after two weeks, you need a little phone sex." Aaron tried to bite back the accusation.

"Don't be crude about it," she replied meekly. "I've missed you. I hoped you missed me, too."

"I have, damn it. I just thought we have a lot to talk about before . . ."

She chuckled in his ear. "I thought it was the girl who usually wanted to talk too much. If you don't feel comfortable," she teased, "maybe you can listen in. I have to be quiet. My folks are sleeping down the hallway."

"Jesus! That'll be a challenge. Staying quiet. And you won't be alone. When are you coming back, Ellen?"

"Oh, didn't I tell you? Oh, my goodness. It has been a while. Sorry, I've got a hand under my sweater toying with a nipple. If you're going to play with me, why don't you fondle your balls for me?"

"Christ," he moaned, cupping his balls in the palm of his hand. "You seem experienced with this. How many boys did you bring to your room?"

Ellen giggled. "Only a couple. It was a challenge. Nearly got caught. You can imagine my fingers tenderly squeezing those precious gems of yours. I'm using my other hand to rim my navel. Do you think I'd look better with a belly ring or with a tattoo?"

"Why not both?" he muttered. "When are you getting back

to the Cities?"

"That's why I'm so keyed up. If I can get some sleep to-night, I'll start back in the morning."

"Beautiful," he said, skimming his shaft between thumb and forefinger. "You want to come by the house for dinner?"

"Maybe," she said, somewhat harshly. "There. I've pushed a finger into my pussy. Too bad it's not as long as yours. Now, where were we? Oh, right. I want you to meet me in Studio B at five o'clock." She chuckled. "We can take it from there."

"All right. Home seems more intimate, but if that's what you want. How long are you staying? When do you have to go back for the fall term?"

"I've got my legs spread wide and my sweater pulled up over my boobs." She sighed into the phone. "I'm working my finger in and out. Are you skimming your cock?"

"Yes."

"Good. I'm glad you're not just listening. I won't be going back for the fall term. I resigned."

"What?" His hand stilled and his heart skipped two beats.

"Don't forget your cock. I'm moving in with Mike and Tina until I find a job and a more permanent living space."

"Fantastic." Aaron glanced at her pictures on the wall try-ing to stay focused and in control of himself. What was she saying? "I could help with both."

"Let's not get ahead of ourselves," she cautioned. "Oh, damn. My clit is begging to be touched."

"Do it."

"I will. Aaron, we'll talk tomorrow, but don't use the M word with me, please. I'm not ready for that. Understand?"

His brain pounded with a hundred hammers rapping on his skull. *No marriage. Not ready.* Did that mean she might be ready someday? He didn't have a clue what she meant. "I un-derstand," he lied. Hopefully, he'd understand more when he could see her face to face.

"Right now . . ."

He could easily imagine her pausing to yawn.

"I have to get some sleep. We can talk more tomorrow. Come with me, Aaron. Don't let me do this alone."

"I'm with you, babe." Aaron swallowed and fisted his cock in time with her panting.

"I'm stroking my pussy . . . my clit. Holy crap," she squealed into his ear. "Are you coming with . . ."

"Yes. Oh, shit." He lurched forward as his cock erupted. He milked it furiously as Ellen's screams echoed across the miles. His hand slowed. He chuckled. "So much for quiet."

"Imagining you splashing all over my boobies was too much for me." She giggled. "I'll probably enter the kitchen in the morning to applause. My folks are rooting for you. Too bad I'm not there to help you clean up. Tomorrow."

"Tomorrow," he said softly. "I can't tell you how happy I am to hear from you."

"Tell me tomorrow. Oh, by the way. Wear your dark robe when you come to me in Studio B."

Aaron began to smile. "A photo shoot?"

"Of sorts. I can hardly hold the phone any longer. Good night. Sweet dreams. Bye, love."

"Bye." His eyes widened as her words sank in. "I love you," he added, but the connection had already ended.

Again he got out of bed to head to the bathroom, only this time, he had a lighter step to match his light-headedness. He wasn't sure where all of this was going, but it seemed clear that the process had not been aborted. They were still sorting out what might be possible for them.

Marriage seemed highly unlikely in the near future, but there were other options he could live with quite easily. Tomorrow promised to be a very long, nerve-racking day.

Checking and double-checking her camera equipment and settings, Ellen was surprised by her own calm. Now that she'd made her decision, all she had to do was convince Aaron of the wisdom of her plan. She smiled as she brought the couch into focus through the lens. She wasn't too worried about it, but then she could be quite convincing.

She'd dressed for her role with considerable care. Smoothing out the mid-thigh polo dress over her hips, she unfastened one more snap. The one just above her navel. She also undid the bottom three snaps, leaving three to hold the fabric together. There'd been no need to bother with non-essentials when she dressed, so she wore no undergarments.

She'd probably thought this seduction through as thoroughly as Aaron had planned the Japanese meal. But then she'd had over two weeks to think and scheme. And she'd been planning this since before she left the city for the prairie.

Ellen ran a finger over her serpent belly-ring and chuckled. He thought she should have a belly ring and a tattoo. She'd gotten both the morning after she left Aaron's bedroom in a huff. Both body adornments celebrated her new life. She was aware the serpent was an age-old symbol of sexuality, and the colorful butterfly on her right buttocks spoke to the ongoing transformation she'd felt taking place for weeks. Even Tina didn't know about the ring and tattoo. They were Ellen's own doing.

She glanced around the room. Just as this was her own doing. Only Aaron knew she was expected back today. She'd known before she left the Cities what she had to do with her former teaching job and her house. It had taken much longer to sort out what to do with Aaron.

Would he accept her on her terms? She shivered. Once she locked in on a goal, she seldom considered failing. That had always been true. Why should Aaron be any different?

The door squeaked and she looked up to see it open.

Aaron nodded as he entered the room. "Welcome back." His eyes sparkled, but he didn't smile.

Was he that unsure about what to expect from her? That was good. It gave her the edge. She remained behind the camera. She wanted to dash into his arms, but that would spoil the effect of what she ultimately wanted. This was a time for deferred gratification.

With professional composure, she returned his nod. "I'm glad you could make it for your photo shoot, Mr. Brewster."

"Ah," Aaron responded with a half-smile. "I can play along. Well, Ms. Jeffers, what sort of pose did you have in mind? May I say you look absolutely stunning in that dress?"

Ellen's heart fluttered. "You may," she murmured. "Why don't we have you sitting on the couch, for starters?"

"Like this?" He settled on the couch and crossed his legs at the ankles. The robe only gave way slightly.

"That'll provide a nice test to be sure I have the proper settings."

She bent over the tripod and focused the camera, clicking a close-up on Aaron's face, backing it off to include his entire body, then further to include the full couch. "Give me a range of expressions. Humor. Intensity. Anger. Dreamy. Ah, you do dreamy so well. Good."

She stepped around the tripod and approached the couch, shooting him a puzzled look as if she couldn't decide what she wanted next.

"No assistant today, Ms. Jeffers?"

She shook her head. "I don't need assistance."

"I'm sure your assistant will be disappointed that she's no longer needed."

"I didn't say that." Ellen went rigid. What the hell was he implying? Or was he merely trying to tease? "I don't need her this evening."

"But you still expect her to help you with your various" —

Aaron wet his lips and smiled a little — "apertures from time to time."

She nodded. "I've discovered that help with aperture settings can be enhanced by multiple partners. Sort of like not relying on only one lens for a photo shoot."

"Yes, I can see how one lens might become rather restrictive."

"Now, why don't you slide around, Mr. Brewster, so you're lying on the couch." Ellen pulled out a pillow. "You can use this for your head." She leaned over, helping him. Her breasts came within inches of his nose.

He inhaled. "You do smell exceptional today. Like prairie grasses."

A jolt shot through her body. It took all the control she could muster not to yank open his robe and ravish his body. She lifted his left arm and placed it over his brow before gulping air and stepping back.

She retreated behind the camera and peered through the lens. With half his face blocked from her view, she couldn't read what he was thinking. "That's good. You may open the robe. Place your right hand over your left nipple and raise your right leg so the sole of your foot is resting on the couch."

He tugged on the sash with his free hand. The robe parted as he positioned himself according to her instructions, and his shaft jutted toward the ceiling. She gasped. "Damn."

"Something wrong?"

"I wanted a picture with him flaccid."

"Too bad. This is what you get."

She snapped several shots. "Fondle him for me, Mr. Brewster. That's right. Now I'll take some free-held shots. Don't move."

Satisfied she had enough, she straightened and grimaced. "This is good, but I really did want some flaccid shots."

"Sorry, I can't help you there."

"Don't move," she grunted. Hurriedly, she knelt beside the couch and took him in her mouth. Without a bit of finesse, she eased him into her throat and began stroking him with one hand around the base of his cock as she bobbed up and down. Increasing the suction on his shaft when she felt him expanding, Ellen congratulated herself both on her efficiency and her devotion to her art. She'd get her picture of Aaron flaccid.

"Jesus," Aaron moaned as he began to spurt. He'd done nothing to help her while maintaining his pose.

She swallowed, keeping up with him. When he finished, she stood and wiped her mouth with the back of her hand. "Now, don't think about me, Aaron."

She dashed to the tripod and took shot after shot. She chuckled as the limp cock began slowly to lengthen and rise. "Like the serpent," she mumbled.

"What?"

"Nothing. Are you thinking about me again?"

"How can I not?" He dropped the arm blocking his view and stared at her. "Do you think Caillebotte had to bring off his mistress to get the expression he wanted in his painting?"

Smirking, Ellen stepped around the camera. "I hoped the pose wouldn't be lost on you."

"How could it not? I've spent hours studying that painting, and then you've posed for me several times on this same couch. Is there a message here somewhere for me?"

She nodded. "It'll become clear in a moment. I want to show you something first." She unsnapped two more buttons, revealing the serpent belly ring.

Aaron whistled softly. "It's perfect for you. The serpent symbolizes kundalini — sexual energy."

"I know. That's why I selected it. That's an energy I'm only beginning to tap." She gave him a half smile. "I hope."

She turned away from him, bent over, and flipped the dress over her back. She glanced over her shoulder to see a huge smile appear on Aaron's face. He sat up.

"Wow! Stunning. Beautiful. Just look at you," he said, standing behind her and running a finger over the butterfly tattoo. "You did these before you left. You knew what you wanted before you got to the prairie."

Ellen stood and turned toward him. She watched his gaze follow her fingers as she unfastened the remaining button and let her dress fall entirely open. "I knew what I had to do to be me. I knew I had discovered a passion that couldn't be ignored. I knew I'd move here. But I didn't know what to do about you. You scared me."

"I didn't mean to scare you," he countered, reaching out to graze her cheek.

"I know you didn't mean to, but you did. I'm not ready to get married again. If that's what you have to have, then you need to find someone else."

He shook his head. "I'm done looking. I've found what I want, what I need. What do you want, Ellen? What can we work out?"

"I want you," she said, running a finger over his chest. "I want Tina. I want Mike. I want what we had during that Japanese meal and more, so much more."

Aaron chuckled. "I haven't heard anything I don't want yet."

"My dad gave me the solution."

"Your dad? What do you mean?"

"He suggested that I not get married again before thoroughly trying to live with the guy. Divorce is too hard on the entire family not to know what one is getting into first."

"First? So you're not ruling out marriage."

She shook her head.

"I like your dad more and more."

Ellen brushed her lips across Aaron's and eyed him cautiously. "I'm willing to be your mistress, Aaron, if you're willing to be mine. I'm not sure what a male mistress would be called."

Aaron shook his head and laughed. "A live-in mistress?"

"If you want. Yes."

"Super."

"But I won't be a kept woman," Ellen insisted. "I expect to earn my way. Here at the studio or somewhere else."

"We can work on that — no problem."

She saw his features darken. "What's wrong? What else do you want?"

"It's remote, I know." He screwed up his mouth and forged ahead. "I've watched Tina and Mike work on their baby-making so often maybe I'm overly concerned. And I trust birth control, but what if?"

Ellen gulped. "Go on."

"What if you do get pregnant? I won't have you taking our baby away."

"Shh," she whispered, hugging him tight. "That won't happen. I won't get pregnant. But if I did, we'd make it work." She leaned back against his arms. "When did you discover you wanted to be a father?"

"When I was in the darkroom and the image of you studying your breast in a motherly way began to emerge from the fixer."

She kissed the tip of his nose. "Patience. As a famous photographer once said, all of this is part of a process. You should know that I do want to be a mother, and you're the kind of father I've imagined for my baby from the time I was a little girl."

He kissed her hair and held her quietly.

"Just don't rush me. I'm going through lots of changes. Becoming a mother is one I can wait on." She beamed up at him. "At least for a while. Now, why don't you show me how much you love me?" She shrugged off the dress, rose on her toes, and nibbled at the corners of his mouth. "Would you like a closer look at my butterfly?"

"What do you have in mind?"

She held his fingers as she turned to climb on the couch, then knelt and waggled her butt. She slapped the butt cheek with the tattoo. "Why don't you come in . . ."

He plunged in before she could finish her sentence.

She arched her neck and chortled. "That was quick. Just hold me for a moment. Do you still like my butterfly?"

"It only enhances your beauty."

"Maybe I should get another."

"I love you, Ellen. I don't care how many butterflies you get. You are the most lovely creature I've ever known."

"And I love you. You know, you can be quite romantic." She slid back and forth over his cock, then paused and turned to grin at him. "I've already had you in my mouth this evening. Fuck me slow and easy for a while, and then finish in my ass."

"You certainly sound like a woman with a plan. Maybe you'll want to take up choreography."

"Maybe I will." She moaned as he began to move inside her.

"What else do you have planned for the evening?"

She chuckled and squeezed her inner muscles. "I thought we might go back to your place and have another of your famous light meals."

"With Tina and Mike?"

She shook her head. "Not tonight. Tonight is just for us. Tomorrow I'd thought we'd call them and invite them over to our place."

"Our place. I like that a lot."

"Me, too. I understand we need to get a picture of the four of us for our bedroom gallery."

"We'll work on it," he said, picking up his pace.

"Good." She dug her fingers into the couch. "Right now, why don't we concentrate on us?"

Excerpt

Merry stared in disbelief at her daughter. "What did you say?

"I said, Mom, why don't you get that vibrator out of the old cross-country ski sock and try it out? I'll bet you never opened it!" Tiffany stood in the kitchen with her hands on her hips, glaring back at her mother. "You're becoming more difficult to be around, Mom. If you don't want a man, at least take care of your needs yourself."

"How did you know about the vibrator?" Camille had bought it for her years ago. She'd never bothered to open it. Using it would have sent her on a deeper guilt trip. How could she satisfy herself, if she couldn't satisfy her husband? She'd forgotten the damn thing was still buried in a sock deep in a drawer, away from prying eyes. Or so she'd thought.

Tiffany cocked her head to the side. Her close-cropped blonde hair looked so sophisticated. Merry was a little jealous of her daughter's looks and carefree spirit. How could that be right?

"Mom, adolescents pry. Don't you remember? You don't

know how many times I checked to see if you'd opened it. I wanted to try it out so badly, but I knew you'd find out if I opened it." Tiffany lips turned up in a half-smile. "If you must know, I haven't checked in a number of years." She arched her eyebrows in a smug look. "I never had to. I got my own."

"When?"

Tiffany shrugged her shoulders. "Sixteen, I think. Yeah, you got yours when I was fourteen.

Merry slumped against the kitchen island. She couldn't believe this conversation. "How?"

"Aunt Camille. She understood."

"I'll bet she did." Merry froze. "Has Camille ever hit on you?"

"Mom, of course not. No way, no how! She's like family. I may get about a fair amount, but I've never thought of Camille in that way. Why?"

Merry cringed under her daughter's close examination. "Nothing."

"Nothing. Bullshit!" Tiffany smiled a knowing look. "Now wouldn't that be something. You and Aunt Camille. That'd be perfect."

"How can you say such a thing?" Merry put on her oven mitts, opened the oven door, and pulled out the dinner rolls.

"Those look great, Mom. If there's anyone who can help you get beyond the past several years, it's Camille. She's a gem."

"But she's bi."

"What do you think I'm talking about? Do I look like an idiot?"

"Of course not." Merry shook her head and removed the oven mitts. "Sometimes I think the world is passing me by. I'm not sure I could date in today's environment even if I wanted to."

"You'll manage. Let me drain the pasta. Whatever you do, don't rush into a—quote—lasting relationship. You need some time for yourself. To explore. To decide what you want — not what some man wants."

"You sound like the voice of experience. I thought these mother-daughter conversations were supposed to go the other direction."

Tiffany chuckled. "You were always a year or two behind with them."

"Oh."

"So maybe we're making up for them now."

"You know I tried my best, but with your father —"

"I know, Mom. Believe me, I know. Let's enjoy this new-found mother-daughter relationship. I really do believe I've gotten to know you much better since Dad died." She frowned. "I'm not saying it was good for him to die."

"Of course not." Merry moved to enfold her daughter in her arms. "But he died. And now there's only us."

"Not true, Mom. Yes, there's us, and there's whoever I let into my life and whoever you let into yours. I've always thought Camille had the hots for you. She has such a tight body. It must be from all the jogging she does."

"Tiffany." Merry tried not to sound exasperated. "I wish you wouldn't talk about Camille that way. There's nothing between us."

Tiffany's mouth twisted into a smile. "I'll bet that's not her fault."

Merry threw up her hands. "So now I'm at fault for not going to bed with Camille?"

"Don't go psycho on me, Mom. I didn't mean it that way."

Merry closed her eyes. She squeezed the bridge of her nose. Where was this conversation going? She opened her eyes and stared at the blank look on her daughter's face, then pointed the serving fork at her. "Okay, Miss Know-It-All, have you been to bed with a female?"

Tiffany laughed and hugged herself. "I was wondering if you'd find enough courage to ask. Yes — not often. But it was lovely each time. Less hassle and pressure than I've found with most guys."

She placed an arm around her mother's waist. "It's okay, Mom. If you want to be with Camille, do it. If not, that's okay, too. Though I personally think that would be a loss. But the most important thing is, get out of this house and away from your bedroom. Have you ever thought of moving to a different bedroom? There are six in this big old house. I'd move, if it were me. I've always liked the old solarium — you know, the dance room."

"Really? I haven't stepped into that room for ages." Merry smiled wistfully. "We did have some good times in there."

"You were always a better dancer than me, Mom. Do you ever wonder how your life might have been different if you had gone on to Julliard instead of having me?"

"I'd make the same choice. You are the most special person in the world to me, Tiffany."

"But—"

"No buts. Dance was a career option I chose not to take. We don't even know if I'd have been any good at it."

"Julliard must have thought so, to offer you a full ride. Anyway, there's that big old room. Pretty much empty last time I peeked in there. I love the way it opens onto the gardens and that you put in three mirrored walls for my dance practice." Tiffany stuck the tip of her tongue out at her mother. "Those mirrors have all sorts of possibilities."

"Huh?"

"Erotic possibilities."

"Oh. Tiffany, will you stop, please!" She paused. Why hadn't she thought of the solarium? It had been her favorite room before she'd turned it over to Tiffany. Maybe she should consider moving her bedroom. She could always remove the mirrors. She glanced at her daughter's telltale grin. Or not. "I'll think about the solarium. It does have a beautiful view of the back gardens. Maybe that'd help some."

"Hell, I might even sell the house, if it were me."

Merry's hand flew to her mouth. "I couldn't do that. This place is part of my soul."

Tiffany nodded. "I understand, just don't let it be a mill-stone. If you're going to keep it, then bring lovers here so it truly becomes your place—not something you share with a ghost."

"Tiffany! That's enough! This conversation is finished. If I want any more advice regarding my love life, I'll ask."

"That's fine, and please do. Let's eat." Tiffany grabbed a plate and began ladling food. She glanced back up at her mother. "Remember. Lower right dresser drawer all the way to the back. In a big old cross-country ski sock, the silver bullet awaits."

Merry couldn't stay vexed at the young woman who beamed at her with such hope and confidence. How had Tiffany survived those difficult years to turn into such a fine young woman? Merry had tried to be the best mother she could, even with all the demands on her time. Camille had helped a lot. She'd gone to school plays even when Merry couldn't. She'd helped with a lot of homework assignments. And apparently, she'd been a better sounding board on sexual matters. Of course, that wasn't saying much.

Camille. Merry sighed and watched her daughter pull out a chair at the dining room table. She couldn't seem to get away from the woman. And she had her daughter's blessing! Wasn't that a hoot?

At least the supper conversation had been less intrusive. Merry surveyed the leftovers. She'd have enough for lunch tomorrow. "Do you want to take some leftovers back with you?"

Tiffany shook her head. "You know how much I hate leftovers. You enjoy them." She stood to clear the table. "Do you want me to bring the books over this month, or do you plan on stopping by the shop?"

"I'll come by. I like spending time at the shop. You have some very creative people working for you." Merry beamed at her daughter. "Have I told you lately how proud I am of you and your business acumen?"

"Yes, just about every time we talk. You know I get it from both you and Dad. You'd think with two accountants for parents I'd be able to do my own books."

"You could do them, if you wanted to. You just try to keep me involved in the business some."

"Well, you should be. You're the partner who provided the start-up money. I'm sure Dad never heard about that."

Merry ducked her head. "No, there was no need to trouble him about such things at that time."

Tiffany glanced at her watch. "I've got to run, Mom. I've got a date at nine."

"At nine. Isn't that awfully late for a date?"

"Hardly. Who said there was a rule about when a date should start?" Tiffany grinned broadly at her mother. "When you do get back on the dating scene, you need to try a couple of young studs and maybe even some older guys. Don't get stuck in old routines."

"Enough! Run along and let me think in peace and quiet."

"Okay, Mom. I love you. Give Camille a hug for me when you see her next."

"Right." Merry watched the door close behind her daughter and then retreated to her kitchen to finish cleaning up.

It didn't take long before she had the dishes put away and the kitchen spotless. She'd been unable to put the conversation with Tiffany out of her mind — or, for that matter, the lingering taste of peaches that still mysteriously clung to her lips.

She'd been in the middle of a huge decision when that detective had arrived. What to do about Camille?

What had her daughter said? Lower right-hand dresser drawer, way in the back, stuffed in a red-and-white cross-country ski sock.

ABOUT THE AUTHOR

Award-winning author Adriana Kraft is a married couple writing Sizzling Romantic Suspense and Erotic Romance for Two, Three, or More. Whether readers open our romantic suspense or our erotic romance, they can expect characters they care about, hot sex scenes, and a compelling story. Our suspense stories deliver one man, one woman, danger and intrigue. Our erotic romance is edgier and nearly always includes ménage or polyamory, sometimes with two women and a man, sometimes with two (or more) couples.

Readers can count on our Romantic Suspense line for "warmth, blazing hot sex, and well-developed characters" (Romance Junkies Reviews) as our hero and heroine battle outer threats and inner demons to stay alive and fall in love.

We write our Erotic Romance stories to entertain, of course, but most of all we write them because we believe in happy endings for all who fall in love, whatever their gender, sexual orientation or numerical combination. Here you'll find multiple partners, three-way, four-way and more, swing lifestyle, lesbian, bisexual, ménage and polyamory, in both contemporary and paranormal settings: "scorching hot ... refreshing ... something to read when you want straight up hotness" (Long and Short Reviews)

Together we have published more than fifty romance novels and novellas to outstanding reviews. We love hearing from readers at adrianakraft99@yahoo.com, and here is our website:

When It's Time to Heat Things Up https://

adrianakraft.com